AMETHYST

AMETHYST

T. G. Styles

ISBN: Softcover 978-1-5245-8368-2
eBook 978-1-5245-8367-5

This is a work of fiction. Names, characters, places and incidents either are the product of the author's imagination or are used fictitiously, and any resemblance to any actual persons, living or dead, events, or locales is entirely coincidental.

Any people depicted in stock imagery provided by Thinkstock are models, and such images are being used for illustrative purposes only.
Certain stock imagery © Thinkstock.

Print information available on the last page.

Rev. date: 02/10/2017

To order additional copies of this book, contact:
Xlibris
1-888-795-4274
www.Xlibris.com
Orders@Xlibris.com
747094

CONTENTS

CHAPTER ONE

LIFE

I didn't know much about my parents and what I did know only came in fragments; glimpses of a past. The more time that passed the less I remembered of them. The last memory I have of them was them placing me in their bed and putting pillows all around me, as if to hide me. I remember hoping and wanting to see someone before going to bed that evening but that person's name and face, like that of my parents escapes me. After my parents finally got me to sleep the next thing that I remember is awakening to find myself locked in their room, my cries for them falling on deaf ears. At least that is how I remember it though my memories are a little hazy, but that is to be expected with it being nearly 17 years ago. I would often wonder why they had left me and never returned for me because I knew that they loved me or at least I thought that they did.

My life up until this point had been anything, but normal growing up in an orphanage in India for I was the only child with pale skin, blond hair, and blue eyes. I was a sight to behold. They would often call me Alexandra the white demon because I would show up at the scenes of various crimes and accidents, mysteriously drawn there by something that to others seemed to think proved that I was a demon that only brought disaster to those around me, yet at each accident or crime I would show up at no fatalities were ever reported.

When I turned 18 I decided to move to America hoping to lose the nickname of Alexandra the white demon and just live a normal life, but I chose the wrong city to settle down in; there was too much crime and I once again found myself in the middle of the crimes and accidents unable to explain how I had gotten there. The only thing that got me through was my faith and the overwhelming feeling that someone as well as God was watching over me waiting for the right moment to return to me.

Now at twenty years of age I Alex Seraph will be starting a new chapter in my life as I enter college in the small town of Iola, Kansas which I hope is far enough away from the larger cities so that I won't find myself in as many unexplainable situations.

I've been in school for a few months now and I have perfected the art of "being invisible." The only person other than the teacher who even knows I exist is my friend, Natalya. She's a sweet girl. She may at times talk too much, but that's what I like about her. There's never a dull moment with her. Her soft blue eyes are the perfect complement to her dark strawberry blond hair. She's adorable, and her pale-peach skin matches everything perfectly. She is and forever will be my best friend - almost like a sister to me.

The college has two groups that seem to rule the school, so to speak. The first group, and perhaps the most impressive, is made up of young, painfully handsome guys. They are so beautiful – as if they were carved from the same molds as the angels themselves. The leader of the group is named Gabriel … even his name is regal! He has blond highlighted hair that seems to sweep across his face just above his eyes in the perfect way. His eyes are to die for – sometimes a deep chocolate brown and other times a crystal clear blue. They make me dizzy every time I see them. And his body is chiseled perfect and strong – almost as if sculpted by a master carver. I can barely breathe when I think about him.

The others in the group are quite good looking – similar to Gabriel with perfect hair and piercing eyes, but not quite as perfect as Gabriel. No one could ever compare to Gabriel. They never talk to anyone except the teachers and each other and are all straight A students. They're kind-of anti-social – not anything like the other dominant group on campus.

The dominant group is made up of almost entirely of girls – except for their leader, who is a guy. His name is Eros**.** I suppose he has a handful of other guy friends he hangs out with, but mostly his group is made up of girls. Eros is quite handsome, as well, with short black hair and nearly licorice black/brown eyes. His tan skin exudes an almost god-like persona – giving him an allure unlike any other. The women of his group are just as appealing as he is, even with their hair colors ranging from the lightest of colors to the darkest. I suppose that's why I don't think about any of the other guys he hangs out with because they're quite ordinary next to Eros and his group of girls. They almost seem to get lost amongst the women of the group – fading into the background.

Two beautiful groups of people, and none of them ever pay me any mind. Dreaming about them is all I can do. I'm satisfied with where I'm at in my life, though. And for the first time ever I have a true friend in Natalya. She is the only one who truly understands me and puts up with my crazy quirks. She likes me for just being me – no strings attached.

I was staring mindlessly at Gabriel, pondering life and the many joys that filled my world, when I was roughly shook.

"WHAT?!?"

Oh no! That came out a lot louder than I had intended it to.

My cheeks flushed red as all eyes turned to me. Sinking into my chair I heard someone mumbling something.

Were they talking to me?

I glanced up from my desk.

Oh man ... it was the teacher and he was talking to me. What was he saying? He was asking me a question.

"How long does it take for the light to travel from the surface of the sun to the earth, and how many meters per second does it travel?"

Okay, so what's the answer? It has to be something we've gone over, but what?

I began to review our classes over the past week.

What did we learn?

My mouth dropped open, I hadn't heard one word he had said the entire week.

I could hear people quietly laughing at my misery. But just as tears began to well in my eyes from embarrassment, someone whispered to me.

"Eight minutes 17 seconds – and 299,792,458 meters or 186,000 miles per second."

I took in a deep breath and blurted the answer out.

"Eight minutes 17 seconds – and 299,792,458 meters or 186,000 miles per second."

The class fell silent. A soft smile touched the corners of my lips and my flushed cheeks began to normalize, but I could still feel stares from the others in the class. How was I ever going to thank Natalya for this one? I turned to her and gave her a quick wink and then set my attention back to the teacher. My smile widened as I noticed that even the professor couldn't believe I had answered the question correctly.

The rest of the class period I beamed with delight. After the remainder of my classes that day I ran home to our tiny one bedroom apartment that was only a few blocks from campus and threw my books to my makeshift bed. Then I jumped on the couch and tightly wrapped my arms around Natalya's fluffy center.

"Oh! Thank you. Thank you. Thank you! You are a complete and total lifesaver."

I pulled back to look her in the eyes and saw nothing but confusion in her eyes.

"What's wrong?"

"I don't understand …" She said hesitantly, pulling away and walking across the small living room to the kitchen bar. "What are you talking about and why are you thanking me? And how did you know the answer to the question that Professor Ramos asked you?!"

I was going to jokingly punch her in the shoulder because I was sure she was teasing me.

She always was such a kidder.

My hand loosely folded into a fist when she continued on absently to herself, almost as if she were disturbed by the impossibility.

"There is no possible way that you could have known …"

She stared at the ground as if trying to fit the pieces of a puzzle together. Natalya held up one finger and turned to my bag plopped upon the couch. Leaning over she pulled my Physics textbook from my bag and quickly thumbed through it.

She ***was*** *joking, right? She had to be. There was no other explanation.*

A large grin worked across my face and I jokingly punched her in the head.

Her round body sunk into the couch with a creaking noise – it was far too extreme of a reaction for such a light tap on the head. Sure, she wasn't expecting it, but her body shouldn't have crumpled like that. And yet she seemed completely un-phased as she continued thumbing through my beat-up textbook.

What's so interesting about that stupid book? Wait – do we have a test coming up?

I tried to remember what the professor had said in class today, but no matter how hard I tried I couldn't recall him ever saying anything about a test, unless he had said it before I'd started paying attention to him.

"You're such a kidder Natalya. You really had me going there for a minute."

My smile began to fade as she looked up and furrowed her eyebrows.

"What are you talking about? I'm not joking about anything."

Her seriousness eked through every pore upon her face. She was telling the truth.

But how? I clearly heard someone tell me the answer.

I shook my head, not wanting to believe she hadn't told me the answer.

"What are you talking about? I clearly remember you telling me the answer."

My eyes pleaded with her to admit it was true.

If it wasn't her that could only mean one thing – I had finally snapped. I had always figured this might happen, I just didn't think it would be so soon – crazy and at only 20 years old.

My self-loathing was interrupted by Natalya's response.

"I didn't give you the answer. I couldn't have … I didn't know the answer."

"What!?"

Shock flooded over me. I was dumbfounded. She knew answers to everything – she was literally a genius. It wasn't possible that she didn't know the answer.

"I didn't know the answer," she said again. "How could I? We're not supposed to study anything about light travel from the sun to earth until the end of this semester."

She pulled the book off her lap and jabbed her finger at one of the pages. She looked as if she were broken, and all I wanted to do was fix her.

"There's a simple explanation for why I knew the answer and you didn't," I said dejectedly.

She looked up at me and there seemed to be a glimmer of hope twinkling in her soft blue eyes. A crooked, self-deprecating smile spread across my face as I squatted down in front of her and tried to balance myself.

"I'm crazy."

"What!?"

"Yes that's what it is."

I tried to shake my head, but that just set me off-balance and I smacked down on my butt. I chuckled at myself and continued as if nothing had happened.

"I'm crazy … it's as simple as that."

"What do you mean you're crazy?" She questioned as she began to try to help me pull myself off the floor.

"Well …" My voice was strained. "Wha … what I mean … is that …" An ornery look flashed in my eyes. "I … hear … voices …"

As I said the last word I pulled Natalya to the ground beside me. We chuckled and rolled onto our sides.

"What do you mean you hear voices?"

"Well, I heard someone whisper … although it was kind of loud. I heard someone tell me the answer to the question. I thought it was you but I guess I was wrong … now that I think about it the voice was that of a man, so clearly it couldn't have been you. Man it sucks going crazy!"

I sat up and shook my head.

Natalya patted me on the shoulder and gave me her best comforting smile.

"I already knew you were crazy … but there's nothing that we can do about that."

"Gee, thanks."

Her grin widened.

"Anyway, enough with stating the obvious. Don't you have a birthday coming up in a few months?"

"Man … I was really hoping that you would forget that."

My face scrunched up in disgust.

"Why? Birthdays are wonderfully happy and …"

She continued to drone on, as she sometimes did. When we first met I admit that it irritated me, but I eventually learned to tune her out. When I thought she was done I gave her my answer.

"I don't like birthdays because it only further reminds me that I'm alone – no parents, no family, and no one to love …"

A tear softly touched the corner of my eye.

"Oh but you do," Natalya said as she wiped the tears from my eyes. "You have me!"

"I know that I have you, but I was meaning …" I bit my lip and quickly glanced up at her before returning my gaze to the floor.

"Oh! You're talking about a guy to love!" She nudged me in the ribs. I could feel my cheeks flush red once again. "But not just any guy … am I right?"

I shook my head and played dumb, "I don't know what you're talking about." I stood up and began to walk from the room.

"Oh yes you do!"

"NO I don't!" I snapped, more harshly than I'd intended.

"Relax Alex. I was only trying to cheer you up."

"Yeah, well, he doesn't even know I'm in the same class as him," I said dejectedly, "let alone on the same planet …"

"He does so know that you're in the same class as him, especially after your embarrassing endeavor today …"

Her face scrunched in awkwardness as my stomach did an uncomfortable flip.

"Did you really have to bring that up again? I was just beginning to forget about it …"

"But how can you forget about something as embarrassing as …" She stopped mid-sentence when she realized what she was saying. "… I'm sorry … I bet you're wanting to forget about that." After another awkward pause, she tried valiantly to change the subject. "So … I've decided to take you out for your birthday! It's in a month and a half … or was it two?" Natalya smiled a sheepish smile. It was one of the things I loved about her – she could change directions in a conversation without so much as losing a beat.

I grinned back at her, "Nat … you know I love you, right?"

"Of course you do. How could you not?"

"I truly don't know how I could, but I think if I tried really, really hard I might be able to not like you." I said matter-of-factly, trying to keep a smile from touching my lips. Natalya's mouth dropped open and all that came out was a disgruntled grunt.

"Anyway, I really don't want you to make a big deal about my birthday … 'cause it really isn't that important."

"Not that important? Not that important!" She shouted. "How can you say that?" Tears began to fill her eyes. "Maybe it's not that important to you but … but it is to me! It's very important to me."

"Why?" I asked, honestly confused by how adamant she was. "Why is it so important to you?"

"It's important to me because you're the first true friend I've ever had."

More tears formed in her eyes, and I grasped her in my arms. It was as if she were inside my head. "I completely understand what you mean and if it means that much to you I will be utterly happy with whatever. And, yes … it is in about a month and a half or more percisly one month, one week, and three days." My eyebrows danced across my forehead as I gave her the exact amount of time till my birthday.

"Okay sense today is January 4th and your birthday is in one month, one week, and three days than that means that your birthday is February14th." A smile touched her face, "I never thought of it before, but your birthday is on Valentines day, that's kind-of cool."

"Don't remind me," I mumbled irritated that it had to be that day.

She pulled me to my feet and began to jump up and down, "Oh, Alex it's going to be fun, so cheer up! So what do you want to do?" She excitedly questioned as she continued dancing around.

Strangely my head began to spin and my heart started to violently beat inside my chest as I tried to answer her question.

"Whatev … whatever you want t-to d-d-doooo …"

And then everything went black.

* * *

I slowly opened my eyes to find myself in a large temple.

How I knew that it was a temple I am not entirely sure, but I figure that it has something to do with it being a dream.

The temple had extremely high ceilings with openings; that I assumed were windows lining the top of the room, a large, thick curtain ran across one side of the room and a large intricately carved stand that had incents burning on it. On the right and left of me were tables with small wooden bowls that had bread resting inside them. Behind the tables where golden candle holders that held seven candles at a time. The light from the candles dimly flickered as I continued to examine the temple room that had elaborate stone carved walls.

It seemed to be completely dark outside the temple, no light shined in through the opening at the top of the room. When suddenly there came a painful howl of agony that echoed through the night, as though the beast where grieving. I began to walk towards the large stone doors when the ground began to violently shake and a great burst of wind tore through the temple snuffing out all of the candles and splitting the thick curtain at the back of the temple in two. As I tried to steady myself the ground beneath me began to crumble and I seen Gabriel offering his hand, heartache seemed to consume his expression. My heart began to vigorously pound and my chest began to ache causing me to immediately awaken.

* * *

My face was lined with sweat and my breathing was rapid and shallow when I awoke, I glanced up at the clock it read 3:00 AM as I thought about the dream. I'd never been so terrified in my entire life. It felt so real, but my dreams always felt real. It was a dream I'd had frequently though Gabriel hadn't ever been in the dreams before. No matter how many times I had these dreams; terror always seemed to plague me. I'd never really found earthquakes to be all that scary, and yet every time I had this nightmare the only things I felt was fear and heartbreak.

My thoughts were interrupted by a soft, "A-hum." I rubbed my eyes to find Natalya sitting on the arm of my makeshift bed. "Are you okay?" She questioned with concern plaguing her voice.

I rolled away from her to face the wall. "I'm fine …" I lied as my heart continued to pound almost from my chest, only making it feel all the more sore. I could feel Natalya move awkwardly across the bed and place her hand upon my damp sweat-saturated forehead.

"You're lying to me," She stated with an authority that caught me off guard.

I pulled her hand from my forehead.

"I don't know what you're talking about."

"Alexandra, I have known you for some time now and I think that I know you well enough to know that you are lying to me."

She continued to drone on about how well she knew me, and suddenly her words struck me as odd. After all, she'd only known me sense the beginning of college. I counted on my hand how many months it had been – only four. Admittedly we'd become pretty good friends over that time period, but the more I thought about it the more I remembered times when she knew things about me that I hadn't ever told her. I assumed it was because she was just really good at reading people, but the truth is I guess I didn't know her as well as what I thought that I did. With her being the only real friend that I had ever had I didn't want to admit to myself that I really didn't know her as well as I told myself that I did.

My thoughts gradually drifted away from Natalya and on to my dream and Gabriel. It only seemed like weeks since school had started, but I did tend to zone out in classes where Gabriel was present. He was so amazingly breathtaking that my thoughts went blurry just thinking about him. I shook my head and tried to push the thoughts of Gabriel aside.

That was harder than I expect, especially with him not really giving me the time of day.

Now back on track I refocused upon what Natalya had said.

Wait! What had she said? She had called me by my birth name. But I've never told her my birth name. So how did she know?

I interrupted her yammering.

"How did you know my name?"

She looked at me perplexed.

"Alex, I have known you since the beginning of school," she replied. "I should know it by now. After all, you are my best friend."

She placed her hand upon my shoulder as if to console me. I pulled her hand from my shoulder.

"No, how did you know my birth name? I've never told you it before."

She bit her lip and quickly said, "The teacher called you by it when he asked you for the answer to the question, and I just thought that it was so pretty it kind-of stuck, I guess." She grinned sheepishly at me and continued, "So what were you dreaming about?"

“It was nothing really.” I paused for a moment and hesitantly continued. “I was standing in a large, abandoned temple and then suddenly the ground began to violently shake and darkness consumed the temple.”

I looked at Natalya she was so engrossed in the description of my dream, as if I were telling her the most important thing ever. “As the ground shook with great power and a great forceful gust of wind blew through the temple tearing the curtain in two that hung upon one of the walls. I looked up to find Gabriel offering his hand to help me up and as I reached towards his hand I woke up.”

I waited for a moment. The silence was deafening.

“Pretty stupid, right?” I chuckled. “But it still made my heart pound.”

“What do you suppose the dream meant? Or maybe it was a memory of an event that you need to remember? No, maybe it’s a vision of the future?” Natalya questioned as she looked into my eyes excitement filling her expression.

“I don’t think it meant anything and it defiantly wasn’t a memory or vision of the future … it was just a dream.” I pulled from her and walked to our tiny square kitchen for a glass of water. I gulped the large glass of water down.

Natalya walked up behind me and placed her hand upon my back. “I think that there is more meaning to your dream than you want to admit." She leaned around me to look at me and reaching up she touched my forehead once again. "Oh Alex! You're ice cold!" Pulling her hand from my forehead she touched my hand. "Your hands are cold, too!"

"That's not possible, I am burning up … can't you see the sweat?" I raised up my arm and pointed to my chest, revealing embarrassing sweat patches. My face wrinkled in disgust, "I think I'm going to take a long shower so I can relax. I'm still a little shaken up from that crazy dream." Natalya shook her head as I made my way to the bathroom.

I stood in the hot steaming shower, unable to clear my head. Something was going on with me but what I didn't know what. I remembered back to the first time I'd had the strange dream – right after my parents died.

I wonder if it did have something to do with them. Maybe Natalya was right and the dreams really did have a meaning behind them.

I tried not to dwell on it, and as I came back to reality when I realized my hot shower had gone cold. I hopped out of the sower and eventually settled into bed, but not before checking on Natalya. I smiled as I heard her snoring on the other side of her bedroom door. She truly could wake the dead with her snoring. You could almost feel the door vibrate with every breath.

The next morning I laid in bed not wanting to get up. The sun irritatingly peaked through the curtains and I pulled my blankets up over my head and began to drift back off to sleep. I could feel the haze of the dream coming on again, though, and not wanting to have that terrifying dream again I began to say, “No, no, no …” over and over again – trying to will myself not to have the dream again. It wasn’t working … the haze of the dream thickened, and just before it took over completely I felt the soft touch of a hand upon my icy hot forehead, pulling me from the fog of the dream.

“Are you okay?” Natalya quietly questioned.

“I’m fine … My stomach’s bothering, that’s all …” I said as I curled up into a ball.

“I understand now why you didn’t go to class today.”

“What are you talking about?” I asked. “Today is Saturday. There’s no class today.”

I know I’m not feeling well but there has to be something wrong with her, if she thinks that today is Monday.

“No … today is Monday,” she said. “You slept the entire weekend. You were really beginning to worry me …”

Beginning!?!

“Beginning!?! I was asleep for over two straight days and you’re saying I was ***beginning*** to worry you?”

How could she **not** *have been more worried about me? I am worried about me – I'd lost over two days!*

It was far beyond my comprehension. As I struggled to understand what had happened to me, just on the edges of my memory seemed to be a hazy explanation – the answer was elusive, just flashes of incoherent thoughts and nothing that made sense of my apparent coma.

"Well, what I mean is I knew you were okay because you were still breathing," Natalya said.

"Oh. That's great," I said sarcastically. "I slept for two plus days straight and everything was okay because I was still breathing!?"

How had she come to the conclusion that everything was fine just because I was breathing? Sometimes I really didn't understand her – how she came to her logic – but then again, she did march to the beat of her own drum.

CHAPTER TWO

CHANGE

It had been a week since I'd had the crazy dream, but I could tell that there was still something wrong with me. I continued to sweat abnormally off-and-on throughout the week – my skin icy to the touch while my insides boiled. The pain that came with it was beyond anything I'd ever felt before – it almost felt as if my bones were trying to burst from my body. I started to think I was going to have to give in and go to the doctor. There had to be an explanation for the crippling pain and the debilitating sweats. The only positive to the experience was that I'd stopped hearing the voices, so maybe I wasn't going crazy after all.

As I headed to class I began to think about the upcoming weekend. It was Friday and I would have the weekend to relax. I didn't know if I could handle another day in class, especially with ***him***.

Gabriel.

It continued to puzzle me why he was in my dream. It almost made me feel as if I knew him. I must have lost track of time as I tried to make sense of it all because suddenly I found myself in class, called upon spontaneously by the professor again to answer a question that I had no idea the answer to.

"Alex, what is the approximate temperature of the surface of the sun?"

Horror flooded my mind. I'd done it again! Everything was silent. Frantically I waited for the answer to come, but my mind was blank. Mr. Peterson looked down at his desk as if he was disappointed in me.

Eros leaned forward and softly placed his hand upon my shoulder. I turned to look at him. His smile could make the strongest of women go weak in the knees. He flashed me a smile and said, "5,778 Kelvin or 5,505 degrees Celsius."

"What?" I questioned not realizing what he was telling me.

He inched closer and I glanced back at Gabriel. He almost looked mad, but that was probably just wishful thinking. I shrugged it off and turned my attention back to Eros.

Man, he smells nice.

His lips softly whispered against my ear, "5,778 Kelvin or 5,505 degrees Celsius."

Shock consumed me, but I didn't respond as I became enveloped by his scent, heat and fire.

Heat and fire? No, that's not right, it was more of a fiery brimstone that gave off the spicy aroma of roasting cinnamon.

"That's the answer to the question Professor Peterson is asking you," he continued, this time more insistently.

"Oh," Was all I whispered before blurting out the answer. "5,778 Kelvin or 5,505 degrees Celsius."

Eros relaxed back into his chair and Professor Peterson's mouth dropped open once again.

"That's right … good …" He nodded his head and continued with his discussion.

I turned back to Eros and shyly smiled at him before turning back to the open Physics book lying on my desk.

After class Eros leaned forward and tapped me upon the shoulder, "You're welcome …"

I stared at him dumbfounded until it clicked. "Thank you …" I stuttered.

He half smiled.

"No problem," he said as he leaned closer and winked at me. "It was my pleasure." He stared at me almost as if he were trying to read my soul. I smiled back at him and he turned away as if he had been searching for something and had come up empty handed.

"Yes, well … I had better be going," he said as he began to walk from the nearly empty classroom, but just before leaving he turned around glanced at Gabriel. Then, redirecting his focus to me, "We should hang out sometime." He raised his eyebrows and with an almost devilishly incredible smile continued, "You know … just the two of us."

"Why?" I asked as I raised my eyebrows in confusion. "I mean don't get me wrong I am flattered that you're asking, but…why?"

Shock consumed Eros' face, "I've never had anyone ask me, why I was asking them out." He said as a look of interest touched his face.

"There's a first time for everything, traditore," Michael said with a thick Italian accent upon the last word and a crooked smile upon his face. Michael had sand blond hair, blueish green eyes, and a muscular build.

I didn't know he knew Italian.

Red anger flashed in Eros' eyes, but quickly vanished as he turned his attention back to me, "Well, I suppose that I am asking you out because…" Suddenly his expression change there was an almost darkness consumed his look as he ran his hand across my cheek, "Because I think you're hot and thought that we might make a nice couple." He said as his eyebrows danced across his forehead.

I wrinkled my nose and arched my eyebrow, “Okay?”

He stepped closer to me, smiled, and began to pull me towards him, as though he intended to kiss me.

Instinctively I backed away.

“I’m sorry if I was too forward.” Eros said as his look softened and he let me go. “It doesn’t have to be a date we can just hang out and get to know each other a little better.”

I stared at Eros for a moment.

What is wrong with him? There is something off with him, but I can’t quiet place my finger upon it. It almost seems as though he has two personalities.

“Okay, it sounds like it might be interesting to hang out.”

“Great! I’ll call you later,” He said as he winked at me and left the classroom.

I can’t believe that he actually asked me out. Especially sense before today I didn’t think that he even knew I existed. Wait! How is he going to call me? I never gave him my number.

* * *

Thoughts continued to swirl in my mind as I walked home that chilly afternoon. I was thinking about the odd scent from Eros when a different strange smell caught my attention.

There's something familiar about this scent, but what? It was an intoxicating scent, with a mesmerizing allure.

I moved closer and closer to the smell, my stomach beginning to growl. I hungered for whatever it was giving off such an amazing aroma. I thought I was getting closer to it, excitement rising within. That excitement was dashed in a breath, however, when I turned the corner and saw a terrible automobile accident right in front of me.

Oh no it's happening again.

I rushed to the car, which had been impaled by a large tree, and examined the situation. There was a mother and her two small children in the car.

I immediately pulled out my cell phone and called for help, knowing I couldn't do this alone. After making the call, I left my phone connected with the operator. I didn't have time to figure out where I was, I had to help.

I examined the children first as I pulled their tiny frames from the lump of a car. The first child was a small boy. He seemed okay – in fact, better than okay. There wasn't even a scratch on him. But as I pulled the girl from the car I realized she was bleeding from the head. She incoherently looked around as if in shock at what had happened.

"It … it came out … out of nowhere …" she mumbled as she smeared blood through her curly red hair.

I took off my jacket and tore the sleeve off of my shirt to wrap around her head. "Are you guys okay?" I questioned the boy. He seemed to be more coherent than his younger sister, but that quickly changed. He began to yell over and over again, as if he, too, were in shock

"Mama! Mama! Mama!"

I turned and looked back at the car. I'd almost forgotten about her. I set the kids down on a large flat rock nearby, checked the girl's cut one last time, and then rushed back to the car.

"Ma'am, are you alright?" I questioned, moving closer to the car. Fear grabbed me as I moved closer and closer to her. The branch from the tree had not only impaled the car, but had also pierced through her shoulder as well as a slightly larger branch going through her side, approximately where her stomach would be. I stared down at her, unable to decide what to do. My mind seemed to be thinking about every possible solution simultaneously. I hadn't realized my mind could move so fast. Without thinking about what I was doing, I tore open the car door and looked down at the branches that ran through the woman, pinning her in the car. I hadn't realized that the children were watching so closely and as soon as they saw their mother they started frantically screaming.

"It's okay," I said consolingly. "I'm going to help her. Everything will be fine."

I promise.

Everything after that seemed to move so quickly that I didn't even realize what I was doing until it was already done. The next thing I recall was hearing the siren of an ambulance, and then someone placing his hand upon my shoulder.

"We'll take it from here ma'am."

I nodded my head and numbly walked to where the children were sitting. They quietly crept over to me, each grabbing one of my hands and laying their heads upon my arms.

One of the EMTs made his way over to the three of us. He looked so familiar, but I couldn't put my finger on where I knew him from. He held out his hand and asked the young girl to go with him. She looked up at me as if to ask if it was alright. A small smile spread across my face and I nodded my head.

The young boy snuggled deeper into my side and I wrapped my arms around him and stared at the young handsome man as he quickly and carefully worked upon the little girl. He seemed to be very good at his job, even at such a young age.

He can't be much older than me.

It was like watching an artist at work, but an artist in the medical profession. It seemed as if the girl couldn't even feel him stitching her forehead as they cheerfully talked back and forth. Once finished, he returned her to my side.

"So you are Alexandra – No, you like to be called Alex right?" He questioned as he ran his fingers through his dark blond hair, with golden highlights.

"How…" I began to question.

"I'm in Professor Peterson's class with you. I sit in the back with Gabriel, Michael and the others. I'm Raphael." His light blue eyes shined as he spoke.

Shock flooded my mind.

Why is he talking to me?

"So can you tell me how this happened?"

"No I … I didn't see how it happened … I just came across it while I was walking home from class." I said as I nervously began to bite my nails.

Raphael gently grabbed my hand and pulled it from my lips.

"So, you live around here?"

I began to say yes as I looked around.

Where am I, anyway?

I didn't know any of the street names.

"I … I …Where exactly is here?"

"You're at 32nd and Abram."

"What!?" I exclaimed. "Last I remember I was walking … Nevermind. I'm just glad I was here to help."

“Ooookay?” He said, slightly confused. “So, how did you know to cut the branches on both sides before removing her from the car?”

“What are you talking about? I didn’t …” I had no idea what he was talking about. As I tried to recall the moment, a strong arm slipped around my shoulders.

“What happened here?” The smooth voice questioned as Raphael’s face wrinkled in disgust at the man enfolding me in his arms. A strong smell of spicy cinnamon filled the air around us.

Wait, I know that smell.

I turned to find Eros.

“Where did you come from?”

“I live not too far from here, and when I heard the ambulance I came to see what was going on.”

Raphael’s eyes narrowed.

“I’d better be getting back to work,” he said gruffly. He began to walk past me when he stopped. “I’ll see you at school, Alex.” Raphael held out his hand and the little girl placed hers in his and quickly grabbed her brothers’. “Come on kids, let’s take you to see your mother.” Raphael gave me one final look that almost seemed to say, “Don’t trust Eros, he’s bad news.” And with that he turned and left, children in hand.

"So what was that all about?" I questioned as I turned to look at Eros a kindness seemed to shine in his eyes as he look at me.

There's something about his eyes, something that seems familiar to me, but what is it?

I stared into his dark eyes.

He half smiled, his look changing when he spoke. "It was nothing … he's just an old rival." An almost evil look consumed his eyes, but quickly dissolved as he continued. "Anyway, I realized after you'd left class that I didn't get your number, so I was really excited that I saw you." He grabbed my hand and sweetly kissed the back of it. My cheeks flushed a deep red, "So can I have it?"

"Have what?"

His smile widened, "Your number …"

"Oh … that's right."

I pulled my hand from his grasp as he pulled a notepad and pen from his pocket. My thoughts bounced around as I nonchalantly wrote my number on the paper. I handed my number over to Eros – my stomach almost seemed to churn as the paper left my hand.

It's just nerves, right?

I watched him place my number into his pocket. Then he leaned over, picked up my coat and sweetly draped it over my shoulders. I shyly smiled as I began to twist my hair between my fingers.

He really is sweet.

"Anyway, I had better be going. I have a lot of homework, but I will call you later … if that's alright with you?"

"Sure that would be fine," I said as I nervously glanced up into his ebony-brown eyes. His hand brushed the hair from my eyes and with a wink he turned and walked away.

I watched as he disappeared around the corner before I began to make the long trek home.

How I did I get so far from my place?

It seemed like only mere minutes had passed sense I raced towards the hypnotic scent. I closed my eyes and took in a deep breath. The scent seemed to be gone, washed away in a flood of a hundred others smells. I shrugged my shoulders.

Oh well.

I walked for quite some time when I felt a faint vibrating coming from my pocket, "Hello."

"Are you alright?" Natalya frantically inquired.

"I'm fine."

"Really? Because it is nearly 10 o'clock! I was expecting you hours ago." Concern plagued her voice.

"I'm sorry …" I looked up at the street sign in front of me. "I'll be home in just a few minutes," I reassured her as I hung the phone up.

I looked up at the sign one last time, knowing I was a good 15 or 20 minutes away by car, let alone just walking. I began to jog as a strange feel washed over me.

I am being watched.

My pace picking up faster and faster with each step. Before I knew it I was at the apartment. I raced up the stairs to our door, and as I fumbled with the keys Natalya opened it.

"I thought you said it would take a few minutes! I wasn't expecting you so soon. It's only been …" She looked down at her watch, which was on a chain around her neck, and tapped the top of it as if it were broken. Her eyes widened as she continued, "It hasn't even been two minutes. Normally when you say it's going to be a few minutes it takes at least 10 to 20 minutes. So this is quite a surprise."

"What?!" I shouted loudly.

How could it have only been a few minutes?

My mind flooded with thoughts and questions going in every direction, but not one explanation made any sense. I looked around one last time before closing the door, the strong feeling of watching eyes preoccupying my thoughts. Growing up I had often felt as though someone was watching over me however there was something different about the feeling something that almost seemed murderous about it. I took in a deep breath as I closed the door as a strange citrusy smell wafted into the room. I walked to the couch and plopped my books on it as I mumbled, “There’s something very strange going on with me.” I looked up, expecting a response from Natalya, but to my surprise she’d silently made her way to the kitchen and started fixing me a plate of leftovers. I shrugged my shoulders and took in a deep breath. Something smelled good. “What-cha makin?” I questioned as I walked closer to the smell that drifted from the kitchen.

“Oh this … I was just browning a roast for dinner tomorrow. I’m gonna slow cook it for tomorrow’s supper.”

“But I thought you were making me a plate of leftovers?” I inquired as I stared at the seared meat upon the stove.

“I did …” She turned and flung her head in the direction of the microwave. “It’s there in the microwave. I just haven’t turned it on yet to heat it up.”

I hesitantly walked over to the microwave.

Maybe that’s the delectable smell I was smelling.

I opened the microwave door. I stared down at the greyish and yellowish lumps that sat alongside some sad looking green beans.

Those are green beans, right? They look a little brown …

I hesitantly poked the yellowish lump.

"What is it?" My face wrinkled in disgust at the plate before me.

"Oh … it's just meatloaf, mashed potatoes, and green beans … can't you tell?" She glanced over her round shoulders at me as if to say duh.

"Right … I can see that now that I'm looking at it."

Those are mashed potatoes and meatloaf?

There was an awkward moment of silence, and then taking a deep breath I continued. "Anyway, so what do I put it on to heat it up?"

"Maybe two minutes and thirty seconds … or you could eat it cold if you like … You know, put it on some bread with butter and have a meatloaf sandwich. That's the way I like to eat it."

My stomach churned at the thought of what she was describing. I quickly hit the cook button. "I think I'll just warm it up."

"Alright …" She nonchalantly said as she continued to seer the roast on all sides.

I stepped closer and stared down at the blood red meat. It smelled so delectably delightful that my mouth began to water. I licked my lips and closed my eyes to further embrace the smell. My senses tingled as every fiber of my being longed to have a bite of the freshly seared meat. Shock flooded me when I opened my eyes to find Natalya staring at me.

"Is there something you were wanting?" She questioned as she looked at me, trying to pull away from me as much as she could.

I stepped back and bit my bottom lip, "Sorry, it just smells sooo good." I mumbled taking in another deep breath of the tantalizing smell. I could feel the flavor of the meat dancing upon my tongue.

"Really?! Because …"

At that moment the phone rang. I quickly scooped it up, happy for the distraction. "Hello?"

"Hi … I was hoping you were home by now," a velvety voice said. "This is Eros …"

"Oh … right! You said you were going to be calling. So what's up?" My stomach tingled with anticipation – or perhaps it was still the smell that filled our tiny apartment, I wasn't quite sure.

"Well, I was calling to see if you were interested in hanging out tomorrow night."

"Tomorrow night? Well … I don't think I have anything planned." I turned to Natalya as if to ask if there was anything going on. I placed my hand over the phone and I questioned. "We're not doing anything this Saturday are we?"

She shook her head, "Not that I know of."

"Okay, I just wanted to check." Flustered, I returned to the conversation with Eros. "Yes … I … I think I can do that … or I mean we can hang out tomorrow. If that's alright?" I nervously played with my hair, pulling it in and out through my fingertips.

"Alright then I'll see you tomorrow."

"Okay …" I nervously laughed. And with one last "Bye," he hung up.

Slowly I hung up the phone and a stupid smile spread across my face.

Maybe I can find out a little more about Eros this Saturday?

I pulled my plate from the microwave and numbly walked over to our small two-seat table. Unaware of anything else, I began to shovel food into my mouth as Natalya fiddled with the roast. A moment later she shoved the pan aside and briskly walked to where I sat at the table. I barely even noticed her sitting there beside me as I thought about tomorrow night, intrigued with the idea of finding out more about Eros.

Maybe I will find out why he seems so familiar to me?

Scooting even closer Natalya asked, "So who was that?"

Her words sounded fuzzy as they came out as I continued to think about what tomorrow might bring.

Natalya raised her voice and poked me quite roughly in the shoulder. "SO WHO WAS THAT?"

My ears seemed to ring from her words. “It was no big thing.”

“That’s not what I asked. I asked you who it was?”

“It was …” A dumb smile spread across my face. “Eros.” I sighed.

Natalya’s eyes widened, “Did you just say it was Eros?”

I nodded my head, “Yep, Eros.” A small part of me ached when I said his name, as if something about him just wasn’t quite right.

It’s probably just nerves.

Natalya snapped her fingers in front of my face. “HELLO! Earth to Alex!” She rapped upon my head. “Is there anyone in there?”

I rolled my eyes – she really could be quite irritating with very little effort. “What do you want Natalya?” I rudely questioned. I gave her a dirty look, but seeing the hurt in her eyes a pang of compassion touched my heart. “I’m sorry. You didn’t deserve that.” I maneuvered around the table, dragging my chair with me clumsily, and flopped my arms around her shoulders. “I don’t know what came over me. What were you saying?”

She shook her head, “It doesn’t matter …”

“Yes it does. I really want to know what you were saying. Please?”

"I just … well I was wondering what happened to you. I mean, you're just acting so different. Getting calls from Eros and coming home late. It wouldn't have bothered me but you were over four hours late and you didn't even explain why."

I thought for a moment, trying to word it just right. I took in a deep breath and quickly explained. "It was nothing, I just came across an accident, saved a mother from death, talked to Raphael, and gave Eros my number. No big deal." I looked up at Natalya to find her mouth gaping open. "What?" I questioned as I closed her mouth with my finger.

She swallowed hard, "I've never heard you talk so – wait a minute. Did you just say that you spoke with Raphael and saved a woman's life?"

"Yes … so?" My eyebrows rose, not realizing the question.

"So since when does anyone from Gabriel's group ever talk to anyone except the teacher and each other?"

I shrugged my shoulders, "I don't know; he probably only talked to me because he wanted to know how the accident had happened."

"So why was he at the accident? Wait – why where you there?"

"I just came across it on my way home from campus, and he was one of the EMTs that responded. You know it was quite amazing the way he stitched the girl up. It was almost as if she couldn't even feel him doing it. I am telling you Nat, I've never seen anything like it before. He was truly amazing!"

Natalya interrupted before I could go any further. "So how did you save the woman's life?"

"Excuse me?" I questioned, being shocked by the quick change of subject.

"How did you save a woman's life and why did she need you to save her life?"

Is she serious?

"She was in an accident and that's why she needed me to save her." My tone was a little condescending, but Natalya didn't seem to notice.

"Well duh … I already knew that she was in an accident, but what where her injuries?"

"Oh," I mumbled as I tried to remember her injuries. My brain seemed to recall it almost immediately. "Well …" I moved my arms around as I explained. "A large tree had fallen upon the car and a couple of the branches from the tree …" My stomach turned as I began to recall the entire ordeal, "… impaled her. They went directly through her, pinning her to the back of her seat." Natalya's mouth dropped open. I knew she was imagining the entire thing – she always did have such a good imagination.

"And just how did you save her?"

"Well I …" Visions of the process began to run through my mind as if it were a movie.

* * *

I quickly tore the back door off its hedges and went to work on removing her from the car. After snapping the branches from the tree my hands tore through the seat of the car as if it were paper. Her lifeless body began to fall. Catching her with one hand I began to pull the limb from her shoulder. A wince of pain escaped her gray lips as blood began to seep around the edges to the limb. I tore off my other sleeve and tightly wrapped it just above the wound in her shoulder.

"I'm sorry, but this is going to hurt." I whispered as I placed a stick in her mouth and pulled the limb from her shoulder.

* * *

As a tear rolled down my cheek I felt a hand wipe it away, "Alex … Alex what's wrong?" Natalya questioned.

I shook my head.

"Please don't make me relive that," I whispered as another cheek escaped the corner of my eye.

Natalya nodded her head.

“I think I’m going to turn in for the night.”

I pulled myself from the table. I staggered to the couch, not even bothering to pull out my bed, and sank into the folds of the pillowed couch. Natalya remained completely silent as she covered me with a blanket and left the room. I began to drift off to sleep – the haze of the day fading away.

CHAPTER THREE

BETRAYED?

My heart began to beat faster and faster. The agony was nearly unbearable as I raced through the night. Tears began to fill my eyes, causing the sand upon the ground to blur into a muddy haze. My heart felt as if it would burst through my chest. I looked toward the sky as the moon and stars began to turn black, and yet my eyes could still see all around me – even in the pitch black. I scanned my surroundings and my eyes fell upon a large temple in the center of town. I had to get there, but it had to be several miles away. The only question now was how to get to the temple.

Suddenly a great pain began to come over me. My bones felt as if they were tearing through my skin. I gasped for air, unable to breathe through the pain.

As I woke up, I rubbed my chest, absently remembering the pain that had been in my dream.

Wait – it really is sore!

Again my heart began pounding faster and faster. The faster it beat, the great the pain grew. My bones once again seemed to slice through my skin. Everything began to blur, when out of the corner of my eye Natalya rushed to my side.

What does she have in her hand? Is that a syringe?

A moment later I felt s slight prick and my vision went black.

Again I woke up, but this time I found Natalya at the end of the couch, her head resting in her hand with my legs in her lap. I stretched my arms over my head, arching my back and letting out a grunt.

"What are you doing in here?" I questioned as her eyes groggily opened.

"You had a dream and started screaming, so I came to calm you down," she said, concern edging her voice. "Don't you remember?"

Flashes of the horrifying nightmare and pain coursed through my mind. I shook my head. "No … I don't remember that," I lied. My stomach churned at my deceitful words. Not wanting to let her see my lies, I clenched my teeth and glanced at the clock on the kitchen counter, it was already 10:30 a.m. I turned back to Natalya, "How could you let me sleep so late? I have lots of things to do before I see Eros tonight." I pulled my heavy legs from her lap and with a frustrated huff I walked to the kitchen.

As I pulled a glass from the cabinet Natalya walked up behind me, "You had such a hard night I just though you should rest."

I gave Natalya a hateful look and headed to the bathroom, "I'm taking a shower." I snapped at her and slammed the door behind myself. I turned the shower on and began to take my shirt off when I noticed something in the mirror. Stepping closer to it I pulled my shirt up revealing my back. A gasp escaped my lips – I was black and blue and it wasn't just on my back. I pulled my shirt up further, the bruises covered my chest and shoulders as well.

Why can't I feel them?

I walked to the door and numbly opened it, the shower still running.

At Natalya's door I placed my hand upon the nob, but halted when I heard her whispering, "No she's in the shower."

I opened the door ever so slightly as she continued her conversation.

"Yes, she began to transform last night, but something went wrong … I don't know. It was almost as if her body was rejecting the transformation, like it was hesitant to change … I know, but it could be because she's female … I've never seen anything like it though … no … but hers didn't look the same and yours when you transform … you're probably right. Well I had to use it on her…I didn't want her to… of course I'll keep you updated."

I couldn't believe what I was hearing.

Had she done something to me? That's why she was coming toward me with something in her hand? It must have been what she injected me with, but what was it?

So many things were going through my mind.

"Alright … see you then. Bye." Natalya said.

I rushed back to the bathroom and quickly jumped into the shower.

How could she do this to me? I thought that she was my friend?

The hot water poured over my black and blue body. Steam engulfed the entire bathroom. I lost track of the time, but it didn't matter… My mind just couldn't grasp the fact that Natalya was betraying me.

Did I do something to upset her? Or maybe she never truly was my friend? I had to do something, but for now I was going to pretend I hadn't heard anything. I will pretend that nothing between us has changed. Yes that's what I will do.

I sunk to the bottom of the tub and relaxed my back into the curve of it. I began to drift off to sleep when there came a soft tap on the door.

"Alex, are you okay? You've been in there like an hour-and-a-half," Natalya questioned, concern in her voice.

A huff of air escaped my lungs, "I'm fine. I was just getting ready to get out."

"Alright … but if there's anything that you need just let me know, okay?"

"Will do," I mumbled. The water had begun to cool down by now anyhow. I pulled myself from the tub and wrapped a towel around myself while wiping off the mirror. I wanted to give my bruises one last look. Shock consumed me, all of my bruises were gone.

That can't be right! I had seen them, hadn't I?

Confusion flooded my brain. Maybe I'd imagined the whole thing. Maybe I truly didn't hear Natalya betray me. I was so confused. I shook my head and decided to forget the whole thing.

It was all just a hallucination from the hot steam of the shower. Yes that's what it was nothing more.

Pulling my wet hair into a loose ponytail, I opened the door to find Natalya standing right next to the door. It startled me.

“You nearly gave me a heart attack, Nat!” I exclaimed, trying to catch my breath.

“You have a phone call,” She said flatly, pointing in the direction of the phone as it lay upon the table.

Who would be calling me?

She answered as if she could read my mind.

“It’s Eros.”

He will be a nice distraction from that disturbing hallucination.

A smile spread across my face, “Oh!” My excitement could be heard through my nervous cracking voice, “Hi.”

“Hi … I am sorry but … I’m going to have to cancel tonight.” His voice seemed to have anger in every word.

Or was that hate burning in every word?

“Okay, but …”

“Don’t worry …” A laugh escaped his lips. “We’ll still hang out, there’s just a pressing matter I must attend to. But I’ll call you soon to reschedule, alright?”

“Okay …” Disappointment dripped from my voice.

“I’ll call you. Okay?”

“Whatever,” I said, making doubly sure he could hear the disappointment in my voice this time.

“I’ll talk with you soon. Have a good night.”

There goes my distraction.

"Whatever," I whispered, hanging the phone up, and not allowing him to say anything further.

Seeing the anger and hurt in my eyes Natalya walked to my side and placed her arms around my shoulders. I shrugged them off and flopped onto the couch. I laid there for a moment and decided to go for a walk.

I can't stay in this house any longer.

"I'm going for a walk," I mumbled as I headed for the door, only to be halted by Natalya stepping into my path. "What are you doing!?" I said as I clenched my teeth tightly together.

Natalya bit her lower lip. "Do you really think you should be going out in a state like this?"

Hate began to build up inside me.

How dare she talk to me like that.

"You have no say in what I do!"

I shoved her aside, causing her to fall to the ground as I slammed the door.

Anger burned inside me. In my 20 years I hadn't known I was capable of such, such emotions.

RAGE! ANGER! HATE!

But that realization wasn't the worst part. No, the worst part was that I could feel it burning and growing more and more inside me – as if it were giving me strength. I ran, not knowing where I was going and not caring. I only thrived upon the hate that swelled inside me. Suddenly I stopped as a great pain coursed over my body.

I held my breath, trying to will the pain away. My face turned red hot as I further deprived my lungs of air, but it didn't seem to make a difference. As the pain increased, so did my anger, which only made the pain that much greater. The pain and anger fed on one another, and the revelation of their co-existence inside of me was discomforting. I looked at my surroundings, trying to force my mind away from the anger. There were trees everywhere as I crumpled to the ground. Waves of pain surged over me again, covering my entire body. I looked at my hands and it seemed as if my bones began shifting and enlarging. The skin upon the back of my hands began to tear open exposing dark black flesh. My breathing became heavy and beast-like.

"What's happening to me?!?!" I screamed – agony in my voice as the pain consumed me. I saw someone rushing to my side faster than humanly possible, and my vision blurred into darkness.

* * *

When I woke up, I didn't recognize the room in which I was laying. I scanned my surroundings, hoping there might be at least one thing I could recognize, but there was nothing. Everything was in perfect order in the white room, from the curtains to the floor nothing was out of place. There was a peaceful presence that filled the air, and the scent that enveloped the room somehow reminded me of Gabriel. It was intoxicating. I closed my eyes, wanting to further embrace the smell, and snuggled back into my pillow. I pulled the soft blankets up to my neck when I heard a quiet knock on the door.

Not wanting to answer, I rolled to my side, hoping that whoever it was would leave. Instead I heard the door open. The intoxicating fragrance immediately increased tenfold. I listened for the footsteps across the floor and heard none. Suddenly there was a gentle touch upon my hand. Softly, whoever had come into the room unwrapped my hands – I'd been concentrating on the room so much that I hadn't even noticed that my hands had been wrapped with tight cloth. Whoever it was, their touch was so soft that I assumed it was a nurse and I was in some sort of hospital. Softly the person brushed the hair from my face and sat in the chair in the corner of the room. I wanted to open eyes but I became overcome with peacefulness that filled the room and eased me back to sleep.

*   *   *

My eyes fluttered open as I stretched – arching my back. Almost immediately I noticed someone sitting in the corner of the room. I turned, prepared for anyone other than the person that I saw.

Gabriel.

My heart began pounding faster and faster as he intently stared at me. The pain began to course over my body once again when I heard a familiar voice.

"Calm down, everything is going to be fine – but you must remain calm."

Hearing the soothing, familiar voice should have calmed me down, but it only further unnerved me, for it was the same voice I heard that day in class.

Pain swelled inside my body when Raphael rushed into the room. "Alex! Calm down, everything is alright! Just calm down."

I looked around him to the corner where Gabriel was sitting, only to find that he had disappeared. "Wha …Where did …wasn't …" I was so distraught that I couldn't even speak.

Raphael looked in the direction in which I was staring. As my confusion grew, the pain slowly subsided.

"Good … just remain calm. You're doing great." Raphael said as he gently moved his hand to my cheek, as though he was checking my temp. I looked into Raphael's kind, patient eyes. "Are you feeling better?" He asked as he touched my shoulder. It almost felt as if he was sending some sort of signal through my body, causing me to feel more at peace than I'd felt in years.

I shook my head, "Yes …" I paused, wanting to ask him where I was, but didn't know how to go about it.

"So you're probably wondering where you are." His kind eyes only further soothed my worries. "You're at our place."

"Who's?"

"Mine. Gabriel's. Michael's. … And the others."

My heart nearly skipped a beat at the mention of Gabriel's name

*It **was** him!*

"Really!?" I said, unable to contain my curiosity.

Raphael laughed and continued, "Yes really …" And as if he knew my every thought, he answered my next question. "Yesterday afternoon Gabriel came across you in the trees just along the edge of our property line. He saw the pain in your eyes and … and well now you're here." He flashed his pearly whites and gave me a wink.

As he began to walk from the room I prompted another question. "Raphael?"

"Yes?' He said, keeping his body toward the door and looking over his shoulder.

A nervous breath escaped my lips, "Do you know what's happening to me?"

He came back to my side, touched my shoulder and continued, "I wish I could tell you more but I can't. To be honest I'm not entirely sure myself. I mean I'm a hund- …" Raphael halted his explanation in mid-sentence and turned to the door where Gabriel was now standing.

"Where did he come from?" I questioned.

His beautiful face seemed to say so much without saying a word, and as if Raphael knew what Gabriel was saying he nodded his head. "Anyway, we had better be getting you back home. Come on, I'll take you."

"Alright, but can we pick up something to eat? I'm starving!"

Raphael smiled and a chuckle escaped his lips, "Yes we can."

"Good cause I feel as if I haven't eating in weeks."

We stopped to get a hamburger, which I inhaled, barely leaving enough time to breathe. Raphael stared at me with wide eyes. I wiped my mouth with the back of my hand, "What?" I questioned, furrowing my eyebrows.

He shook his head and blinked his eyes, "I don't think I've ever seen anyone eat quite like that."

I moved my gaze to the ground as my face began to warm, "I'm sorry, it just …" My voice lowered all the further. "I couldn't help myself. The meat was just so perfectly cooked." A sigh of ecstasy escaped my lips and my mouth began to water as I thought of the meat.

"Really? 'Cause mine was undercooked." His face wrinkled in disgust. "Extremely undercooked." He lifted his burger to show me, revealing the nearly raw meat.

I began to salivate as I stared mindlessly at the meat.

"You gonna eat that?"

Raphael began to hand the hamburger to me. As he started to say something else I almost took off his hand as I ravenously grabbed the hamburger – inhaling it mere moments after taking it from him. Raphael didn't say so much as a word, he just calmly acted as if the way I was reacting was a normal thing.

After we left the restaurant, Raphael walked me to the apartment and up to the door. When I made an off-hand comment about him being a gentleman, he said, "I know I don't have too, but I want to."

Natalya flung open the door before I could even place my key in the lock and roughly locked her arms around me.

"Where have you been? I've been so worried," she demanded, crushing my head into her shoulder. "You've been gone for like 36 hours! I called the police a few times but all they said is, 'She has to be missing for 48 hours before we can do anything.' And they were quite rude about it, too! I mean, it's not like I did anything wrong – I was just a concerned citizen. So what if I call 24 or more times?"

What?

"You called how many times?"

"I don't know … 24 … maybe 48 … I kind of lost count." Her voice wavered for a moment before rushing on. "Anyway none of that matters now that you're home." She tightened her kung-fu like grip on my neck.

My face began to turn red at the lack of oxygen. Raphael stepped closer and placed his hand upon Natalya's shoulder. "I think you're choking her," he said with one eyebrow cocked.

"Oh, sorry …" she mumbled as she pushed me from her arms.

I gasped for air as Raphael gave me a quick once-over, and then with a courteous nod he turned away. Just before leaving, he turned back to me and with a sweet calming smile he questioned, "See you at school tomorrow, right?"

"Yes, I'll be there," I said as my cheeks flushed pink.

A chuckle whispered through his lips. "Good," was all he said. "Oh, and Natalya I'm sorry that I didn't give you a call and let you know that Alex was alright. I should have."

Nat's cheeks blushed a faint pink, "Oh, it's okay," She mumbled.

Then, with one last breathtaking smile, he softly closed the door behind him.

A shiver rushed up my spine as I watched him leave through the open curtain. Natalya just stood dumbstruck in front of the door. I took in a deep breath, "So what do you want to do today?"

"No, you totally can't do that," She said shaking her head.

"Do what?" I questioned.

"You've been gone for more than 36 hours and then when you do you're with the hottest guys on…I mean one of the hottest guys on campus?!?!? What happened!?!?"

Flashbacks of the horrifying transformation of my hand and the excruciating pain flooded my mind, followed closely by the phone conversation that Nat had had the other day.

A pulse of pain vibrated over me as the feelings of betrayal once again consumed my thoughts.

No I can't think about that, not now stick to the plan of forcing the hallucination of her betrayal from my thoughts. Good. Now what do I tell her?

I took in a deep breath, relaxing my heartbeat.

"Not much, really. I was walking for hours when I became faint – you know … because I hadn't eaten– and just before passing out I saw Raphael walking toward me to assist."

My stomach turned with every additional lie, but my heart stayed the same as if it just came naturally to me. I continued, digging myself further and further into a black pit of deception. "When I came to I was in a hospital bed. The doctor decided that he wanted to keep me overnight for observations, and now here I am." I bit my lip and held my breath, waiting for Natalya's reaction.

"Oh … well I'm glad that you're okay. Did the doctor give you any medication to take?"

"No."

"So why did you have Raphael drive you home and not me? 'Cause I would have. You know that right?"

A smile spread across my face. This lie was going to be easy, and yet my stomach still seemed to be twisted in guilty knots. "I know you would have, but have you seen Raphael?"

"Yes …" Her words were drawn out slightly and she seemed as if she where daydreaming. "No more explanation required." Her eyes seemed to light up when anyone spoke about Raphael.

I sauntered over to the couch and plopped upon it with a sigh.

Natalya sheepishly made her way to the couch, "So what's he like?" She shyly bit her bottom lip and continued, "Raphael, I mean."

"I don't know – he's just a nice, cute guy. What more is there to know?"

A large smile worked its way across her lips. “Yes …” she murmured.

I hesitantly smiled at her.

It was just a hallucination. Just a hallucination.

“Natalya I didn’t know you felt this way about Raphael,” I said, trying to make the excitement swelling in my voice.

Natalya’s grin faded. “I don’t know what you’re talking about?” She nervously squeaked.

A spiteful burst of laughter escaped through my lips as I tried to maintain the appearance that there was nothing wrong, “I’m sorry … but … you’re … not very good at lying.”

“I have no idea what you’re talking about,” she said with a huff, but then, unable to contain her laughter, she exploded into a fit of giggles. “It’s not fair … you … know me … too … too well.” Her high pitched laugh; somewhat like an animal squeal which caused all the spite in my laugh to disappear as I began to truly laugh with Natalya rolling around beside me.

After laughing so hard that it caused us to slide from the couch to the hard floor, we laid there trying to catch our breath. My body seemed so worn out. My cheeks hurt from laughing so hard – I couldn’t remember the last time I had laughed like that.

“I think I need a nap after that,” I said with another little chuckle.

“Me too …” Natalya said, stifling a giggle. “You think we could take a short nap and then figure out what we wanted to do today?”

“Yes …” I mumbled as I pulled myself upon the couch and stretched back into the cushions.

“Aren’t you going to pull your bed out?” She questioned.

I shook my head and rolled further into the full cushions.

CHAPTER FOUR

BLUE

Early the next morning I did something I hadn't had the nerve to do since the night of the accident.

I went to the hospital.

Though I'd considered checking on the woman from the car a couple of times before, I just couldn't seem to find the courage to face the implications of what saving her might mean. But I had to know if she was okay.

I made my way to the hospital doors. Nervously I walked through the hospital halls. The smell of disinfectant overwhelmed me, making my head swim and contributing to the churning of my stomach. I decided the only way to get over the sickening feeling was to not think about it.

That's not working.

I started holding my breath, pausing only long enough to stop and ask for directions.

Okay how am I going to do this?

I needed to ask her, but I didn't want to take in the deep breath necessary to ask the question – for fear that I might lose my lunch, which was not sitting well in the first place. I closed my eyes, prepared to ask my question and, hopefully, contain the contents of my stomach.

"Can I help you?" The nurse asked condescendingly

"I um … I was just …" No matter what I did, I couldn't get any words to form. As I stuttered on, the nurse's grimace turned into a soft sweet smile. Then someone placed a hand gently upon my shoulder.

I whirled around, prepared to release my pinned up nervous energy as the person caught my arm in a firm – and strangely hot – hand. The look on my face must have been pure murder because the first thing Eros said was, "I figured you were still upset with me, but I didn't think you were that upset … and you are a lot faster than you look," Eros ran his hand down the remainder of my arm and interlaced his fingers with mine.

"I … I … I didn't know it was you …" My gaze fell to the ground, embarrassed by my thoughts. I could feel my cheeks beginning to flush pink as his hand lifted my gaze.

"You are fine … come on," he said as he began to lead me further down the hall.

I remained silent as he led me to an elevator and pressed the button to take us to the top floor.

Where are we going?

The elevator dinged a moment later, and without a word Eros led me out of the elevator and further down the hall, his jaw tightening as he stopped in front of a room.

"What is he doing, he does know who's beyond that door."

I looked around to see where the angry woman's voice was coming from, but there was no one around only a strong citrusy scent that filled the air around us.

"It seems that he has lost his way."

The hair upon my neck began to stand on ends as the citrusy scent increased and malice consumed the voice as it continued.

"…and this girl is the source of his downfall."

Maybe the voice is coming from the other side of that door?

Curiously I stared at the door, Eros let go of my hand and nudged me ever so slightly toward the door. I stepped back, not knowing what I was being led to.

"It's alright …" He reassured me, running his hand though my hair and nodded me towards the door.

"… aren't you coming with me?" My words pleaded with him, not wanting to enter the room alone.

"No … I think it would be best if I waited out here for you."

"... but I don't ..."

"Alex, just go ... trust me, everything is going to be fine." He nodded his head in the direction of the door once again only more insistently this time.

Once more I took in a deep breath and slowly opened the door. The deep breath was a mistake because the smell – which had a moment before been masked by the cinnamony scent of Eros and the strange citrusy smell– returned in all its ugliness and my vision became blurry, making it difficult to see where I was going. I staggered into the room as if I were drunk, and just before falling to the floor strong arms grasped me, keeping me from plummeting to the ground. A different scent enveloped me as I tried to make sense of what was going on.

"Are you alright?" A strong voice asked.

"Yes, I'm fine ... just got a little dizzy ... that's all." I closed my eyes and let out a slow, steady breath.

"Here, sit down," The voice said, leading me to a chair.

I slowly opened my eyes to a handsome gentleman with light blond hair and soft blue eyes.

"So, are you feeling better now?" He questioned as he handed me a tall glass of water.

"Yes ... thank you," I replied politely as a soft smile spread across my face.

Suddenly the door flung open and two children rushed through the door. In a matter of seconds they tightly wrapped their arms around me.

Shock flooded me.

Who are these kids and why are they hugging me?

My eyes plead with the gentleman before me, but before he could say anything the children looked up at me and images of the accident raced through my mind. They were the woman's children. But who was the handsome man before me? Absently, I wrapped my arms around the kids, returning their hugs.

"So, are you guys doing better?" I asked, looking down at the two entangling me in their arms.

"We are good and mom is doing much better!" They chimed, one right after the other almost as if they had heard me at different times.

The handsome young man stepped forward and stretched his arm out in front of himself. "I am Derrick. It's nice to finally meet the woman who saved my wife's life."

I flushed a deep red as I shook his strong hand, "It really was nothing … I mean anyone would have done the same thing if they had been the one to come up on the accident as I did."

A crooked smile creeped onto his chiseled face, “Maybe so,” he said, “but it was not just anyone – it was you and I am eternally grateful.” He pulled my hand up to his lips and sweetly kissed it.

“Derrick …” A soft voice whispered.

He released my hand and made his way to the hospital bed. “Yes, my love?”

“Will you … bring her to … me?” Her words were hushed, as if she wasn’t getting enough air into her lungs.

“Yes,” He said, turning back toward me. Then, walking over to me, he held out his hand. “My wife would like to see the face of the woman who helped save her life.”

My heart began to pound.

I wonder what she might say.

I placed my hand in his. Slowly we made our way to her bedside. This was the first time that I had seen someone that I had save after the actual day of the accident.

A soft smile laid upon her face as I walked toward her. She was moderately beautiful with nearly black hair and dark brown eyes. “How can I ever … ever repay you for what … what you have done … for me … and my family?” Her breaths seemed to come in short gasps as she spoke.

“There is no need,” I started to say, fumbling for words. “I wanted to help … and I wouldn’t have had it any other way.”

"I know you … you wouldn't h-have, but it still … doesn't ch-change the fact th-that I would like t-to repay you f-for your …kindness. But I know … that God will … g-greatly bless you f-for what y-you have d-done. And f-for future re-reference I … am Isa … Isabella …" She held her weak hand out in front of her, the pale-white fingers hovering just above her heart.

"Nice to meet you Isabella, I'm Alex," I said as I gently placed my hand in hers and softly shook her hand.

She's so weak.

Her eyes began to close, her smile fading, and the doctor entered the room, "I think it's time for her to rest," he stated as he began to take her vitals.

We began to exit the room when the doctor grasped my hand. Turning around he handed me a piece of paper, "This is from the young gentleman that was waiting in the hall for you."

"Oh, thank you." I'd almost forgotten Eros was even here.

"My dearest Alex, I regretfully had to take my leave ... something came up, but I will talk with you later. Eros"

Disappointment consumed me as I read the note.

Derrick gently placed his hand upon my shoulder. "Are you alright Alex?"

"Yes, I'm fine. Just a little disappointed with my … well, I'm really not sure what he is to me, but I wanted to get to know him a little better. I guess we can talk another time because he had to leave …"

Derrick smiled. "Well his loss is my gain," he said. "Would you like to join me for a cup of coffee?" He raised his eyebrows and widened his eyes, causing me to smile. I couldn't help myself from nodding.

"Sure. That sounds nice."

Down in the cafeteria, Dartanian placed a cup of coffee in front of me. "Cream and sugar?" He questioned.

I shook my head, "Just cream."

He nodded his head, grasped a handful of cream-filled cups and handed them to me.

"Thanks … so how bad are her injuries? ... I mean, I know she's doing better but how extensive are they?"

His eyes filled with pain.

"Well, the tree that fell upon our vehicle as you know crashed through the car – one straight through her shoulder and the other through her side which punctured her lung. It's a miracle that you arrived when you did. The doctors said that if you hadn't been there when you were and did what you did she would have been dead." He grasped my hand and gave it a squeeze. "But she is in a lot of pain. It rips my heart out every time I see her wince in agony." A tear touched the corner of his eye.

A flash of his wife wincing in pain as I tried to free her from the car flashed through my mind, along with the visions of Raphael working on the young girl. I glanced over at her – specifically the place on her head where she should have had stiches – but all that I saw was a tiny scar, as if it had happened months ago rather than days. And that is when it came to me without thinking.

"What if you had my friend examine her?"

A soft smile crept upon his face.

"I would welcome any help you might be able to give."

I took a deep breath and continued. "His name is Raphael and he goes to my college. He is a very good friend and I am sure he will help in any way possible. And I know it will help for him to examine her because … well this is going to sound crazy but I think he had healing powers or something cause …" I looked up at Derrick's face to find a huge smile upon his face that stretched from one side to the other.

"What?" I demanded, interrupting my praise of Raphael's abilities.

"You're friends with Raphael and Gabriel?" he asked.

"Well ye- … wait, how do you know Raphael? And I never mentioned Gabriel!"

"Let's just say that we go way back. And I think you're right, it will help to have Raphael examine her. And it will be nice to see the guys again – it's been years since I have even spoken with them. Thank you for bringing him up … you're a very surprising woman, you know that Alex? Very surprising indeed. But there is still one thing that I have been wondering."

"And what's that?" I asked.

"How did you come upon the accident?"

I began to absently stir the cream into my now lukewarm coffee with the thin black straw Derrick had given me. "I'm really not sure … I remember smelling something. I was following its scent when I came upon the accident."

"I see …" he said as he shook his head. "Well, my children and I are in debt to you." He gave his children a glance, both of whom were sitting a few tables over blowing the paper from their straws at each other.

I smiled. "They're really sweet kids," I said as I watched them playing.

"Thank you."

"So how old are they?"

"Well, Jordan is seven years old and Annabel is five." His face seemed to light up when he talked about them.

"So where did Annabel get her red curly hair? Your side or Isabella's?"

"Neither. Annabel is adopted. We cannot have girls," he said, looking down at the ground in disappointment.

"Oh, so your wife is unable to have any more children … I'm sorry …"

"No, she can have more children, but she really wanted a girl and I am unable to give her that."

Confusion consumed me as I stared at his downcast face. "What? I don't understand. So you're the one unable to have any more children?"

Derrick stared at the table as if he were wondering how to word what he was going to say. "I can have more children … however I cannot … produce girls."

I stared at him with confusion.

"The look upon your face tells me how confused you are. Okay let me try to make my explanation easier …"

Before he could finish, we were interrupted by the soft clearing of someone's throat. A gentle smell of white chocolate enveloped me as I turned around to find Raphael standing beside me.

"Raphael! Where did you come from?"

"I was taking a coffee break. What are you doing here?" Raphael asked me.

"I came to see how Isabella was doing."

A smile spread across Raphael's face as he noticed who I was sitting with. "Derrick," he said warmly, extending a hand, "it's been years since I've seen you. And the kids are yours?"

Years? That can't be right. Raphael isn't any older than me, right?

I shook off the strange thought as I watched Derrick stand up and shake Raphael's hand. His eyebrows were raised and a chuckle escaped his lips as he nodded to his children. "Yes, they are my little angels."

A large grin spread over Raphael's face, but quickly faded, "And what of Isabella?"

Derrick glanced at me and smiled, "She's alive … and I have this beautiful woman to thank for that."

"She's an amazing woman …" Raphael wrapped his arm around my shoulder. "And there is a whole lot more to her than meets the eye."

Derrick nodded his head, "I do believe you're right."

I could feel my cheeks flush a deep read.

"Raphael, I was wondering if you could examine Isabella?" I asked, eager to change the subject. "I really think it might help with her pain."

"And why do you think that?"

I took in a deep breath as flashes of the aftermath of the accident ran through my mind. "… Because I remember when you were working on Annabel … it was as if she couldn't even feel you working on her. So I don't know I just … well … it couldn't hurt, could it?"

"You're right, it couldn't hurt for me to take a look at Isabe-"

Before he could finish, a red light began flashing and the chilling words, "Code Blue" began to be repeated over the loud speaker. "Code Blue! All available personnel to the third floor."

Chills ran down my back and fear grabbed me. I looked over at Raphael and Derrick.

"I'm sorry. I have to go," Raphael said.

"You don't think it's Isabe-" I began.

"No," Derrick interrupted. "It's not her."

"Are you sure?" I asked.

"I'm sure … it's alright, Alex. She may be weak, but she is stable. There's nothing to worry about."

"Okay …" I mumbled, still nervous about the Code Blue.

Raphael gave Derrick a firm hand shake that led to a one-armed hug. Then he wrapped his arms around me tightly and said, "I'll see you at school tomorrow, right?"

I rolled my eyes, "Where else would I be?"

A crooked smile worked its way onto his face. “Okay, see you then,” he said. Just before Raphael left the room Derrick ran to his side and began to whisper something to him. Raphael shook his head a look of fear in his eyes.

What are they talking about?

“Are you sure that they are after her?” Derrick questioned.

“Pretty sure.”

“But, why?”

“Not sure, but it should be alright. Gabriel keeps a pretty good eye upon her.” Raphael looked up at the flashing lights. “I’m sorry Derrick but I’m going to have to talk with you at a later time, I really need to head to the third floor.”

“Of course,” Derrick stated as he gave Raphael one last hug. “And if you need my help once they make their move let me know.”

“Alright, I’ll talk with you later.” Raphael patted Derrick upon the shoulder, “I’ll see you at school, Alex.” He said as he left the room.

Who were they talking about?

Annabel walked up behind Derrick and tugged upon his shirt. “I’m tired daddy,” she mumbled as he picked her up, and she tightly wrapped her arms around his neck.

“I’m going to have to be getting these two in bed,” he said as he walked to my side and I glanced over at the clock, “It was great meeting you and I hope to see you again soon." Turning away from me he called out to his son. "Come on Jordan, it's time to head home."

Annabel leaned over and gave me an awkward hug from her dad's arms, followed shortly by a tight squeeze from Jordan. I leaned over to better embrace his hug. "Thank you so much for saving my mom," he whispered as a tear rolled down his cheek.

"I'm glad that I could help," I said, trying to maintain a tough exterior.

Derrick gave me one last nod. "Thank you," he said, his words hushed as Annabel's eyes seemed to drift closed.

I slowly walked through the hospital trying desperately to find where I'd entered. Finally after about 15 minutes of aimless wondering I found it. When I walked through the exit doors I found Natalya waiting patiently for me.

"How did you know where I was?" I asked, confusion plaguing my words.

Anger pulsed over me as Natalya stared at me.

Stop Alex! It was just a hallucination because if it wasn't then...

I shook my head not wanting to think about what it would mean if she really had betrayed me.

"Raphael called me and said that he thought you might need a ride."

A smile worked its way upon my face with great difficulty, "Oh, Nat –What would I do without you?"

"I don't know," she replied with a smile in her voice, and when I look up there was an ornery look shining in her eyes as she opened the door. "I got something for you … just call it an early Birthday present."

In the front seat of the car was a small box. I picked it up and set it on my lap as Natalya made her way to the driver's side.

"Aren't you going to open it?" her bottom lip began to quiver ever so slightly as if she were going to cry.

"… but it's not my Birthday yet" I said as I tightly clenched my hand into a fist.

"I know, but I just couldn't wait. Please open it … it would mean the world to me if you would."

She raised her eyebrows in question as her bottom lip quivered all the more.

"Alright. I'll open it," I said, I let out a slow steady breath as I tore open the wrapping paper to reveal a ring box. "Um … what is this?"

"Just open it up and see," excitement beamed with her every word.

Reluctantly I opened the box uncovering a ring with the word "Friends" on it. I looked up at Natalya, "Thanks Nat … it's great."

"It's a thumb ring … and look," she said as she shoved her hand toward me, "I have the other one … See! They're a match. Mine says, 'best' and yours says, 'friends.' Do you get it? Best friends!" She really seemed sincere in her word as she spoke them.

"I get it … and thank you," I said as I placed the ring upon my thumb and held up my hand for her to see.

"So are you ready to head home?" She questioned.

"Yes, I'm ready … it's been a long day."

Natalya nodded and started the car.

On the drive home I silently stared out my window and watched the trees pass by. The peaceful monotony of it made me tired, but just before my eyes began to close a bright almost neon blue caught my eye, pushing all of my sleepiness away. I scanned the horizon, hoping to catch another glimpse of the beautiful blue, but no matter how hard I looked I couldn't see it anywhere. Lightning streaked across the sky, lighting the ground below. Natalya pulled into our parking lot as I continued scanning the surrounding trees.

"Alex … aren't you coming in?" She asked as she nudged me in the shoulder.

"Yes … I'm sorry …" I began to get out of the car. "I just … I thought I saw something …"

"Oh. Well … what did you see?"

"I'm really not sure –" I began, and then I caught site of it again. Excitement swelled inside me. "There!" I whispered, excitedly pointing my hand in the direction of the two beautiful lights. "That's what I saw! What do you think it is?"

Hopping out of the car, I quickly started to walk toward the lights. After only a couple of steps, however, Natalya grabbed my arm.

"It's probably nothing," she said. "Just … just some kids messing with flashlights."

"No it can't be that," I said. "I mean – just look at the color. It's almost hypnotic …"

I pulled my hand from hers and began to walk toward the lights once more. And then suddenly they disappeared.

"Huh …they're gone … what do you think they were?"

Natalya didn't answer, and after a moment of searching the trees some more I finally gave it up and turned toward the stairs to our apartment. Halfway up to the door a thought dawned on me.

"I got it!!" I shouted.

Natalya grabbed my arm and placed her finger to her lips as she tugged me through the door, hushing me on the way. "You got what?' She asked as she quietly closed the door behind us.

"They were eyes!" I said, a large grin stretching across my face.

Natalya rolled her eyes, "No, Alex they weren't eyes …"

"Yes they were I …"

Natalya walked over to the counter and dug through one of the drawers. Walking back to my side she placed a small flashlight in my hand, "No, Alex they weren't."

I pressed the button on the bottom of the light. A neon blue light flashed in my eyes nearly blinding me. "Oh …" I murmured as I walked over to my couch and began tossing the cushions onto the floor.

Lying in bed I continued to think about the blue lights.

I know that they were the same color as the flashlight, but I can't help it I know they were eyes, but if I'm right and they are eyes then what kind of beast would they belong to?

My thoughts wondered from the blue eyed beast to myself and my hands tearing open to reveal black flesh. I rubbed the back of my hands where it had torn open, there wasn't even a scar left; just a memory of the horrific pain.

What if I am like that beast? Would I be good? Or would I be evil?

CHAPTER FIVE

VOICES

Once again the dream came. Pain seized my body as I raced toward the temple. I crumpled to the ground as my breathing became shallow, and then I heard a familiar voice. I peeled open my eyes to find Raphael his sweet white chocolate scent enveloping me as he stood before me.

"Alex. It's alright," he said. "Alex! Hurry! We must get to the temple – it has begun."

He turned and began to transform before my eyes, but into what?! His body began to pulse and enlarge as the bones in his arms tore through his flesh revealing large clawed paws. Pain consumed his posture as the bones in his back jig-sawed, his shirt ripped from his enlarging back and before his transformation was complete he motioned for me to follow him, without turning to face me, and let out wail of pain as he disappeared behind the cover of the hills.

"Wait!" I thought as I ran after him. "Don't leave me here by myself."

Pain ravenously vibrated over me, but I had to catch up with Raphael. More quickly than should have been humanly possible, I found myself at the city with the temple. Standing in front was Raphael, back in his human form and a finger on his lips.

"We must blend in now," he said. "Transform back into your human form."

* * *

Panic caused me to wake up in an instant.

Human form? What did he mean, human form?

I looked down at my hands and let out a sigh of relief.

Transformed? What was I thinking?

I hadn't transformed into anything, it was just a dream. Yet it felt so real.

I continued to mull over my dream when I realized that Natalya was standing up against the wall, her eyes wider with fear.

What's wrong with her?

"Are you okay Natalya?" I leaned towards, but she pulled away, as if she were scared of me. "Did I do something wrong?"

Natalya shook her head, "No, I thought I saw your eyes turn re … nevermind me ... just thinking too much, that's all. Are you okay? I got up to go to the rest room and it looked as if you were having a nightmare."

"I'm fine. It was nothing. Just a bad dream. Nothing to worry about." I looked over at the clock, which said 3:30AM. "I think I'm going to get some more sleep before classes in the morning."

"Yes … I should too … See you in the morning." Natalya quickly turned and left the room, disappearing into the darkness.

I laid in bed for awhile, thinking about the dream. Just before falling asleep I heard a noise from Natalya's room. Sitting up, I dragged myself to her room to see if everything was okay. Just before knocking, I heard her phone buzz. I stopped short and put my ear to her door to listen.

"Hello?" She whispered. "Yes, she's asleep. Of course I'm sure … well – she began to transform! … No! That's the thing! It wasn't normal! … No! I've never seen anything like it before. … No …No, her eyes were re …"

I leaned closer, hoping to hear a little better. The movement caused me to stumble and I accidently bumped her door, which swung open and thumped against her wall. I stumbled further and lost my balance, tumbling onto her floor. Quickly I scrambled to my feet, expecting to be greeted by an angry glare. To my surprise, however, that she didn't even ster. Almost as though she was sleeping.

I was sure that she was talking to someone.

I tiptoed from her room as I silently closed the door behind myself.

I truly am going nuts. It's the only explanation for hearing voices.

I lay back, praying I wouldn't have the same horrifying dream again. I didn't need the stress. It took me a long time to fall back to sleep, but eventually sleep did come.

When I woke up, it was to the jolting sound of a blender. I rubbed my eyes and staggered to the kitchen, where Natalya was blending her breakfast together. Turning to me, she shut off the blender as I stared in disgust at the brownish yellow mixture. She pulled two glasses from the cabinet and filled them to the top.

"Want some?" She questioned as she shoved the cup in my face.

My stomach turned at the site of the vile brown liquid sloshing in the glass.

"What is it?" I asked, trying to contain my vomit as the nauseating smell nearly knocked me out.

Was she trying to poison me?

"It's a smoothie!" She chirped, a little too enthusiastically for this early in the morning.

My head pounded with her every word. I massaged my fingertips across my forehead. "Do you have to talk so loud? And what's with you always waking up in the morning all smiles? It's not natural." I glanced once more at the vile stuff in the glass as she placed it on the table. "What's in it?" I gagged.

"Oh nothing much – just eggs, bacon, juice, toast, sardines … You know, the usual."

I could feel my stomach acid quickly making its way up my throat.

Seeing my face turn green, she continued.

"Oh don't worry, I totally cooked everything before placing it even in the blender." A half smile spread across her face as she cocked an eyebrow. "I added a secret ingredient." She motioned for me to take a drink. "Come on – just try it." She pushed the glass a little closer to me.

She is trying to poison me.

"It's got all the things you'll need to help you ace today's test."

Test!?!

My eyes widened. "There's a test today? For what class?"

"Mr. Harman's class, he told us three times before class was over Friday."

"I never heard him say anything about a test."

Natalya shook her head, "That's because it's the class with Gabriel and Eros in it."

"Yes, but what has that got to do with anything?" She raised her eyebrows all the further as she took a big gulp of the vile matter she was trying to pass off as a smoothie. My nose wrinkled in disgust as I continued, "You're right … that's probably why I didn't hear Mr. Harman say anything about the test." I bit my lip and flashes of Gabriel flooded my mind. "My mind becomes mush with Gabriel anywhere close."

Natalya nodded her head once again. "Well, drink this … it'll help." Her eyes seemed to sparkle with anticipation.

Well I guess it can't hurt, right? After all if she is drinking it that means that it can't be poisoned, right?

I took in a deep breath. "As long as it doesn't kill me." I whispered as I reluctantly grabbed the glass off the table. "Well, here goes nothing." I tried not to breathe as I placed the full glass to my lips. It was worse than I thought. I tried to make myself swallow, but it was not easy. I swallowed with all my might, but it still seemed to go down like a cheese grater upon my throat. I placed my hand over my mouth as it tried to work its way back up.

A larger than normal smile spread across Natalya's face, "So do you like it?" Her eyes were so full of hope.

I took a drink of water and swished it around in my mouth a few times, "So what's the secret ingredient?" I said, trying to keep my mind off the horrifying texture of the smoothie. I shook my head, trying to push the terrible drink from my mind as Natalya walked to the trash.

"It was some sort of French delicacy." She pulled a jar from it and attempted to pronounce the name. "It's … cavieary … yes that's what it says. Cavieary."

She handed the jar to me. Horror flooded my being. "It's not cavieary, it's caviar."

"Oh, so what's caviar?" She questioned as she stared intensively at me.

"It's … well it's … caviar is …" There was no delicate way of putting this – and she had nearly drank the entire glass. "It's fish eggs." I mumbled under my breath.

"What?! I didn't catch that." She said as she finished off the last few swallows of her smoothie.

My mouth dropped open.

"So what is it?" She inquired as she closed my mouth with her finger.

"It's … it's …" I truly dreaded telling her.

I can do this.

I took in a deep breath to build my confidence. "It's fish eggs," I mumbled once again.

"You know, Alex, you really need to learn to speak up, cause all I heard was something that sounded like fish eggs and I know that, that can't be right."

I looked at her with a sheepish grin. "That is what I said."

"WHAT!?" She screamed. "AND YOU JUST LET ME DRINK THAT VILE MATTER?!"

"What would you have had me do? Tear the glass from your hands?"

"Uh, yes …"

I could see it in her eyes. She was going to make this into a big thing. I held up my hand and pointed to the clock on the wall. "I have got to get ready for class because if I don't get ready now then I'm going to be late." I turned and walked toward the bathroom. Just before entering I turned to Natalya. "I should have told you sooner," I said, "but I didn't. I'm sorry …" And with that I closed the bathroom door.

I took a shower and after putting on my jeans and a long sleeved, striped shirt I quickly ran a brush through my hair, grabbed my bag from the living room floor and raced downstairs to where Natalya waited in her junky maroon car.

The car made a strange clunking noise as we made our way to campus. When we arrived, Natalya pulled into a parking spot and standing in front was Raphael.

A large smile spread across my face as Natalya's seemed to flush pink. "What are you doing here?" I asked as I stepped from the clunker of a car.

"Hey …" His smile made my heart jump. He truly looked happy to see me. It was nice having more than just one friend. "I told you I would see you at school. Anyway, come on I'll walk you girls to class." He motioned with a nod of his head.

I walked to his side with Natalya trailing behind.

Raphael slipped his arm around my shoulders, "Man you smell nice, real nice."

"Thanks …" I said glancing over my shoulder at Natalya. Her head hung as if she had just lost her best friend.

Then, almost as if Raphael knew how his actions had made her feel, he stretched his arm behind and grabbed Natalya's hand. "Come on Nat …We don't want to leave you out." His smile touched his entire face.

"Okay …" Natalya whispered, her eyes sparkling with delight.

In Mr. Harman's room Raphael pointed to *their* corner. "How about you girls come and sit beside us?" He inquired, never letting go of Natalya's hand until we were at our seats. "In fact, would you girls like to hang out after classes today?" Raphael questioned as he nervously ran his hand through his hair.

"Sure tha …" I said, my eye catching a glimpse of Gabriel in all his splendor. My words caught in my throat and my thoughts became jumbled in my mind. I turned back to Raphael, "What was that?" I asked, trying to focus on something other than Gabriel's ice blue eyes.

Raphael shook his head, "I was just wondering if you and Natalya would like to hang out after –"

Suddenly he was interrupted by a rough throat clearing – almost as if someone was growling. At the sound I saw Gabriel tense, as if preparing for a fight, and his eyes turned a chocolate brown in color. Fleetingly I wondered how his eyes could change colors so dramatically. When I turned to see who had made the noise, to my surprise it was Eros.

He flashed me a smile, revealing his ivory white teeth.

"Hi …" I stupidly smiled. I looked back awkwardly at Raphael. Who was I kidding? I had forgotten all about Eros … that is until this very moment. I looked back at Eros as my cheeks flushed pink, and I bit my lip waiting for him to say something.

He ran his hand through his black wavy hair, "So how about we hang out?" He asked as he leaned forward, his lips whispering against my ear and causing shivers to run down my spine and goosebumps to crawl up my arms. "Maybe today … after classes?" He glanced up at Raphael and Gabriel as if to taunt them.

Was it just me or was there something slightly creepy about how he said that?

Intrigued by the look he gave Raphael and Gabriel I agreed, "Sure …" I breathed.

Raphael placed his hand upon my cheek, turning my head to face him. "But you were going to hang out with Natalya and me." His eyes almost looked as if there was heartbreak in them.

"Yes, but you guys can hang out without me. We can all get together some other time, can't we?"

Raphael closed his eyes as if to calm himself, "Yes, we can all hang out another time."

"Are you okay?"

"I'm fine." He turned and looked at Gabriel, his eyes almost seemed as if they were asking for forgiveness.

"You're sure?"

"Yes, I'm sure. We will do it another time, no worries."

A smile spread across my face, "Okay …" I turned back to Eros' ebony eyes. "Sounds like a plan."

"Alright, I will meet you in front, at the main entrance."

"Okay …"

Eros placed his hand upon my cheek, “You want to come and sit with me?” He asked.

I bit my lip.

Sit with him?

I glanced back at Gabriel. Irritation seemed to consume his chiseled features, “Sure,” I mumbled in a nervous almost cracking voice.

He ran his hand down my shoulder and grasped my hand, causing chills to dance upon my skin. I turned to Natalya as my cheeks flushed pink and we walked to his side of the classroom. There were girls plaguing every seat. Eros motioned with his head and three seats opened up with a mad scramble. I had never seen such authority, and with only a nod of the head. He truly had a power over people. He even seemed to have some sort of control over the teachers. He led me to my seat and swiftly slithered into his, still holding my hand.

As we sat there, I could feel the difference in the temperature. For some reason this side of the room seemed to be at least ten degrees colder. How that was even possible I didn’t know, but it was. I began to shiver as my skin went from warm to ice cold. Eros didn’t even seem to notice the goosebumps blanketing my arms. Looking at him, I felt as if someone was staring at me. I began to examine those around me, all of whom seemed to be staring at the teacher. Then I caught a glimpse of Gabriel from the corner of my eye. I turned to him and shock flooded me. He was the one who was staring at me. Caught off guard I quickly turned away.

Why is he looking at me? And why does he seem angry?

I mulled these questions over and over in my mind and my heart began to race. Pain started to consume me once again – the familiar pain I'd come to know all too well. I bit my lip, trying to conceal it.

Then came the soft, sweet voice:

"It's alright, Alexandra. Just breathe ... everything is going to be fine."

I knew I was crazy. I should not want to be hearing voices. Yet it seemed to calm me somehow, slowing my heart rate. I took in a deep breath and sighed in relief as the pain subsided.

I tried to understand why the voice calmed me and why I would have these attacks, but none of it made any sense, After a moment I realized I was no longer holding hands with Eros. I wrapped my hands around my arms in an attempt to warm up and glanced once again at Gabriel. I couldn't help myself, but this time he didn't look angry anymore. He almost looked as if he was trying to hold back a smile, which was far better than an angry stare. I'd never seen this expression on him before. It made his already painfully handsome face seem even more irresistible than ever. A shiver of pleasure coursed down the back of my arms and a smile spread across my face as I flushed pink.

I continued to stare into Gabriel's soft blue eyes as he stared back into mine. His eyes seemed as if they were searching for something, something he was unable to find. There was a look of curiosity pooling in them, creating more questions about him to race through my mind.

We stared at each other for several minutes, when the look in his eyes changed.

What happened?

A moment later Eros wrapped his arm around my shoulders.

I turned to him, smiled, and glanced one last time at Gabriel. Anger had returned to replace the curiosity in his eyes. I quickly turned away, not wanting to see him with anger fuming in his sultry eyes. It almost pained me to see it.

I had to get him off my mind. I turned back to Eros and stared at his almost god-like tanned skin. He turned to me and smiled as he ran the back of his fingers across my cheek. A flush of heat pulsed over my body. Only a moment ago I had been cold beyond belief and now I was hot, even burning to the point of being uncomfortable. Eros pulled me closer and the look in his eyes changed from a kind one to a slightly sinister one as he traced his fingers from my shoulder to my elbow. My mind flew in a million different directions – the teacher, Gabriel, Raphael, Natalya … and mostly Eros.

There is something strange about Eros, but what I can't place my finger on it. That will change after classes are over.

To my dismay, the teacher called upon me. Unlike the two times before, this time I actually heard the question, but that didn't mean I knew the answer.

I waited a moment before speaking, hoping to hear the sweet voice once again. It almost seemed as if I had spoken to the voice asking it to give me the answer.

Sodium Chloride and Ammonium Chloride.

The voice came soft and sweet.

I belted out the answer with no hesitation, knowing it had to be right, The voice was always right.

Eros looked at me with a half-smile and nodded as if to say, "Nice …"

A large smile spread across my face, I was good and I knew it.

I felt pretty good about myself as I stared down at the test paper – proud even. Then, another voice began talking – sweet and pleasurable like the first voice, but somehow different.

"Alexandra ... why do you boast so? After all, it was not you who answered the question, was it?"

The smile on my face faded. The voice was right. I hadn't answered the question. I continued to wonder about these things as Mr. Harman dismissed the class.

Eros stood up and motioned for me to follow him. "Come on, I'll walk you to your next class."

I stood up, still a little shaken about having heard a new voice in my head. Eros smoothly slipped his hand around my shoulders and pulled me to his side. I couldn't help but smile. I took in a deep breath, enveloped by Eros' sweet hot smell. How a man could smell so appealing was more than I could comprehend. It was unimaginable.

A girl stepped up beside Eros and cleared her throat. I'd seen her before hanging out with Eros and his groupies, but she never really seemed to fit in – almost as if she didn't want to be with them. "Alex, this is Chrystal. She asked me to introduce you to her."

She bit her lip. "I'm in Advanced Physics class, with Professor Peterson?" Her voice was so quiet and timid that I strained to pick up her voice through the scuffle of the students.

"Nice to meet you, Chrystal," I said as I pushed my hand around Eros to shake hers. She shyly moved her hand toward mine, and to my surprise she firmly shook my hand.

There's more to this girl than met the eye.

"Alright," Eros said as he gave my hand a squeeze. "I'd better be headed to my next class." He turned and began to walk away when he stopped and wrapped his arms around me once again. He pressed his lips upon my neck, causing shivers to run down my spine, and whispered, "I'll see you after classes today." With a soft peck just behind my ear he turned and left.

That was kind-of odd.

Chrystal motioned to me, "Can I sit by you?" She softly questioned.

"Sure. Sounds good," I said as I searched the room for Raphael, who I knew was in this class. When I spotted him and waved, a smile flashed in his eyes and he motioned for me to sit beside him. I quickly walked to a vacant seat next to him.

To his left sat Michael, I slipped into the chair beside Raphael, not wanting to get the attention of Michael. He always seemed to have an almost angry look upon his face, though why I had no idea. I turned to Chrystal, who was still standing at the front of the class, and motioned for her to come over.

She stared at me hesitantly. I furrowed my eyebrows and motioned for her to come over once again. She took a deep breath, almost as if she had to build her courage, before coming over.

Chrystal shyly slid into the seat next to me and slouched down as if she were trying to become a part of it.

I smiled.

“This is Chrystal,” I said, introducing her to Raphael.

Raphael looked at me as if he were disappointed

Why is he disappointed?

Before I could dwell on it, the moment passed and a second later he had politely taken Chrystal’s hand.

“I’m Raphael.”

“Nice to meet you,” Chrystal said.

Raphael turned to Michael and nodded his head in his direction, “This is Michael.”

The anger in his eyes seemed to bubble as he gave a tight nod of the head.

Chrystal held out her hand with a small, almost sweet smile upon her face. “I’m Chrystal,” She said with a sparkle in her eye.

Michael nodded his head once again, then turned back toward the front of the class.

I leaned closer to Raphael’s “Why does Michael always look as if he is angry?” I asked, hoping to get a little more insight into why Michael was so different from Raphael.

A half smile graced Raphael’s face. “He is … well … he just has a lot of anger built up.”

I nodded my head, “Oh … but … why?”

“That is a question for another time,” Raphael replied evasively. Then, leaning closer to me, he whispered into my ear. “Don’t worry, I’ll let you in on the secret soon enough.”

“Alright …” I mouthed, curiosity coursing through my veins.

CHAPTER SIX

THE DATE

The rest of the day almost seemed to drag on – as if time were almost standing still. I never before realized how many classes I actually had with Chrystal, and now that she'd made a new friend she seemed to follow me around like a lost puppy.

I stared at the clock as time slowly ticked away. The last few minutes of the day seemed to linger on as if in an endless loop, repeating itself over and over again. Finally the professor waved his hand and dismissed class, which was the sweetest gesture I had ever seen.

I turned to Chrystal and bound from my chair, racing out the door.

Why does my last class have to be so far from the main entrance?

I tried to contain my excitement. I didn't want Eros to think that I was desperate or anything. It was all I was worth to keep my pace to a quick walk. Chrystal chattered on about class and the thesis of Plato as my heart began to pound.

Why are you getting all worked up?

A sharp pang in my chest reminded me what would happen if my heart started pounding to hard – a crippling pain and agony that overwhelmed my being. I stopped walking for a moment and staggered to the nearest wall.

Chrystal rushed to my side. "Alex, are you okay?" She questioned, concern welling in her eyes.

I clenched my teeth together, trying to absorb the agony. I looked at Chrystal, pleading with my eyes for her to help me.

She turned and searched for someone to help. While she was looking, the soft sweet voice came out of nowhere to comfort me.

"It's alright Alexandra … breathe … just breathe … everything is going to be fine. Help is on its way. Just breathe …"

There seemed to be fear and concern in the beautiful voice – a concern that I hadn't heard before. Suddenly, someone placed their hand upon my shoulder. I turned, still tightly clenching my teeth, to find Natalya.

My bones felt as if they were trying to tear through my skin and my back felt as if the flesh was being ripped from my body, leaving my bones exposed. I looked down praying that my skin wouldn't tear open revealing the black flesh from before.

Natalya placed her hand on my back. "It's alright Alex, I have it." She pulled a syringe from her pocket as she gave me a wink.

What is that?

Flashes of the other night when Natalya had used the syringe on me before raced through my mind.

"I have your medicine," she said as she plunged a syringe into my shoulder.

What is in that syringe?

Ice tore through my veins, extinguishing the pain in every corner of my body. I breathed a sigh of relief and goosebumps rose upon my skin. "Thank you …" I mumbled.

Thank God it worked.

I let out a sigh of relief as I straightened up.

"What just happened?" Chrystal questioned, not believing what she had just seen.

I looked at Natalya, curious as to what her answer would be. "It's nothing really … Alex just, just …"

Raphael came up behind her and finished her sentence. "Alex just has as illness that … plagues her body at times … nothing serious … and nothing to worry about."

"I'm just glad that I grabbed her medicine this morning," Natalya said. "I don't know what would have happened if I hadn't been here to help."

I rolled my eyes. "I know Natalya you are a saint … I don't know where I would be today if you hadn't come into my life … probably lying somewhere dead in a ditch, that's where …" I said with thick sarcasm.

"Oh stop it …" Her cheeks flushed a soft pink as she jokingly punched me in the shoulder.

Don't touch me!

Anger pulsed inside me, but quickly faded when the soothing voice spoke once again.

"Relax, Alex everything is going to be fine."

I nodded my head and let out a slow steady breath.

"Well, thanks guys. I have to go meet Eros," I said quickly, turning away to continue my trek toward the entrance of campus. Natalya, Raphael, and Chrystal all followed closely behind in silence.

At the main entrance I walked impatiently back and forth, inventing reasons why he was late. Fifteen minutes later, when he hadn't shown up, I decided that I was not going to wait any longer. I turned to Natalya, Raphael, and Chrystal. "Well, he's not showing and I'm not waiting," I said as I began to make my way to Nat's junker of a car.

Raphael's eyes filled with pain and he grabbed me by the hand, halting my escape. I turned to him as my eyes welled with tears not from hurt, but from frustration. Eros pulled me into his chest as Michael walked by, "What's wrong with her?" He angrily belted out as he walked to Raphael's side.

Anger burned inside me, but before I could tear into Michael, Raphael spoke up. "It's because of inconsiderate, thoughtless, no good jerks like Eros and you're just like him; not caring who you hurt!"

Shock flooded me at the anger in Raphael's usually kind voice.

"WHAT?!" Michael bellowed.

"You heard me," Raphael gently unfolded me from his arms and shoved Michael in the shoulder.

Anger fumed in Michael's eyes. "How dare you speak to me like that," he said, violently poking Raphael in the chest. "Don't forget your place, mongrel."

I'd never seen Raphael like this – anger spewing out with every word. "Don't call me that!" His voice was low and almost dark as he glared at Michael and a neon blue flashed in his eyes.

I know that blue.

Flashes of from the other night blanketed my mind as they continued, they paced around in a circle, countering each other's moves. I couldn't believe what I was seeing – it almost looked as if they were getting slightly larger with every circle they made.

Does he transform into a blue eyes beast?

Suddenly, as if from thin air, Gabriel appeared and stood between the two. Anger still fumed in their eyes and it almost sounded as if they were growling at one another. Michael winked at Raphael and Raphael leaped for Michael, only to be halted by Gabriel – who merely place his hands on both Michael's and Raphael's chests. It seemed as if he made no effort at all, but pain flashed in each of their eyes for one brief moment before returning to normal.

Anger no longer plagued Raphael's eyes. As if Gabriel's touch had someone zapped the anger away, he was now consumed by the peaceful demeanor he almost always possessed. He walked back to my side and smiled.

"So are you going to be okay?" He nonchalantly questioned as if nothing had happened.

I glanced over at Michael, who was now talking quietly with Gabriel.

"Wha … what just happened?" I asked as my eyes bounced from Michael to Raphael.

"Oh, it was nothing … I was just mad that Eros hurt you and Michael has traits that remind me of Eros and … well, my anger for Eros overwhelmed me. That's all … nothing too serious."

"No, I understand that part I was meaning …" My words were interrupted when someone placed their warm arms around me and the familiar scent of spicy cinnamon consumed me. The moment the arms slipped around my waist an angry look once again consumed Raphael's eyes. I was starting to become used to that look, so I knew immediately it was Eros behind me. As if a mirror to Raphael's look, my face wrinkled with anger.

"And where have you been?" I demanded, pulling Eros' arms from my waist and turning on him with pursed lips and the most scolding look I could manage.

A devilish half smile graced his face. "Sorry, my last class ran late," he said as he ran his hot fingers down my cheek.

Shivers pulsed through my veins as his fingers made their way down my arm to my hand where he interlaced his fingers with mine, I pulled my hand from his grasp.

He's lying.

"Really," I questioned as I raised my eyebrows.

Something in his look changed and his head fell in disappointment, "No, not really…I'm sorry." He looked up at me his eyes pleading with me for forgiveness, but as if he flipped a switch his look once again changed. "So are you ready to go?" He asked as he ran the back of his fingers across my cheek sending a strange cascade of vibrations down my spine.

What is wrong with him?

I bit my lip as I thought for a moment.

Do I really want to go somewhere with him?

A kind gentle smile touched his face, a smile that made me feel almost as though we were lifelong friends.

"Yes …" I said as all negative thoughts about him disappearing. "I'm ready to go. I'll see you guys later …"

"Good," Eros said as he grabbed my hand and began to pull me towards the parking lot.

Raphael grabbed my free hand. "What?!" I rudely inquired. "Sorry," My eyes pleased with Raphael to forgive my rude outburst as I turned to face him, Eros' grip upon my hand slightly tightened as if he thought Raphael was trying to take me from him.

"What where you going to ask me before Eros interrupted us?' Raphael asked, his eyes almost pleading me to stay.

I thought for a moment.

That's right I want to know if he transforms into something and if he does what was it that he transforms into?

"I'll talk with you later …" I turned as Eros pulled me in the direction that we'd been walking.

As we walked away I heard Raphael say, "Alright, I'll talk with you later." Concern seemed to drip from his words as they whispered through his lips.

I couldn't get the sound of his hurt voice out of my mind as I walked at Eros' side toward his car. I shrugged it off, however, and tried to engage in a conversation with Eros.

"Wow!!! Is that your car?!" I questioned as we walked up to a crimson red Porsche.

"Yes, it's mine … do you like it?" He asked as he opened the passenger side door for me.

"Yes …" I breathed.

A short laugh escaped his lips as he shut the door behind me. Eros sleekly slipped into the driver's seat almost instantaneously from the moment that he closed my door.

How'd he do that?

"So … what's the plan?" I stuttered, unable to speak as I breathed in his hot, sweet scent.

"Oh, don't you worry about a thing … you're going to love it!" He said with a sly grin upon his face.

* * *

"Don't peek …" Eros said as he led me – blindfolded – to our destination.

"I'm not …" I scolded. My heart began pounding faster as he pulled me into his. This was the first time I had been this close to a guy.

What do I do?

I silently said a thank you prayer as my heart began to violently thunder and I felt the medicine once again begin to work its way through my burning veins.

I wonder how long it'll last.

He continued to lead me forward people loudly spoke around us and a strong smell of popcorn, roasting nuts and fried food filled the air. I let out a frustrated huff when someone ran into me, not even bothering to say 'excuse me.'

"Can I take this…" I began as Eros pulled the blind fold from my eyes.

Wow!

"It's a festival…" Eros excitedly said his eyes glowing with anticipation in his voice.

Lights lit up the streets and each of the booths that lined them. There where rides of all kinds from the tea cup rides to the Ferris wheel, I could hardly believe what I was seeing. A smile touched my face as I continued to take in all of the sights of the festival.

"So what's the festival celebrating?"

"I'm not entirely sure, but I think that it to celebrate Martin Luther King day." He tightly grasped my hand as his eyes widened, "Oh you have to try this!" He shouted as he pulled me towards one of the booths, "Two fried Twinkies please." He held up his hand as to indicate how many he was wanting.

The irritated girl looked up at Eros and her look immediately changed, "Hi." She mumbled as she stared at Eros with a twitterpated smile upon her face.

"Hi," Eros cocked his eyebrow as though he was wondering if she had heard his request. "So how much is do I owe you?" He asked as he pulled me up next to him.

She shook her head, "What?"

"How much do I owe you for the two fried Twinkies?"

"Oh, sorry," She mumbled as she typed it in on her cash register, "That will be eight dollars." She rested her head in her hand and continued to stare at Eros.

Eros handed her a ten dollar bill and began to look around at some of the other booths as we waited for his change and the fried Twinkies. Irritation began to pulse in his eyes as the girl continued to stare at him, but quickly faded as he leaned forward commanding the you girls attention, "Can we please have our fried Twinkies."

"Of course," she mumbled as she turned around and quickly made the fried Twinkies. When she turned back around she handed two fried Twinkies to Eros as well as his ten dollar bill. "It's on the house." She said as she wink at him.

"Oh, well thank you," Eros said as he picked up the folded ten dollar bill and a small piece of white paper fell out. He pushed the bill into his pocket and handed me one of the Twinkies. "You have to try this!" He exclaimed not even noticing the paper that had fallen from the ten.

"Thank you," I said as I picked up the paper, thinking it was a receipt.

Wait Eros didn't have to pay for the Twinkies.

I looked at the paper and glanced up at the girl as she glared at me, a shocked half smile worked its way upon my face, "You have got to be kidding me."

"What? You don't like it?"

I handed him the folded up piece of paper.

Unfolding it a look of confusion touched his face, "Did you get a new number?"

"Nope, that's her phone number," I said as I pointed towards as she smiled and batted her eyes at Eros.

An almost devilish smile moved over his face, but disappeared when he glanced in my direction. Eros let out a huff and handed the number back to the girl, a look of complete heartbreak consuming his face. "It seems you dropped this young lady," The tone in his voice changed as he continued. It almost sounded as though he was disgusted with himself, "You really should be more careful with your personal information, you don't want it to fall into the wrong hands." He turned back to me with a crooked smile, "Come on let's go on a ride!"

It was strange the way that Eros was reacting; it was almost as though he was a little child that was getting out for the first time, everything brand new. His eyes were wide as he dragged me all around the festival, going from ride to ride and booth to booth.

We were having a great time when something changed anger pulsed in his eyes, "Wait here…" Eros sternly said as an almost red seem to flicker in his eyes, "I promise I'll be right back." His muscles tightened and he kissed me on top of the head.

Eros hadn't been gone long when I felt as though someone was watching me. Chills danced down my spine as the wind gently blew a familiar citrusy scent towards me. I began to walk into the wind when I heard a voice the same voice that I heard that day in the hospital.

"Is he at the meeting place?"

"Yes," A new voice chimed in. ***"He arrived a few minutes ago."***

"Why does the master want her?" Anger and hatred pulsed in her words.

"I'm not sure, but I assume that it has to do with the guardian's interest in her."

"Why are you still here? Isn't there something that you are supposed to be doing?"

"Of course."

The scent moved closer causing fear to pulse over me. I began to step back when there came a horrified scream. Unable to help myself I began racing towards the direction from which the scream had come. The closer I got to where it had come from the tantalizing scent from the day I had come upon the accident. I took in a deep breath and continued to towards the direction of which the scream had come from when I came to large crowd. I looked where the crowd was staring to find that the Ferris wheel had begun to tear apart. I weaved myself throughout the crowd towards the front. When I heard a few officers talking amongst themselves yet even though they were on the other end of the Ferris wheel I could hear them as though they were standing next to me.

"We were able to get everyone off of the Ferris wheel except for the two children at the top."

"Well then get them down."

"We can't no one safely make it to the top. A few people tried, but their attempts where unsuccessful, they were injured pretty bad."

I glanced in the direction of which the officers had turned their attention, there was an officer with sever cuts covering his body. Suddenly a frantic woman shoved through the crowd, "My babies, please save my babies!" She pointed up towards the top of the Ferris wheel.

Two young girls sat crying at the top of the Ferris wheel as they tightly clung on to each other. Without thinking I quickly made my way to the bottom of the Ferris wheel and looking up my mind calculating the perfect way to the girls. I weaved in and out, over and under until I was at the door of the cart that the girls were in. I opened the door and the bar that I was holding onto broke quickly I grabbed the nearest bar and flipped on top of it. Screams of panic rang out all around me. I steadied myself and once again opened the door placing my hand out towards the girls, "come on."

One of the girls moved her shaking hand towards me I quickly grasped her hand and pulled her into my chest, "I'm coming back I promise." I reassured her. Tears began to pour from her eyes as she nodded her head and clung to the side of the cart.

Carefully I made my way back down the Ferris wheel; I was almost to the bottom when the Ferris wheel shifted causing some of the broken bars to come tumbling down around us. I leaped to the ground and protectively cupped myself around the child as the bars violently pelted me. Once the falling debris stopped was dug out from under the bars.

"Are you okay?" they questioned.

"I'm fine," I said as I began to head back toward the remaining girl, only to be halted by one of the officers.

"You can't go back up there, it's too dangerous."

I angrily pulled my arm from his grasp, "I promised her."

"Yes, but…"

"Don't tell me what I can't do." I gave him and angry glare and quickly made my way up to the girl, much faster than the last time.

I held my hand out to the girl as the Ferris wheel shifted again, the supports beginning to creak and bend. I looked down at the supports as they began to turn white from the strain.

We don't have much time.

I swiftly grabbed the girl and pulled her into my chest, "Are you ready for this? I'm going to need you to hold on very tight."

She nodded her head and tightened her grip around me as the Ferris wheel began to crumble behind us. I didn't know I was capable of moving so fluidly; flipping and dipping in and out over and under. With about ten feet to go I leaped from the Ferris wheel because all other options disappeared giving no other choice. I landed in a crouched position upon the ground one hand wrapped around the girl and the other upon the ground.

Numbly I escaped from the crowd as the EMT's examined the girl. I didn't want to answer any questions about how I did what I did; after all I didn't even know how I had done it. I walked back to the place that Eros had told me to wait and sat down on a nearby bench.

I guess there are some good things about morphing into a monster.

"What happened to you?" Eros questioned as he gently ran his hand across my cheek wiping some blood away.

I shook my head, "It was nothing…" I looked up at Eros, "Would it be alright if you take me home? I'm kind-of tired."

Concern consumed his eyes, "Yes." He said as he grasped my hand and led me towards the car.

The ride home everything that had been happening in the past few week consumed my thoughts, causing anger to burn inside me. I remained silent not wanting my anger to spew out.

At the apartment the door flung open and Natalya stood with her arms folded and her foot impatiently tapping upon the floor. "And where have you been?" She impatiently questioned, anger bubbling in her eyes.

Her anger did it releasing all of my pin up anger, “It’s none of your business where I have been and how dare you speak to me like that!” My words angrily spewed out, hate filling my voice. Pain touched Natalya’s expression and remorse swelled inside me.

An evil look of accomplishment touched Eros’ eyes, “I had better be going. It’s getting late.” He said as I glanced at the clock on the wall over Natalya’s shoulder read 2:06AM.

Eros hugged me close.

“Okay,” I huffed, the anger still burning within.

A strange look consumed Eros’ face as he leaned in passionately kissed me.

I stood stiff and unmoving shocked by Eros’ forward actions. That was what I had expected him to be like the entire night, but when he actually did a feeling of disgust churned in my stomache.

“I’ll see you at school.” He said as he winked at me and left our apartment.

“Oh man that was completely gross,” Natalya wrinkled her face in disgust. “It looked like he was trying to swallow your face.” She opened her mouth as wide as she could to show me what she meant.

I rolled my eyes. “You really should not do that. It makes you look like a baby seal trying to swallow your own face. Besides, don’t you know that if you make faces like that for too long it will stick that way … forever …" I lowered my voice upon the last word for a little dramatic flair.

"Nuh uh …" She said as she rubbed her face just to make sure.

"It's true … you didn't know that?" I could barely contain my smirk, my mouth slightly turning up at the edges. I stretched my arms over my head and quickly changed the subject. "It's getting late. I think I'll be headed to bed." I walked over to the couch and clumsily flung myself upon it.

"Aren't you going to pull out your bed?"

"I guess …" I mumbled as I pulled myself from the couch and began my nightly routine of getting ready for bed.

CHAPTER SEVEN

HORROR AND CHANGE

I looked around – my surroundings seemed familiar and yet I couldn't recall where I was. I glanced out the window to see a dark figure moving. It almost looked as if it was a large beast – but it was larger than any animal I'd ever seen. I turned to make my way to the door when I seen Gabriel.

"He hasn't returned," I said as though my words were not my own. "I have to go to him." I gave Gabriel, but the feeling that pulsed over me was only that of friendship, "Please watch over her."

Gabriel nodded his head and I ran for the door.

The wind caressed my face, making my senses tingle. Horror washed over me as the strange scent from the night of the accident and the festival came with the wind; that scent seemed to always be associated with something horrible. I closed my eyes and began to follow the scent, not caring that it lead me straight toward the large beast, I knew it would lead me to where I was needed most. Taking in a deep breath, the irresistible smell seemed to fill every crack and crevice of space around me.

"Join me …" A familiar voice said enticingly.

I opened my eyes to find Eros standing before me. Blood dripped form the corner of his mouth. He held his hand out before him – blood stained his hands. Horror consumed me and my heart began to beat as if it were going to burst from my chest. The smell flooded me. It seemed to make my head hurt and swim simultaneously – I couldn't get it's alluring out of my mind. My stomach almost seemed to ache for it and my soul mourned at its very presence. My heart beat faster and faster, pounding against my ribs.

"Join me …" Eros said again. A sly grin crept across his face as his eyebrow seductively arched. He reached out his hand and grabbed mine. "You've never been one to say no to just a taste."

What was he talking about?

It was hard to keep my mind off the nearly unbearable pain that was rising within my chest.

He traced his lips with his tongue. "Join me …" His sultry look disappeared, only to be replaced with anger, a fiery red burning in his eyes. He turned his gaze down as if to show me where he wanted me to look.

I shook my head, not wanting to follow his gaze. A tear rolled down my cheek, afraid of what I knew I would see. I closed my eyes and hesitantly lowered my head. Opening my eyes slowly I was unprepared for what my eyes beheld. My breath caught in my throat. I gasped for air as my heart raced. A young man laid before me, blood covered his chest. His blond hair had turned a sickly color of brown as his blood spilled over his forehead. I knew him.

How do I know him?

I leaned down, unable to stop myself, and wrapped my arms across the man's chest. Tears began to pour over my face. I couldn't contain my sobs as the pain in my chest increased. Suddenly his chest moved. I looked up at his face and he opened his ocean blue eyes. "Zander…" I cried.

How did I know his name; unless this wasn't a dream and maybe a memory? No not my memory, but maybe someone else's. Could someone be trying to tell me something or warn me of something? Or maybe it is a glimpse of the future?

"He fought admirably, taking out nearly a hundred of our kind before I was able to take him down." An evil grin rested upon Eros' face as he spoke.

"Why?"

Anger billowed off of Eros in waves, "Because he was the enemy you weren't supposed to fall in love with him!" Pain filled his words.

Enemy?

Air gurgled through his lungs and Zander grasped me in his arms, "R … ru … run …" he gasped as he tried to push me away.

Pain now coursed throughout my entire body. I wanted to cry out in agony, but my voice seemed to be caught in my chest, where the pain was the most excruciating.

Was this heartbreak?

Sweat beaded across my forehead. I clenched my teeth tightly together and forced myself to look up at Eros' hate-filled eyes.

"What have you done?!" I cried out as Eros lunged for me. Right before his hands found my throat, I jolted awake.

My breaths came in short gulps and a cold hand touched my arm. Defensively I pinned those hands to the wall. My fingers wrapped around the person's neck and my breaths came out as if I were growling.

No more than three seconds passed before I realized the icy fingers belonged to Natalya. Immediately I released her.

"I'm sorry … I'm so sorry! I didn't hurt you did I?"

Tears began to stream down my face. I curled into a ball on the edge of my bed.

Natalya gasped for air. "I … I think …I'm okay …" She coughed as she sat on the arm of the couch.

"Natalya?"

"What's wrong?" She questioned, seeing the tears streaking my cheeks.

"What's wrong with me? I nearly killed you."

"It's okay … I know you didn't mean it."

Pain began to pour over me once again. I knew she was keeping something from me. She knew something! The strange phone calls in the middle of the night. I had tried to convince myself that it was all a hallucination, when deep down I knew the truth; that she knows more about me and what's happening to me than she is letting on and I was tired of her keeping secrets from me. I looked at her, anger burning in my eyes.

"What's happening to me?!?!"

As if in response to my anger, my bones seemed to want to tear through my skin. The pain was excruciating. And then in to the middle of the pain there came the soft soothing voice I'd been hearing off-and-on over the past week. Only this time it wasn't in my head. It came from a shadowy spot in the corner of the room.

"Nothing is wrong with you.," the voice said. "You just didn't know."

I searched the corner for some discerning features from this strange person, absently noting that the pain had begun to fade.

Who is mysterious figure?

My eyes were completely adjusted and I could see everything, everything except the person.

"Who are you?"

I leaned forward, drawn to the mysterious figure in the shadows.

"I am someone who wants to help you and has been watching over you your entire life," the soothing voice calmly explained.

"But that tells me nothing. What's your name?" I questioned, not even attempting to keep the irritation from my voice.

"I'm sorry, Alex, but I'm not ready to reveal my identity to you yet…" An uncertainty filled his words. "But for now you must relax. Getting anxious and upset will only further irritate your condition."

"And what condition is that?"

A soft laugh escaped the mysterious figures lips, "You're right to the point; just like you were when you were younger." The velvety voice was silent for a moment before continueing, "Your condition is the resolt of a curse." The sound of the voice seemed to calm my rapid heart very quickly as I listened to him. He let out a frustrated huff, "I'm afraid that I must be going, but all will be revealed to you soon." Natalya walked to his side, "I have sensed some tention between you and Natalya and you are right to assume that she knows more about your condition than you, however do not hold that against her she has only been acting upon my behalf. I appointed her to assist you in the delaying of your full transformation." The figure stepped closer, but he never left the mask of shadows.

"Alex, always know that when you need help, it will never be very far. Goodbye."

"Goodbye …" I stuttered, as the mysterious figure disappeared.

I turned to Natalya, "Who was that?" Natalya shook her head. "You know who that was Natalya, don't you?" I demanded, stepping forward threateningly.

Natalya coward ever so slightly, and then as if she had swallowed a confidence pill she stepped toward me and puffed up her chest. "It's not my place to tell you, he'll reveal himself to you when he is ready to."

I glared at her, my heart beginning to beat faster and faster. Pain began to consume me again. I absently recognized that the pain came every time I started to get really angry, but I didn't care at the moment. My anger needed a release.

Fear flashed in Natalya's eyes as she noted my wince of pain. "Relax Alex, everything is going to be alright."

Her voice seemed to grate upon my ears, only further angering me. "Relax? Relax!!" My words came out low and dark, almost evil.

She ran to the counter and pulled out a hidden drawer where she was keeping the syringes full of the medicine to stop my transformation. "Here, this will help …" She said nervously as the pain swelled over my body. She hesitantly leaned forward and proceeded to try and give me a shot.

I looked at her with hate and swung my hand in her direction, knocking her violently to the ground. I stepped closer to her, wanting to take all of my anger out upon her, when something tackled me from behind, forcing me to the ground. I felt a soft pinch and my pain began to decrease, as did my anger as the icy medicine tore through my veins. Each second that passed the icy burning of my veins calmed and the excruciating pain lessened. My heart rate slowed and my bones relaxed – the tearing feeling subsiding the black beneath my flesh reseeding within.

Worn out – as if I'd just run five miles – I laid on the ground, even after I had been released from my tackle. My breaths still came in great gasps, but after lying there a while I rose to a sitting position. Turning to Natalya, I found her and Raphael sitting against the wall across the room.

"Where did you come from?" I questioned, glancing at the clock. It said 7:30 AM.

"I was going to head to school with you girls when I heard a commotion and found you throwing Natalya violently to the ground."

I turned to Natalya, the incident flashing in my mind. "I'm sorry Nat …" My head fell in shame, seeing the bruise upon her cheek where I had struck her. Tears filled my eyes as I stood up, "Just let me get ready and then we can head to campus." I said as I made a detour and pulled some ice from the freezer, placing it in a hand towel I handed the ice to Natalya, "You really should put some ice on that if you don't want it to continue swelling."

In the restroom I once again examined the bruises that transformation had caused the soreness in them completely gone and as I began to stare at the bruises they began to heal before my eyes. Shocked I pulled my shirt down and ran out to the living room, "You guys have got to see this!" I exclaimed excitement in my voice as I proceeded to pull my shirt up.

Raphael's face flushed a deep red and his heartrate accelerated, but calmed when he realized that it was transformation related. “Look at the bruises...They are healing!” I turned my back to them and pulled up my shirt as far as I could, “Are they healing on my back, too?”

Raphael ran his hand gently over my back, “Yes, it is healing beautifully.” He whispered awe in his voice.

A disgruntled grunt echoed through the room, “If you’re done caressing Alex’s back do you think that was could head to campus.” Michael impatiently questioned as he ran his hand tiredly back through his hair.

My face flushed almost as red as Raphael’s and quickly pulled my shirt down, “Why are you here?”

“Believe me I don’t want to be,” He closed his eyes and stretched his arms behind his head. “I was told I had to be here to pro…” His eyes widened as though he had said something that he should not have, “I mean, I wanted to ride in Raphael’s car.”

A gave him an angry glare, “I don’t believe…”

“Man look at the time we really should be headed to school, otherwise we will be late for Mr. Peterson’s class.” Michael interrupted as he pointed over to the clock.

I let out a frustrated huff, “Fine…” I said as I quickly ran a brush through my hair and pulled it back into a ponytail. I slipped into a clean shirt and walked back into the living room where I grabbed my bag and motioned towards the door. "Come on." As we walked out of the apartment I stopped just outside the door.

There it is again; the smell of citrus and the feeling of watching eyes.

I looked around, and couldn't see anything when a great pain coursed over me and a sword tore through my back and out my front. I looked down everything becoming hazy as I stared at the blade covered in my blood. Blood spilled from my lips and I gasped for air as the blade was violently pulled from my body.

Someone leaned in closer to me and whispered in my ear, "I don't care what the repercussions are you're too dangerous to allow to live any longer," The hot citrusy scent completely enveloping me as she spoke. Everything around us seemed to move in slow motion as she licked my cheek allowing her lips to linger upon my cheek. "Too, bad though you are kind-of yummy."

As she released me from her grasp I fell to my knees as I watched my friends run towards me.

"Hold on Alex, just hold on…" The voices around me seemed to dim as my eyes began to shut, the warmth from my blood completely covering my stomach. My body became heavy, and I collapsed to the ground everything going black as I gave in to the darkness of my wounds.

CHAPTER EIGHT

DARKNESS COMES

I lay in dark silence, air gurgling through my lungs with every breath and pain twisting through my veins.

Why is it so dark and why is no one helping me?

It seemed as if I could count the bubbles of air as they tried to escape my lungs through the open hole in my chest. Wanting to plug the hole, I attempted to place my hand upon it. My body was paralyzed and unable to move. I could hear muffled voices encircling the darkness.

"Save her! You have to save her, Raphael …" Muffled movement accompanied the voices.

"I'm trying, but it's unlike anything I've ever seen! It's almost as if her body is attacking itself or fighting within itself! And to top it off she was pierced with a sword of darkness. The poison has already begun to work its way through her blood, spidering out through her veins."

Raphael was right I would feel the poison as it tried to work its way through my body it was as though my veins burning as though it was trying to incinerate me from the inside out.

"So did you find her," Raphael questioned as someone entered the room.

"No I was unable to pick up on her trail." Michael stated an irritated tone in his voice.

There was some commotion and Raphael spoke up, "Then what use are you?" He angrily questioned.

"It's not my fault you know that she has ways of cloaking her presence from us."

"You were supposed to be protecting Alex, but look at her."

"Don't you think I know!" Michael shouted, "That's the one thing that Gabriel asked me to do and because I thought I was too good for it I let him down." Disappointment filled his voice as he spoke.

Suddenly there was a new voice. "That's enough you two." There was a moment of silence before the velvety voice continued, "Is there any improvement?"

It was the same voice as that of the mysterious figure. He'd come to check on me. My heart rate slightly picked up, but the calm in his voice relaxed it once again.

"No – no change. And I can't figure out what's going on with her wound. It's … well it's almost as if her … well …her …"

Natalya picked up where Raphael couldn't continue. "Almost as if her body is battling within itself…"

"I was afraid of that," The velvet voice said. "But it is to be expected."

"Expected because she's a girl, right? And her body is acting differently to the transformation?" Raphael questioned.

His question was met with silence, though Velvet Voice must have shook his head no because Raphael responded.

"It's not? Then what is it?"

Again silence. It was overbearing and seemed to make the darkness encroaching upon me all the more evil and oppressive.

"At least her heart rate seems to be remaining steady?" Velvet Voice said.

"That puzzles me, too," Raphael said. "With the amount of pain she has to be going through, her heart rate should be racing – and yet it remains steady. I've never seen anything like this before."

"Have you given her any morphine for the pain?" Velvet Voice asked.

"No! That's why it puzzles me …" Raphael mumbled.

"Why don't you try giving her some? It couldn't hurt, right?" Velvet Voice said.

There was an almost unnoticeable pinch in my arm and immediately my body seized spasming as if a lethal poison had been injected into my veins. Pain consumed me and my bones tried to tear through my human skin.

No! It couldn't be happening! Not again. I can't morph into the beast. Not with Raphael and Natalya in the room. PLEASE, GOD NO!!!

Agony wracked my entire body and I could feel a tear run down my cheek when there came, the other voice – not the velvet voice of the mysterious person in the room, but the other voice; the one that had come that day at school. The one that carried with it a supreme sense of authority – as if anything it said would come true.

"Anything you ask in my name shall be given to you."

A warmth touched my heart and fanned out from there, causing my transformation to come to a halt. My bones jig-sawed back into place and my heart rate once again slowed. I relaxed back into myself, knowing with a strange sense of certainty that from now on I would no longer have to worry about my transformation. Whoever the voice belonged to, I knew they would help me control, or even halt, the transformation.

"Well …" Velvet Voice said. "That was a bit of a letdown."

"What?!" Natalya questioned, almost as if she knew my very thoughts.

A frustrated huff escaped someone's lips as Velvet Voice continued. "I was expecting a full transformation."

"INTO WHAT?!" Raphael exclaimed in a nervous shriek. "I'm nearly as old as you and I've never seen a transformation resembling anything close to what she was starting to morph into."

There was a pause, and I felt a soft touch upon my hand.

"Look at her injury," Velvet Voice said, a note of wonder in his voice. "Is there any change to it?"

I felt a slight tug upon what I assumed was some sort of bandage, and a gentle hand slowly moved over the wound.

"It is incredible …"

"What?" Natalya questioned.

"Her wound it … well it looks as if it happened months ago … not hours …"

I hadn't even noticed, but the gurgling in my lungs was gone. Something must have happened while in my transformation stage.

"But how?" Raphael questioned.

"There is much more to Alex than meets the eye," Velvet Voice answered vaguely.

"And what is that supposed to mean?" Natalya wondered, her voice slightly elevated in irritation.

"All will be revealed in due time."

A smile spread across my face at the obvious dodging of the question.

"I've heard that before," I said, meaning to say it in my head and surprised at having said it aloud. Immediately I felt arms wrap tightly around my chest.

"Oh Alex, you're okay! Thank God you are!" Natalya squeaked.

I opened my eyes, seeing the familiar white room of Raphael, Michael, and Gabriel's place. As my eyes adjusted to the light, I searched for the face that matched Velvet Voice. My eyes examined every inch of the room in a matter of seconds. Disappointment consumed me, "Where is he?" I questioned, pushing Natalya from my chest and sitting up.

"Where is who?" Raphael asked, looking around the room, as well.

"Velvet Voice," I mumbled as I stood up still slightly lightheaded.

"Velvet Voice?" Raphael asked, a slight chuckle escaping from his lips. I punched him in the shoulder, "Don't make fun of me."

He stumbled slightly from my punch, "You should not be walking around … you have been through quite a bit this morning."

I turned to him angrily.

"DON'T!"

When I saw the concern flash in his eyes, however, my anger dissolved and my heart rate immediately returned to normal. I remembered again that the voice would help me control the transformation. I couldn't explain how I knew it, but I did. I knew it in my heart that he would help me control whatever this was that plagued my body.

Raphael's mouth dropped open. "How … how did you do that?" he questioned, releasing my hand.

"Do what?" I raised my eyebrows in question.

"How did you neutralize your heart rate so quickly? I could feel it rapidly increase and then …" Raphael shook his head in disbelief. "Then as if you flipped a switch causing it to return to normal." His eyes widened with wonder, waiting for my answer.

I shrugged my shoulders. "I don't know … I just did …" I looked down at the floor and placed my hand over my heart, the warmth still present. I glanced up at the watch that hung around Natalya's neck. "It's ten o'clock?"

Natalya looked around the room. "How do you know what time it is?" She questioned, curiosity upon her face.

I walked back across the room, tapped upon the top of her necklace, and cocked my eyebrows as if to say, "Duh…"

"How … you were clear across the room?"

"Guess I have good eyes," I said as I walked back across the room to the door. "We're late for class." Not wanting to remember the horrifying even. I looked down at my shirt. Blood stains ran down the entire front of it, that's when I noticed a dark mark upon my upper chest; just beneath my neck. I walked over to the white Victorian mirror that hung upon the wall, pulling back my shirt I seen a dark cross shaped scar that appeared to have flames growing from it.

Raphael walked up behind me, "I'm afraid that scar will never heal." He said as I continued to stare at the scar. "The blade that you were pierced you with left its mark upon you."

I ran my hand across the raised scare, "Why?"

"Because the sword of darkness is filled with great evil," Raphael said as he patted me on the shoulder.

Warmth pulsed beneath my fingers as I traced the scare.

"Anyway we had better let you get changed so that we can head to class."

After getting dress I searched for Natalya's old junker in the driveway. Unable to find it I gave her a confused look. "Where…" I began.

"I thought we would take mine," Raphael interrupted as I turned to face him.

"Yours? Well, where is yours?"

Raphael cocked his eyebrows and half smiling he turned to face the north side of the house. Then he pointed to a midnight blue 2016 Dodge Charger.

Speechless, I stared at the amazing car "When did you get this?" I asked.

"Yesterday … I drove it to your apartment this morning and was going to surprise you girls when things took an unexpected turn. So how about we go?"

"You don't have to tell me twice!" I said, as I ran to the car. Just before jumping into the back seat I glanced at my reflection in the window and pulled my shirt up to hide the scare upon my chest. Slipping into the car Natalya followed closely behind.

Before Raphael could enter the car, Gabriel appeared to speak with him. The two of them began to have a heated discussion – Raphael frequently shaking his head. I turned my ear toward the two as they talked

"No he cannot come!" Raphael said emphatically. There was a pause and then Gabriel said something else that I couldn't hear.

"What!?" Raphael retorted. "No! We would be in an enclosed area! It would be too dangerous for all of us. What if she … you know … ?"

I strained to hear Gabriel, but no matter how hard I tried I still couldn't hear him. Natalya looked at me as we sat in the back seat and questioned me with her eyes. I shook my head, not really sure what to tell her as I continued to try to hear what was being said.

"… Are you sure because I am not and I don't want to put Natalya in danger like that," Raphael said, waiting respectfully for Gabriel's reply. "Yes, that might work …" Gabriel gently placed his hand upon Raphael's shoulder. "I'll do it, but I still don't feel right about this," Raphael said as he reluctantly nodded his head and walked to the car, slipping into the driver's seat.

"Isn't Gabriel coming?" I asked.

"No …" Raphael said with a tight lip. Turning to face us he continued. "So Nat, would you like to sit up here with me?" A flash of nerves twinkled in his eyes as he looked down at the floorboards of the car.

A sweet smile spread across her face as she nodded her head. "Sure!" she said excitedly, her cheeks flushing a pale pink.

Raphael smiled, "Cool …"

Natalya opened her door and made her way to the passenger seat. Raphael met her, opening the passenger-side door.

How did he get in and out of the car so quickly? I didn't even see him move!

A moment later he was back behind the wheel. Flashes of how fast Eros had gotten in the car the other day flooded my mind, but no matter how hard I tried I still couldn't explain what my eyes had seen.

There are so many weird things going on! Some part of me wishes that I could turn back time, before all of this started; to a time when I only had to worry about being called a white demon and not if I actually was a demon.

We sat silently in his car for nearly 10 minutes and I was beginning tired of sitting in silence there were too many thoughts going through my mind. Unable to stay quiet any longer I spoke up. "Sooo...are we going to go?" I questioned, one eyebrow raised in confusion.

"Yes," Raphael said as if he were irritated about something. "We're just waiting on someone."

"Okay … so who are we waiting on?" Natalya asked.

Raphael's jaw tightened. "Michael."

My stomach did a flip at the thought of him riding in the same car with me. "We are going to be late … can't we just leave without him?"

I do not want to sit next to Michael!

"I told Gabriel I would let him come … and I always keep my word." Raphael looked at me out of the corner of his eye. "Besides, we're already late for class. A few more minutes won't hurt." Anger seemed to underline his words as he breathed them through his clenched teeth.

My heart rate began to increase, “Fine …” I huffed as I tried to focus on slowing my heart rate, saying a silent prayer to the voice I called My Strength.

Almost as if he could hear my heart, Raphael turned and raised his eyebrow, “Nice!” He said, nodding his head.

“What?” Confusion consumed me. What was he talking about?

There’s no way he can hear my heart rate ... can he?

Raphael closed his eyes, almost as if he’d made a mistake. “Um … I …” He glanced out the window and a smile spread across his face. “Michael is coming.” I followed his gaze out the window. I really wish it could have been someone else, anyone else, really just as long as it wasn’t him.

Michael slipped into the seat next to me and with a sly grin upon his face he gave me a wink and then did a double-take, noting the special way in which I’d fixed my hair. “Wow … Alexandra … I wasn’t even sure you were a girl and that outfit is not helping.”

My blood began to boil and my heart-rate doubled. I turned to Natalya and seeing the concern in her eyes I closed my eyes to focus on my breathing. Once I knew I could handle it, I opened my eyes to find everyone staring at me. “What!?” My eyes bounced from Natalya to Raphael, conveniently avoiding eye contact with Michael. Natalya shrugged her shoulders as though she didn't know why they were staring at me either.

"WOW!!!" Raphael said, turning back to face forward in his seat. "Alright, let's get this show on the road."

Suddenly Gabriel appeared at the passenger side window. He looked in at Michael and without a word Michael opened the door and slid out.

"Where is he going?" I questioned, staring after him in confusion. "He literally just got here! And we waited 10 minutes for him to arrive," Irritation consuming my words.

Silence filled the car as I waited for Raphael to answer. Not getting a response, I gave his seat a slight nudge. "Hello … am I the only one in the car?" I glanced at Natalya, who shrugged her shoulders and shook her head, not sure what was going on with Raphael.

Finally, after an extended moment of silence, Raphael let out an almost relaxed huff of air and his posture softened. He turned to me with a smile on his face. "Michael won't be coming back … it's just going to be the three of us. Are we ready to go?"

He began to pull out of the circle drive, "Wait … how do you know he won't be coming back?" I asked.

"Because he's taking his bike."

"What?" About that time a motorcycle raced past the car, doing a wheely toward the end of the drive and quickly making its way out of sight.

"If he had a motorcycle this whole time then why did we have to wait for him!?!?"

No answer was forthcoming, and the ride to school continued in silence.

CHAPTER NINE

NEW VIEW

The ride to campus was pretty quiet. I stared out the window, trying to figure out what was happening. Somethings had begun to make sense but others baffled me; I knew that I was transforming into some sort of monster and that it was because of a curse, but what kind of monster and why it was because of a curse I still had know idea. The horrifying dreams were getting worse and worse.

Especially now that Eros is in the dream.

And to top things off someone was trying to kill me, but the reason why she would go to such extreme measures alluded me.

Who was this woman that smelled of citrus and had murderous thoughts about me?

My heart began to pound as I thought of these things when I heard a soft tap on the window. I shook my head, closed my eyes and took a deep breath. When I looked, to the window, I realized the car was parked at the college. Raphael and Natalya were standing expectantly beside the window. Numbly I opened the car door and Raphael offered his hand to help me from the car.

Slowly we walked to the classroom. I leaned against the wall as Raphael explained to the Mrs. Lee why we were late. He leaned in a placed his hand on her shoulder. Flushing pink, she batted her eyes in his direction.

It was odd how she seemed so smitten with one of her students – hanging on his every word.

Not fair! Just a few weeks ago I spoke with her and she was nowhere near this cooperative. In fact, she was downright rude to me!

She nodded to Raphael, signifying that she was giving each of us a pass. As we made our way to our seats, Raphael asked me if I was going to be Okay.

"I'll be fine," I said in the most optimistic tone I could muster.

The day seemed to drag on, and yet being so engrossed in thought I didn't catch a thing that happened. I especially didn't realize that Chrystal was talking to me most of the day. Eventually, however – after not getting so much as a nod of the head from me – she grabbed me by the shoulders and commanded my attention.

"Alex, what's the matter with you? You've been distant today."

"I'm sorry … I just …" I paused, trying to think of what exactly to tell her. "I have a lot on my mind."

"I got that much … but what is it? What's on your mind?" She looked at me with kind eyes.

It was hard not telling her everything – the nightmares, the excruciating pain, the strange voices in my head, even the attempted assassination upon my life. I felt a connection with her that I couldn't explain, even though we'd only recently started to be friendly with one another. I took a deep breath and then decided to just go for it.

"Okay … you're going to think I' m crazy but …"

My words caught in my throat when I heard the voice – My Strength – speak to me. *"Alex, now is not the time for this conversation. Chrystal is not ready to hear it yet."* Chrystal stared at me in confusion, waiting for me to continue and unaware of the voice of My Strength. *"But I will let you know when she is. Do you trust me?"*

I nodded my head and said, "Yes."

Chrystal cocked one eyebrow.

"Yes what?" she asked.

A small giggle escaped my lips. My Strength's voice not only was a comfort, it lifted my spirits and put a smile on my lips.

"Yes I'm crazy, but you already knew that," I said, grinning sheepishly and shrugging my shoulders.

"Well I may not know you that well, but I would have to agree with you," Chrystal replied playfully. "You are a little crazy."

"So what did I miss?" I said, trying to change the subject. "You know how I am with day dreaming."

Before she could answer, the professor dismissed the class. We gathered our books and made our way into the hall, where Chrystal started to fill me in on the things I'd missed throughout the day.

"Same stuff, different day," she said. "We never really learn anything new in that class." She quickly turned to face me, grabbing my arms. "So, how did your date with Eros go?"

"Wow … that was random." I exclaimed.

Chrystal's head fell. "I'm sorry …" she began.

"No, you're fine … it just caught me off guard. It's no big deal."

A soft smile spread across her face. "So how did it go then?"

I bit my lip and averted my eyes from her stare as we continued to walk to our next class. "Weelll …" I paused for a moment. Her eyes widened in anticipation. "It was terrible."

She looked at me in shock, and then a moment later we burst into laughter.

"Really?" She said after a moment. "That bad? Wow … I never would have thought that anyone that went out with him wouldn't have enjoyed it. I mean, I know when I went out with him …" She stopped in the middle of her words and changed directions. "I mean … I thought that everyone enjoyed their time with Eros … he is quite dreamy …" She trailed off, a nauseatingly dreamy smile on her face.

"Now wait a minute! You were about to say something about going out with Eros, weren't you!"

We turned in front of Building C, where our next class was, and I opened door for her. Together we started down the hall.

"No," she said. "No … I … I didn't say …I …"

Strangely, I could hear her heart rate begin to increase as she stuttered on.

I knew that my hearing had improved but I guess I hadn't realized just how much it actually had improved. One of the ***perks*** *of being a monster?*

"I n-never …"

She stumbled at my side bumping, ever so slightly into me. Her heart rate seemed to increase with every breath. I turned to her, seeing pain fill her eyes.

"A-Alex?" She said as she stumbled into the wall.

"Chrystal!"

She started to collapse, and I caught her just before her head smacked against the hard floor. I scanned the hall. There was hardly anyone in the halls.

"Somebody help!" I yelled, but nobody came to our aid.

I scanned the hall again and found one of the guys that hung out with Gabriel standing idly at the end of the hall; he must have been assigned to watch me for the day. I waved my hand at him, "Please, help."

He stared at me unmoving with an irritated look upon his face as Chrystal's body began to convulse with every pound of her accelerated heart. I bowed my head, not knowing what to do.

"Please help ..." I pleaded to My Strength.

"I am here," He answered immediately. *"Help is on the way ... you just need to stay calm ... everything will be fine."*

"It's going to be okay Chrystal … help will be here soon."

She looked up at me. "Alex …"

"I'm here Chrys … it's alright …"

"Alex … you have … have to … run …" She breathed through clenched teeth.

"No … I won't leave you," I said, confused by her words.

"You have to … I … I can't … protect you …" She gasped as the pain seemed to consume her all the more.

"What? Protect me? Protect me from what?"

"FROM ME!!!" She shouted as her eyes turned red. "I can't hold it back much longer! You have to run!" Agony consumed her tone as she spoke.

"Hold what back?" I asked, truly confused.

She dropped her head and a growl rumbled in her chest. My heart began to pound as her bones seemed to enlarge. Horror consumed me when I realized what was happening.

She is what I am!

The beast that lurked inside me also lurked inside her. I stepped back, overwhelmed.

But what kind of monster do we become?!?!

That's why I felt a connection with her – we were the same. A twisted longing sparked inside me – I wanted to see what she would become!

No what I would become if I gave into the beast lurking inside of me.

Finally I would get some answers, I was repulsed with myself to find an eager anticipation for what was about to happen. I shook my head, trying to chase away such terrible thoughts.

"That's my girl," My Strength said. *"Push the evil thoughts from your mind. Don't allow them to control you."*

Relief flooded over me when He spoke. And then a moment later Gabriel and Raphael were suddenly there, standing at the end of the hall.

"Well what are you waiting for?" I yelled at them. "Help her!"

Raphael turned questioningly to Gabriel. What he said next didn't make any sense to me.

"I can't help her," he bitterly said, shaking his head forcefully. "I won't!"

"What!?" I shrieked, confusion consuming me. "You have to help her!" Anger began to burn inside me as I looked at them standing idly by.

Chrystal continued to convulse in pain, and then suddenly I heard a dark voice come from deep within her chest.

"RUN!!!"

Fear pulsed over me as I stared down at her.

"No!" I retorted defiantly. "I won't run."

Again I looked at Raphael and Gabriel.

"I don't know what's happening, but I know you guys do! Whatever it is, I think you're good people. No I know you are! So how can you just stand there doing nothing? Why won't you help her?"

A tear worked its way out of the corner of my eye.

"You helped me …"

My heart began to pound again, but My Strength was there immediately.

"Calm down," he said. *"Everything is going to fine."*

I looked into Gabriel's beautiful chocolate brown eyes, silently pleading with him to help.

Why won't he do something? Why is he just standing there?

Gabriel stared down at Chrystal almost as if he were having a conversation with someone inside his head. Finally, with a shake of his head and a deep breath he kneeled beside her. He glanced back at me with a peaceful look upon his face, and seeing the distress in my eyes he turned his attention back to her.

Raphael walked up behind him.

"You don't even know if this is going to work," Raphael said. "What if she …"

He stopped talking and cocked his head, as if listening to something or someone, but I could hear no voice.

"You don't know that," he said in response to whomever he was listening to. "Fine, but if you don't mind I'm going to step back – you know, just in case."

He stepped back against the wall, not wanting to be too close to me, either, it seemed.

I watched Gabriel gently place his hand upon Chrystal's chest. Then My Strength spoke again.

"Don't be afraid. I told you everything would be fine. Trust me."

I nodded my head and seemed somehow calm.

Slowly Raphael made his way to my side, he must have noticed my calmed heart-rate and breathing. I watched as an energy – a light, almost … it was hard to describe – seemed to flow from Gabriel's hands into Chrystal's chest. Her body wrenched in pain, every muscle tightening.

I stepped forward, wanting to help somehow, only to be halted by Michael's grasp around my wrist.

"When did you get here?" I angrily questioned.

He gave me an unfavorable look and turned his attention to Gabriel and Chrystal, not saying a word. I let out a frustrated huff and clenched my teeth trying, not to tear into him. I focused my attention back on Gabriel and Chrystal. I watched curiously as her wrenched body began to relax and morph back into her normal size.

Raphael made his way quickly to her side and began to check her vitals. "Huh … that worked … it actually worked …" He turned to Gabriel. "I've never seen that work on her kind before."

Gabriel just nodded his head, stared down at Chrystal for a moment and then turned and began to walk away, followed closely by Michael.

"What do you mean her kind?" I questioned as I bent down and placed the back of my hand upon her cheek.

Raphael bit his lip.

"I … ah … all I … you see it … I …" He lowered his head as if to admit defeat.

"What did you mean her kind?!!?"

Turning to me he continued.

"I'm sorry, I can't tell you anything right now. But I will – promise. … Soon. But at this moment in time you're not ready to hear what I mean when I say … her kind …"

My heart began to pound with irritation.

"Don't get me wrong," he continued. "You've come a long way, and if it was up to me I would tell you everything right here right now. Unfortunately it's not up to me, and until it is your time you'll have to wait."

I closed my eyes and shook my head. It took everything in me to accept what he was saying to me.

"Be patient," My Strength said, compassion in his voice. *"Your time is soon."*

I took a deep breath and then gave Raphael an encouraging smile.

"I waited this long," I said "I guess I can wait a *little* longer."

A second later Eros walked up beside us. We were still hovering over Chrystal.

"And just what do you think you're doing?" He demanded of Raphael, disdain dripping from every word.

I looked up at his beautiful tan face as he stared hatefully down at Raphael.

"What do you think you're doing?" He repeated, this time with even more cruelty.

His ebony eyes seemed to have a slight red tent to them as he hatefully glared at Raphael – almost as if a fire were stoked in the depths of his soul.

Just like the dream.

I stepped back as his body began to radiate heat – a heat so great that it caused sweat to begin to bead across my forehead. I could hear Raphael's heart rate increase as Eros' heat increased.

I tried to hear Eros' heartbeat, as well, but no matter how hard I tried I couldn't hear a thing. It was as if his heart wasn't beating at all. Raphael turned around and stared angrily at Eros.

"I'll ask you one last time," he said, this time adopting an evil smile obviously intended to get under Raphael's skin. "What do you think you're doing?"

He stepped closer as they both seemed to grow in size.

I stepped in front of Chrystal protectively, not sure what I would do if something happened.

"You have to stop them," My Strength said quietly.

"Me?" I questioned unbelievingly. *"What can I do?"*

"You know what to do," My Strength said. A vision of Gabriel stepping between Michael and Raphael the day before flashed through my mind.

I shook my head.

"I can't do that," I said, half-cowering half-crouching into a protective stance over Chrystal, who remained unconscious.

"You can," My Strength said.

"No ..." I mumbled. *"I can't ..."*

Fear consumed me as I stared at Raphael and Eros, growing bigger and bigger in size with every passing heartbeat.

"You can," My Strength said. *"You must. Do it now. Alexandra, you have to. If you don't Eros will kill Raphael."*

I took in a deep breath and closed my eyes.

"Okay, I will try."

Then I boldly stepped between Raphael and Eros. They were so consumed with each other that they didn't even notice I had stepped between them. Slowly I raised my hands over my head and hesitantly touched each of them upon the chest, everything seemed to move in slow motion as I silently spoke with My Strength.

"Now feel My Strength as yours," My Strength said. *"Let it flow through you freely."*

I took in a deep breath and felt a gentle warmth work its way from my heart and out through my hands. It calmed me immediately.

"Now Alexandra, you must prepare yourself," My Strength continued. *"Here's where things are going to get difficult."*

"What do you mean?"

Suddenly a burning pain begin to make its way up my right arm.

"Alexandra, you must listen to me," My Strength said. *"Your faith must be unmovable, or it won't work and you, too, will change."*

"My faith in what?!" I gasped as the pain began to increase all the more.

"In me ..."

"In you?"

"Alexandra, I am more than just a voice in your head. You are right to call me your strength."

Silence fell upon me as the pain increased. An icy pain began to make its way up my left arm, increasing as it inched closer to my heart. It was like night and day, my right side began to boil as if molten lava burned through my veins and my left felt as though liquid nitrogen had been poured through them. Both pains rapidly made their way toward my heart. When they met in the middle, I was suddenly somewhere else.

I stood in a beautiful field full of blue, yellow, and white wildflowers. The flowers' scent was a sweet fragrance that seemed to float upon the air.

Suddenly someone wrapped me in their arms.

"Hello, beautiful!"

Accompanied by a new fragrance that wafted into the air – a hot, sickeningly sweet smell of cinnamon enveloped me. I turned to find Eros with his arms enfolded around my waist.

"Hello …" I shyly mumbled.

Guilt swelled inside me as he sweetly smiled at me.

"So did you finish your task?" He questioned, his smile devolving into a more nefarious grin.

Silence filled the space between us.

What is he talking about?

His sneaky grin faded and was replaced with anger.

"Did you finish your task?" he demanded, heat in his voice. "Has he been eliminated?"

I shook my head. I wanted to say, "I don't know what you're talking about," but all that came out was, "No …"

He angrily stared at me, awaiting my explanation of why I hadn't completed "my task."

"I couldn't ..." I mumbled, confused about what he was asking me but also caught up in the scene playing out before me. Sadness seemed to accompany my words – they escaped my mouth almost as if someone else were saying them.

"Why couldn't you?" He angrily hissed.

Fear flooded over me.

Eros stepped closer, his body enlarging and his ebony eyes turning a slight red in color.

"Why couldn't you do this for me Avangileen?"

Avangileen? Who is Avangileen? That's when it struck me this is another dream, no this is a vision or a memory, but of what and why was I being shown this.

"Why didn't you end his life," he demanded even more harshly

I clenched my teeth together.

"Because I ..."

"You what?" His words almost seemed to burn as they came out.

"... I love him ..." I stated.

Love him? Love who?

"Fine ... but you do know the penalty for betrayal? Don't you?"

"Yes, I know the penalty, but I won't kill him," I said as I slipped my hand in my pocket and pulled out a beautiful ruby necklace and placed it in Eros' hand.

He stepped forward and placed his head upon my shoulder and wrapped his arms around me. Butterflies swam in my stomach, followed closely by an almost sick churning. I took in a deep breath as he continued.

"So be it," he said, disappointment apparent. "But because I like you I have a gift for you."

He pulled me from his chest. His entire demeanor had changed. Hate no longer filled his eyes. Instead he seemed to be in pain. He closed his eyes to hide a tear that touched the corner of one eye.

"I'm going to give you …" He leaned in and kissed me softly upon the mouth. "… a head start …"

Eros pushed me away and cracked his neck. An evil smile formed on his lips, and then he began to morph into a large beast.

"Run," he whispered menacingly.

Suddenly I was jolted back to reality. I felt the fire and ice collide inside, clashing inside my heart. The pain was so great that it caused my body to convulse. My bones began to tear from my body.

"Don't give in to the pain and anger," My Strength said. *"My Strength is sufficient. Trust in me. It cannot overcome you unless you allow it to."*

I used My Strength to push the fire and ice back from my heart, relieving some of the pain that consumed me. Taking in a deep breath, I pushed harder. Finally, with one final push I forced it back into Raphael and Eros, causing them to shrink down to their normal sizes as everything seemed to swirl into a blurry pool of nothingness.

CHAPTER TEN

AN EXPLANATION?

I continued to stand there between Eros and Raphael, my eyes closed, as they reacted to what had just happened.

"How did she do that?!" Eros exclaimed.

"I don't know …" Raphael pondered quietly. "I've only seen one person be able to stop transformation. You know – other than Gabriel – and that was …" Raphael stopped as if his words had been interrupted, but no matter how hard I tried I couldn't hear anyone else.

Apparently neither could Eros though.

"Was who?" He questioned, as though taking the words out of my mouth.

Then a flash of revelation sparked across my mind.

Gabriel must be close by! That's who Raphael listens to when I can't hear anything! That's how he always knows exactly what everyone was thinking. Gabriel can read minds!

I knew I was right. I could feel it as surely as I knew that My Strength was the most true thing in all of existence. I popped open my eyes and quickly searched for him, knowing he'd be somewhere close. Dizzied, I tried to regain my composure as I unsuccessfully scanned the hall.

"Where is he?" I asked, pulling Raphael's attention to me. "Where is Gabriel?"

Eros ran the back of his hand down my cheek.

"Beautiful – Gabriel is not here," Eros said as he grabbed my hand and kissed the back of it. "I've got to go, but I will call you later."

I stopped scanning the hall – absently wondering at how easily I had just memorized every single feature of the nondescript hall in one glance – and redirected my attention to Eros. He was already starting to walk away.

"So who's Avangel–" I began to ask him when I heard him mumbling to himself.

"That's why he wants her."

I began to step closer to Eros when someone placed their hand gently upon my shoulders. I turned to find Gabriel smiling at me. Butterflies fluttered inside my stomach, my cheeks flushed pink, and forgetting everything else I blurted out, "I need to speak with you!"

Gabriel bit his lip and nodded ever so slightly to give me the go ahead.

I looked around and noticed that more students were starting to gather in the hall. It was getting crowded. I looked over and saw that Chrystal had come to and was now talking to Raphael. There were too many eyes watching.

"No, not here," I said to Gabriel. "Alone. It must be alone."

Gabriel gave me a confused look and nodded his head again. Then he stepped to the side and motioned for me to lead the way.

Nervously, I stepped around him and started to walk, only to be halted by a warm hand.

"Alex," Chrystal said in a pleading voice. "I need to speak with you … please …"

I looked back at Gabriel. His eyes were kind, calm, and unbelievably gorgeous. I shrugged my shoulders, and he once again nodded his head, giving me the go ahead to talk with Chrystal. I let out a frustrated huff and turned back to Chrystal.

"Alright, what's up?" I asked.

She softly smiled and quickly grabbed my hand, leading me from the hall. We made our way across campus to the most secluded area, where she let go of my hand.

"Okay … how did you do that?" Her words were slightly rushed with excitement and intrest.

"Do what?" I asked, trying to pass off what had happened in the hallway as if nothing had really happened.

She looked around, making sure we were alone.

"Alex, there is only one other person, other than Gabriel, that I knew of who could stop a transformation as you did."

"Really?" I stepped closer. "Well who is – wait a minute … you said *knew* … what do you mean *knew*? How do you know anything about any of this?"

"The woman I knew was my best friend," Chrystal said. "We did everything together. She sort-of took me under her wing, so to speak, and taught me the ropes of this new life."

"Wait – what do you mean new life?" I interrupted. She bit her lip and pondered my question for a moment.

"There's too much to tell. I can't …"

I placed my hand on her shoulder.

"It's alright Chrys," I said, remembering what My Strength had said about being patient. "I understand that there are things you can't tell me right now."

"No, I'm not saying I can't tell you – only that I can't think of where to begin," she said. "You see, when I became what I am… well it was a very, very long time ago. In fact, I was one of the first to join the group."

Chrystal paused for a moment before continuing on.

“I was just a poor girl from Ancient Rome, roaming the street and barely scraping by.”

Ancient Rome? That can’t be right.

I chose to ignore it and refocused my attention on her story.

“Most days I would have nothing to eat, and when I did eat it wasn’t good,” she continued. “I’d even resorted to eating bugs and palm leaves at one point.”

Her face scrunched in disgust, as if remembering the taste. She took a deep breath she continued on.

“I can still remember the first day I saw Ava,” she said, wonder in her voice. “She was so beautiful. All dressed in her royal robes. I wanted to be just like her – beautiful and elegant. I couldn’t help myself. I followed her through the streets to her house ….that’s where they caught me – the guards. They were all beautiful and regal-looking, as well. But Ava was the only one in the whole city who had female guards. Eros left my fate in her hands … she chose to take pity on me and allowed me to stay with her as her maidservant.”

I’d never seen this side of Chrystal – and though it was quite charming to watch as she excitedly continued her story, I began to worry that she was making things up. Now Eros was apparently from Ancient Rome, as well.

"She was always so kind to me," Chrystal continued. "From the moment I joined her staff I never had to worry about food – there was always an abundance of food, which was something I hadn't known for a long time."

She stopped as a tear began to streak down her cheek.

"But as Passover drew near things began to change. She remained the same, but Eros changed. He seemed so nice and handsome at first. What girl wouldn't have wanted him to want them? Two days before the Passover he … he … well …"

I could hardly believe what I was hearing. I could tell that this was very difficult for her to talk about, and I was pretty sure it was because of something Eros had done to her.

Did he take advantage of her?

Chrystal's eyes widened and then she let out a frustrated huff of air.

"To be continued," she said with an irritated look upon her face.

"But aren't you going to –" I began as someone wrapped their arm around my shoulders.

"I just couldn't stay away any longer," Eros said sweetly, burying his face in my hair and taking in a deep breath.

I tightened my jaw, remembering Chrystal's story. Though I didn't know for sure what he had done, I still was very angry with him. I turned around, ready to tear into him, but was unprepared when I actually saw him.

He's so beautiful!

"I have something for you and was going to give it to you earlier but with all of the comotion – well it sort of slipped my mind," he said.

He continued reaching his hand into his pocket and pulled out a small, hand-carved wooden box. Butterflies swarmed inside me and my heart began to pound, causing a slight flicker of pain.

A smile spread across Eros' face as he handed the box to me.

Slowly I opened the box, which revealed a beautiful ruby necklace. A flash of memory from my vision in the hallway almost made me drop the box and it's necklace.

Eros ran his hand across my face and tucked my hair behind my ear.

"Do you like it?" He questioned as he pulled the necklace from its box and placed it upon my neck.

"It's … it's …" My mind flooded with wonder as I stared down at the mesmerizingly beautiful necklace. "It's beautiful," I said as I looked up into Eros' ebony brown eyes. "Thank you." I softly kissed him upon the cheek and continued to study it.

This neckless belonged to Avangileen; did he want me to replace her?

I peered down at the exquisite necklace as it hung around my neck, "It's beautiful isn't it?" I said, glancing up at Chrys. Anger and hurt filled her eyes as she stared speechless at it.

"Okay, so what class do we have next, my lady?" He questioned as he sweetly kissed me upon the hand.

"What do you mean *we*?" I asked.

"I spoke to the administrator about changing my major."

"Changing it to what?" I inquired as Chrystal grabbed my hand and began pulling me in the direction of our next class.

As we walked down the hall, Eros continued.

"About changing it to scientific engineering," he said, interlacing his fingers with mine. "… so that I can have more classes with you."

"And did she say you could, or is she just allowing you to visit today?"

I stared up at Eros, secretly hoping that he was unable to change his major.

Eros shot me a half smile.

"We'll see," he said, shrugging aside whatever unforeseen roadblocks there might be to changing his major. "Now that I have you I'm not ever letting you go."

He pulled me closer to his side. An almost sick feeling swam in my stomach at the thought of him being with me every moment of the day.

I took in a deep breath as we entered the classroom and immediately scanned it for Gabriel. The moment that our eyes met, I felt as if I were betraying him entering the room with Eros; the pain in his eyes only made the betrayal all the more real, I coward behind Chrystal and Eros, not wanting Gabriel to see me with him. Eros almost boasted as he strutted into the room with me upon his arm.

All the girls fawned over him, and yet at the same time their expressions almost seemed to curse me. The sickness in my stomach seemed to grow with each passing second.

Why am I feeling this way?

"Have a seat," Eros said, nodding his head in the direction of two empty seats. "I need to go and speak with the professor for a moment."

He sweetly kissed me on the cheek and headed for the front, making his way through the crowd of girls. Raphael smiled at me weakly and gave a quick glance in Eros' direction. Then he looked back and me and nodded to the chair next to him. It was empty.

"I saved you a seat," he said. "Right there … beside *Gabriel.*"

My heart began to pound, beating rapidly inside my chest. I nervously bit my lip as I glanced up at Gabriel. Before I could answer, I was interrupted by a deep throat clearing.

"Can I help you?" Eros questioned as he slipped his arms around me and pulled me into his chest.

My heart sunk. I knew I couldn't sit with Raphael and Gabriel. I didn't want another fight.

... or whatever that was that happened in the hallway.

Raphael stepped closer to Eros and an almost sinister look crossed his face.

"What's it to you?"

I could see their skin tightening as if they were in the stage right before transformation. I couldn't let that happen. I stepped between the two.

"Not this time, Raphael," I said, Immediate disappointment flashed in his eyes.

"Okay …" He mumbled as he turned and began to head back to his seat.

I had to say something. I couldn't help it.

"But maybe next time … okay?"

Raphael turned around and softly smiled.

"Okay," He said and walked back to his seat as if in defeat.

All through class I continued glancing up at Gabriel, hoping he might be looking at me as well, but no such luck. Every time I turned to face him he was staring up at the teacher. He seemed distant as he stared blankly at the front of class. My mind was consumed with random imaginings of what could be going through his head. I glanced down at my necklace – there almost seemed to be a glow to it as it hung upon my neck. Before I knew what was going on, people were shuffling around me to get to their next class. I glanced over to where Gabriel had been sitting and to my dismay he was already gone – as though he could no longer take the sight of me.

CHAPTER ELEVEN

GAMES

For our lunch hour we made our way to the local McDonalds where Eros ordered me a burger and fries. My mind was numb trying to absorb everything that was going on. Some things were starting to come together, but still nothing seemed to make sense.

I can't wrap my mind around my strange transformations, the curse that causes the pain of the transformation, how I am connected Gabriel, Raphael, Eros and the others and why had someone tried to kill me?

Eros rattled on about how he enjoyed going to class with me and how he thought this was the right thing for him. Chrystal was still with us at the restaurant. She, like me, seemed to have a lot on her mind and an almost angry light in her eyes. After a few minutes, she stood up and without a word made her way to the restrooms.

"I'll be back," I said, jumping up from my seat and following after her. Walking into the restrooms I found Chrys hovering over the sink. I could hear her heart pounding.

"Chrys – what's wrong?" I asked, placing my hand upon her back. I could feel her bones beginning to shift inside her. "Chrys!" I shouted, turning her to face me.

"You h-have to g-get out of h-here!" Her tightly clenched teeth made it almost difficult to understand the words that she breathed.

"Help her," My Strength whispered.

I bit my lip and nodded my head, placing my hand upon her chest. *"What about the door? Can anyone see this?"* I asked him.

"Do what you have to and let me take care of it," My Strength said as I focused my attention upon Chrystal.

Fiery daggers raced up my arm and pain consumed me as I tried to halt her transformation. My bones began to tear from my body and I stopped breathing when suddenly I once again was transported to a strange place from a different memory.

"You shouldn't be here!" Chrystal said as she tightened her kung-fu like grip around my shoulders.

I looked around. We were an ancient building – columns surrounded the walls and there were large archways that opened to the outer air.

"Eros is going to kill you!" Chrystal said. Her teeth were clinched as a tear rolled down her cheek.

"I know Chrys," I responded, the words coming out of my mouth but not really belonging to me. "But I had to see you one last time before I entered hiding. I couldn't leave without saying goodbye. You're my best friend."

"We have to go Ava! They'll be here any minute!"

Chrystal shot a look over my shoulder and I turned to see a handsome man waiting at the door for me. Something about him seemed familiar and reminded me of Gabriel. That's when I realized I'd seen him before.

He's Zander.

Sorrow filled my mind as I nodded Ava's head and turned to leave.

A cacophony of images bombarded me then – one after another in rapid succession. I saw many images of traveling with the handsome man – we were on the run, leaving Chrys behind as tears streamed down her face. I saw flashes of marriage and a baby, Chrys present in the background of each of the flashes – and then an excruciating pain pierced my heart. Like before with Eros and

Raphael, I used My Strength to push back the pain from my heart and into Chrystal. Her breath caught in her chest and she gasped for air. We were suddenly back in the McDonald's restroom.

"I'm sorry. I'm so sorry, Chrys. I didn't mean to hurt you."

I stepped back to give her some air. She looked up and smiled.

"Thank you Alex," she said with a strange look resting in her eyes. "I don't think I have to worry about unwanted transformation anymore. Once again I have a powerful friend."

"That vision … what was it?"

She shook her head in confusion.

"Vision?" she asked. "What vision?"

There is something that I was supposed to catch, yet I know I missed it something that is an important part of everything that is going on.

I frowned and looked at the floor.

"Nevermind," I said, and then looked up her and smiled. I grabbed her hand and headed to the bathroom door. "We'd better get back. Eros will probably think we fell in."

Chrys laughed quietly.

"By the way," I said as we exited the restroom. "I was going to ask you – would you like to come over to my place after school? You, me and Natalya can hang out."

"Sure!" She quickly said, and I smiled at the excitement in her voice.

An entire line had formed outside the bathroom and everyone blankly stared at us as we walked over to our seats. "What's everyone staring at?" I asked Eros.

Eros raised one eyebrow and stood up to allow us to sit.

"Probably because you and Chrys locked the bathroom door," he said absently as he sat back in his chair.

I wrinkled my face in confusion.

"No we didn't. That door doesn't even have a lock on it."

His smile faded.

"Oh …"

"All I can guess is that it got stuck somehow," I said. I knew the excuse was lame, but I'd realized too late that My Strength had probably kept the door locked in place for me. Trying to change the subject, I pulled my phone from my pocket.

"We'd better be headed back to campus," I said. "I have a class in 15 minutes."

Eros slipped his hand around my shoulders as we headed to the car.

"You mean *we* have class in 15 minutes," He said, kissing me on the cheek and slipping into the car.

The remainder of my classes that day went by fairly quickly, but when I would catch a glimpse of Gabriel, he always seemed to be intentionally distant. I knew it was because of me, and I couldn't help but feel a nagging guilt about it.

After classes Chrys and I made our way to Raphael's car.

"This is his car?" She questioned, not sure we were at the right one.

"Yes, it's his alright," I said with a big smile. "I rode in it with him and Nat this morning."

Chrystal made her way around the car to admire it. A moment later Raphael, Natalya, Michael, and Gabriel walked up to the car.

"Alex, Gabriel is ready to talk with you. Is now a good time?" Raphael asked me as Chrys' head popped up on the other side of the car, giving everyone a shock.

"Well actually now is not a good time for me," Gabriel nodded his head and turned to walk away. Panic flashed over me. I quickly turned to Chrys.

"Can we do this a little later on – at about 6:30?" I asked, and she nodded her head.

"That would be great," she said with a sweet smile.

I jotted down my address on a corner piece of paper that I tore from my notebook and handed it to her.

"I'll see you there at 6:30 sharp."

Chrys waved and walked from my sight. I turned back to Raphael.

"Okay, where'd Gabriel go? I'm ready to speak with him."

Raphael bit his lip.

"He left. I'm sorry," He mumbled. "But we can meet him at the hou– I'm sorry you are going to have to speak with him another time."

Frustration swelled inside me as I thought of what I was putting Chrystal through. I closed my eyes, wanting to shout her name in hopes that I might catch her in hearing distance. Opening my eyes I found Chrys standing before me. My frustration quickly dissolved, replaced by curiosity.

"Hi!" She eagerly chirped.

"Wha … how did … when did you …" No matter how hard I tried I could not get my words out clearly.

Natalya stared at me with wide eyes, "oookkkaaay … so what are we going to do?' Nat said, trying to change the subject from my embarrassing stutters.

A smile spread across my face.

"Well, I guess since Chrys is here we can head back to our place and hang out – if that's alright with you two?"

They both nodded their heads as Raphael's drooped in disappointment.

"So I guess I'm not invited?" He asked.

I walked to his side and draped my arms around his shoulders.

"Of course you're invited," I said. "I thought that went without saying."

He smiled and then winked at me. The look he gave me was knowing – almost as if he'd known beforehand exactly what I was going to say.

We ate dinner together at the apartment, and afterwards Raphael and Natalya volunteered to go to the store to get ice cream.

Once Nat and Raphael left I decided to take advantage of the moment.

"Okay, now that they're gone, can you finish what you were saying before – you know, when you said 'To be continued.'"

Chrystal Smiled.

"All I was saying is tha–"

Before she could finish there came a rough pounding at the door.

"Give me a second," I said hesitantly as I peeled myself from the couch and headed to the door. I was surprised to see Micheal standing in the doorway with his arms folded across his chest.

"What are you doing here?" I questioned as I furrowed my eyebrows.

He let out a frustrated huff.

"I was wondering if I might be able to hang with you, Raphael, Natalya, and that other girl," he said. My jaw dropped. "What's her name? Chrystal?"

"Why would you want to hang out with us?"

Michael's jaw tightened.

"I was told – I mean I thought that it might be f-fun …" He almost seemed to choke upon his words as they hesitantly came out.

You don't need to guard me Chrystal isn't going to hurt me." I whispered in his ear.

"What makes you think that I'm guarding you?" He nervously ran his hand back through his hair as he back away from me.

"I overheard you guys talking when…" I stepped closer and lowered my voice, "When I was stabbed."

"Look I may have failed to protect you this morning, but I won't fail again and whether you like it or not you're stuck with me guarding you so get used to it." Irritation and pain filled his words.

I shook my head.

"Fine, you can stay but don't be such a party pooper …"

An almost awkward smile worked its way upon his face.

"Good. This will be … interesting?"

Michael stepped around me and into the living room.

Chrystal had a sweet smile upon her face as she shyly tried not to stare at him.

"So would you like a drink?" I asked as I walked to the kitchen sink and pulled a glass from the cabinet.

He stretched his arms over his head and arched his back.

"What have you got?"

"Well, we have water, ice water, and …" I opened the freezer to pull out some ice cubes. "Wait – correction. We don't have ice water, so just tap water. So what will it be?"

"I guess I will have … cold tap water, if it's not too much trouble."

I nodded my head as I let the tap run for a bit, allowing the water to get cold.

"Okay so what are we going to do?" Michael asked as he plopped himself down in a lounge chair.

"Well I guess we could play a game?"

I handed the glass to Michael and pulled the remote off of the end table, turning the channel to video.

"I have Epic Mickey, Super Mario, Wii Sports …"

"If it's alright with you I will just watch for now."

I nodded my head and turned to Chrys, "What about you," I asked. "What would you like to play?"

"Well, I've always wanted to play Wii Sports, if that's alright with you?"

As the games began I totally crushed Chrys, annihilating her in the first round. I leaped to my feet. "Yes, I won…" I stated dancing from side to side just to rub it in a little more. Chrys smiled at my ridiculous flopping around and my rude behavior and Michael rolled his eyes.

"Alright …" Chrys said as she pulled her hair back into a ponytail. "I know you won the first round, but I think I've got the hang of it now so …" She paused for a moment and raised her eyebrows. "…Let's do this."

"Yes …let's …"

I sat back down, confident in my abilities as the games began, but in a matter of minutes all confidence was swept away as Chrys effortlessly annihilated me this time.

My mouth hung open at my defeat. How I had gone from winning to complete defeat was beyond my comprehension. I bit my lip and glanced at Michael from the corner of my eye.

His pleasure at my defeat seemed to pulse from every fiber of his being as he confidently stared at the television.

"So have you been put through enough humiliation?" He asked, a half smile irritatingly working its way upon his face.

"What? You think you can do better?" I questioned in an irritated voice as I shoved the controller in his direction.

"No. I don't think I can do better," A larger grin made its way upon his face. "…I know I can do better."

Anger boiled inside at his cocky remark and pain worked its way from my heart, through my chest, and down my back. I closed my eyes and let out a slow steady breath as I pushed the pain back to where it had started. A soft smile worked across my face. I knew My Strength would be proud of me, and when I was sure that I was in control of my body I opened my eyes to find Chrys, Raphael, and Michael all staring at me in utter astonishment, Nat was placing the ice cream in the freezer.

When did they get back?

"What?" I questioned.

"I don't care how many times you do that, it still amazes me," Raphael said, shaking his head. "It just looks so effortless."

"No it's not effortless!" I said, frustration starting to bubble over. I took a slow, deep breath and rubbed my sore chest; I could feel the raised scar beneath my fingers as I continued. "It takes a great deal of concentration to push back the transformation.

Michael gave Chrystal a hateful glair as if he didn't want her to be there, even more-so now that I was talking about my transformation.

"The pain is unlike anything I've ever felt before," I continued. "Almost as if my bones are trying to tear through my skin."

I shook my head, not wanting to think about the pain. I continued without hesitation.

"When the pain flares out from my –"

Before I could finish I was interrupted by a loud throat clearing.

"I don't mean to be rude, but Gabriel was wondering if you were free to speak with him now?" Raphael asked, pointing to his phone.

My heart felt as if it were about to pound straight through my chest. The great pain came once again, and fanned out from my heart, but I didn't care.

"He's here?" I blurted out, placing my hand gently upon my chest as the tearing pain pulsed over my entire body and my scar began to throb.

"No he's not here … He wants you to meet him at our place …"

I began to steady my heart rate, slowing its rapid pounding as he continued.

"And from the sound of it, it's quite urgent."

My heart rate spiked higher than it ever had before. I tightly clenched my teeth, only able to dull the pain slightly. Still, it was enough to hold back a transformation.

Raphael protectively stepped in front of Natalya at the spike of my heart rate, as if he knew a transformation was coming. I turned to Chrystal just to see what her reaction might be. She seemed to almost cower away from me as she listened to my elevated heart.

Finally turning to Michael I found a slight grin upon his almost glowing face, as if he were waiting for me to morph into a hideous beast. I tried to further slow my heart but my attempts were futile. So, satisfied with holding my transformation where it was I started walking toward the door.

"Let's go, then," I said to Raphael. "Come on." I huffed, trying to motion them out the door.

CHAPTER TWELVE

ANGER

At the car Michael gave Chrystal a nod.

"So I guess I'll see you in class," he said as he slipped into Raphael's car.

I leaned over to look inside at him as a wince of pain escaped my lips and my heart rate spiking ever so slightly once again.

"She's coming with us," I stated, almost pushing her into the car next to Michael.

"What?! ... NO … SHE CAN'T!!!" Michael exclaimed, slipping out the other door.

"And why can't she?" I asked, trying to keep my heart rate from spiking any higher.

"Well … well because she can't," Michael stuttered as he nervously ran his hand through his hair.

"That's not a reason … besides, you're not riding with us anyhow you have your own mode of transportation."

I nodded toward his bike.

Michael furrowed his eyebrows.

"About that … I … well I blew out my tire on the way over here."

"WHAT!?" Raphael exclaimed.

"My tire blew out on …"

"I know that, what I was meaning is you don't think that you're going to be riding with us do you? Cause you're not." Raphael interrupted.

Michael leaned closer to Raphael and a crooked smile made its way upon his face. "That's the idea," he said, folding his arms across his chest.

"You can't ..."

"And who's going to stop me?"

Michael stepped slightly closer to Raphael and poked him in the shoulder.

"You?"

Raphael straightened up and puffed up his chest.

"Yes. Me. Do you have a problem with that?"

A bright blue flashed in Michael's eyes.

"I'd like to see you try."

The same blue color flashed in Raphael's eyes but quickly faded when there came a faint vibrating from his pocket.

"STAY OUT OF MY CAR!!" Raphael said as he slid his finger across his phone to answer it. "Hello?" He began. "Yes we are, but … no I can't … but she … well even th … no I won't put her in danger like that, not again … yes but it is already elevated …"

My head fell in shame. I knew he was talking about me and he didn't even have to say my name. Was I really so horrifying that he thought I wouldn't be able to control my transformation? Hadn't he seen me do it a number of times? I rubbed my hand across my sore chest. I knew my heart rate was elevated, but I was keeping it in check. Or at least I thought that I was.

"… I know you trust that she can control it, but what about the other one? We barley even know her." Raphael paused as if he were listening to what the person on the other end of the line was saying.

I glanced over at Chrystal as tears began to well in her eyes, I swiftly slid across the seat, bumping into her side.

"You okay?" I asked

A faint smile worked its way upon her face.

"I'm fine … how about you?"

"I'm good."

In the background I heard someone's heart rate spike, and Michael slid into the seat next to me, pushing me into the center of the car. Irritation swelled inside and anger filled my heart as I stared at Michael's cocky, crooked smile.

"Sounds like I'm riding with you," he said as he glanced in Raphael's direction.

Anger filled Raphael's eyes. He angrily walked to the car and got into the driver's seat and tightly gripped the steering wheel as a huff of air hissed through his teeth. We uncomfortably sat in the car waiting for Natalya. Everyone's nerves were raw, and I worried that another fight might break out between Raphael and Michael, which would cause Chrystal to transform.

"You know what to do," said My Strength suddenly – quiet and authoritative within my head. *"Place your hand gently upon Raphael's chest. Let My Strength flow through you."*

"I can't …" I whispered.

"You can …" Natalya said flippantly as she slipped into the car and closed the door.

Confusion consumed me.

Can she hear My Strength?

"I can what?" I asked, probing.

Natalya smiled and shrugged her shoulders.

"I dunno. You tell me."

"Tell you what?"

I could hear Raphael's heart spike all the further as we sat there discussing what I could and couldn't do.

"What you *can* do ..." She turned her attention to Raphael, almost as if My Strength were speaking through her. "Is he okay?"

Raphael's eyes turned a neon blue in color and his jaw tightened.

"You must do it now," My Strength said.

I turned to Chrystal and saw red flash in her eyes and pain flush over her face. *"You have to help all of them, but start with Raphael. They'll tear each other to pieces. HURRY!"*

A low growl rumbled in Michael's chest. I turned to find him staring at Raphael with a devilish smile upon his face and his eyes turned an ice blue.

There came the female voice once again, along with a strong smell of citrus.

"Whatever you do, do not engage them."

I looked around for the woman but feeling Chrystal's fear as it almost seemed to radiate off her I turned my attention to her. Unable to contain her fear or pain any longer, she tore open the door and slid out. She raced for the nearest coverage of tree only to be halted by Raphael. I stared in shock at what was happening.

"Where do you think you're going?" He angrily growled.

"I don't want to fight," Chrystal said as she tried to slow her heart rate.

Michael walked up behind Chrystal, both Raphael and Michael towered over her as she stood between the two.

Fear grabbed me. I sucked in a deep breath, trying to find courage.

"Now are you ready to help?" My Strength asked.

I nodded my head.

"Good. Then you know what to do. So go do it."

I stepped between Michael and Raphael, and with one last encouraging word from My Strength, I placed my hands upon their chests.

"That's enough!" I shouted in a stern voice. Then My Strength sent a pulse racing down my arms and into their chests. Both convulsed with pain as the currents pulsed into their bodies. Falling to the ground, their bodies violently jerked in every direction.

Terror consumed me.

"What's happening?" I screamed as I stepped back from their shaking bodies.

Natalya ran to Raphael's side and pinned herself across his body.

"Hurry! Do the same to Michael," she said as she tried to stop Raphael's body from convulsing.

I hesitantly looked over at Michael's body as he violently shook.

"C'mon! He could hurt himself!" Nat shouted as she nodded her head in Michael's direction.

I took a deep breath and sat down on the ground beside Michael. I wrapped my arms around his shoulders with great difficulty. Then I moved my body on top of his, twisting my legs around his. Then, letting out a slow, steady breath, I tightened my muscles to try and force him to stop convulsing. After a few minutes his convulsing stopped.

"Is Raphael alright?" I asked as I listened to the rhythm of Michael's heartbeat.

"I'm alright," Raphael said as he sat up next to Natalya and wrapped his arms around her shoulders.

"What about Chrystal? Is she okay?"

"I'm fine," Chrystal's quiet voice came from the car.

"What were you doing?" I asked Raphael, trying to hold back my anger at him.

"I started to become the beast," he said.

"But you didn't transform fully into the beast," I said, using air quotations to emphasize "the beast."

Shame consumed his face as he continued.

"It was bad enough," he said, head lowered. "I couldn't stop myself. It was all I could do to keep myself from killing her. It's part of the curse of our kind, when our heart rates spike and transformation starts we lose control of our…I guess that you could say our humanity?" He glanced in Chrystal's direction indicating that it was the same for her.

Suddenly Michael shoved me off of his chest and onto the ground. Then he jumped up and pulled open the car door and got in.

What's his problem?

I stood up and ran my hands quickly over my jeans, removing some dust and twigs that had stuck to them before making my way to the car.

The car was filled with awkward silence throughout the entire drive to speak with Gabriel. The only sound was the wind blowing through Chrystal's open window.

"So did you enjoy laying on top of me?" Michael asked suddenly.

"What?" I questioned, completely caught off-guard. "I … I didn't … I mean I was just trying to help."

My heart rate spiked again and this time I couldn't hold the pain back.

Is he trying to make me transform?

Michael continued to pick at me.

"So …" I turned to find one of his eyebrows cocked and a crooked smile upon his face, "You want a kiss?"

"WHAT!?!"

My anger swelled and I lost control. The familiar pain consumed me. I tightly clenched my teeth and tried to hold it back, but the transformation was coming – there was no stopping it. The very thing I'd been dreading for weeks – the transformation that taunted me with evil potential for the past few days – was about to come forth.

What sort of monster will I become?

As I succumbed to the inevitable, I did the only thing I could think of. I leaped for Chrystal's open window and somehow twisted myself through it while the car was still speeding down the road. Raphael brought the car to a screeching halt as I landed firmly upon the pavement below.

My bones began to shift, nearly tearing through my skin. I wanted cry out in pain, but remained silent as my fingers dug into the cement as if it were sand gently slipping through my fingers. The skin upon the back of my hands rip apart revealing the black flesh beneath and savage animal like claws; the ripping of my flesh continued up my arms and across my back and chest. The scar upon my chest throbbed as I continued to transform.

This is it. I can't hold it back any longer.

Then – soft and sweet – came the voice of My Strength.

"Don't give in," he said. *"Don't let the darkness take over. Push back the darkness before it consumes your heart."*

My Strength was calm and confident as my heart nearly pounded its way out of my chest.

"I CAN'T!"

"You can," said My Strength. *"I believe in you."* Warmth touched my heart as My Strength continued. *"Let My Strength be your strength."*

The warmth flowed from my heart and fanned out from there, working its way through my chest, over my arms, and down my back. I let out a painful but steady breath as the warmth worked its way further through my body.

Too consumed with pain, I didn't know what was going on around me, but my ears seemed to pick up every noise around me with startling clarity. It was overwhelming – I could hear each individual flap of a fly's wings, each drop of dew falling from blades of grass as it fell to the ground, and each step that my friends took toward me as they vacated the car.

I can hear everything!

The pain was excruciating as my bones jig-sawed back into place. The noises collided inside my mind and a wince of pain escaped my lips as I held in my agony. I repeated over and over again in my head the words spoken by My Strength.

Let My Strength be your strength. Let My Strength be your strength.

The words seemed to hush the noise that surrounded me, allowing my body to relax and further allowing My Strength's warmth to consume me.

After what seemed like an eternity, my body worked its way back to normal, as if this was normal in the first place. Allowing my body to calm completely, I sank to the cold, damp cement below. Laying there for several seconds, I heard the sound of my friends' footsteps growing louder as they came toward me.

"She could hurt you," Raphael said, cautioning the others.

"She won't hurt me," Natalya hissed. "How could you even say that?"

"… Because she has before."

Shame consumed me as I lay motionless on the ground.

"That was different," Natalya said. "She can control it now." A soft hand pressed against my forehead. "She's so cold."

"Cold? What do you mean cold?"

"Touch her … her skin is like ice."

Raphael placed his strong, gentle hand upon my forehead. "You're right, she is like ice … but why?"

Another hand swept across my cheek as Natalya and Raphael tried to figure out what was happening to me.

"So why is she cold?" Chrystal wondered. "I've never reacted like this … my body turning to ice …"

"Why would she react like you?" Michael huffed, his heart pounding violently against his ribs.

"Because she's one of us," She stated, her voice taking command of the situation.

A low evil growl echoed through my ears as Michael continued the conversation.

"No she's not, you Ανόητο γάτα! She's one of us."

"That's impossible! She's a girl …"

Just as I could hear every little detail of the world around me, I could feel the pulsing of their hearts as they argued back and forth, until their hearts beat so rapidly that they sounded like continuous thunder. Afraid that Michael might hurt Chrys, I snapped at him.

"Don't speak to her like that!"

My words were confident and sure as I laid upon the ground, weak and tired.

With my back to Michael Natalya helped me to my feet.

"Be careful Alex … you're still weak and Michael is a trained fighting machine."

"Don't worry Nat, I'll be perfectly fine," I said. "I'm a lot tougher than I look and somebody needs to teach Michael …" I turned to face Michael, unaware of what I might see. "… a lesson."

Strangely, Michael was nowhere in sight.

"Where did he go?" I asked as I searched the surrounding trees. Confusion consumed me when I noticed Chrystal missing as well. I turned to Raphael and Nat. "Where is Chrys?"

Natalya's eyes fell to the other side of the road. "Why did she run off and …"

Before I finished I noticed a pile of discarded clothes lying upon the ground.

Making my way to it, I knelt down to examine the pile. I turned the clothes over and over in my hands, but unable to explain them being torn into shreds I looked to Natalya for an explanation. I held up the clothes in question and simply said, "What happened?"

Natalya furrowed her eyebrows, wrinkled her nose and – unable or unwilling to give me an explanation – she directed her eyes toward the trees lining the road beside me. I stood up and walked closer, pausing and listening for anything strange. Confusion consumed me – there was a faint but steady heartbeat coming from the trees in front of me, but what was even more confusing was the rapid almost painful pounding that echoed from the trees on the opposite side of the road.

I began to head to the other side, when a soft gentle hand halted my pursuit.

"Alex are you okay?" Chrystal asked as she wrapped her arms sweetly across my shoulders in a half hug. "To halt transformation as long as you did and to stop it completely … well it had to be hard."

How did she know that I halted my transformation? I don't think she transforms into a beast, does she?

I glanced at Raphael.

No he must have told her.

"Not only did it have to be hard, but in all of my years I have never seen anything like what you did." Raphael stated in awe.

Embarrassment colored my face as she continued to go on with her flattering. Suddenly a low growl emerged from the tree line, accompanied by the same rapid heart rate. It had to be Michael, he was the only one of the group it could be.

"Michael, if you're trying to scare us it's not going to work," I yelled as I began to scan the trees for his presence. I caught a flash of two neon blue eyes.

"What is it? What do you see?" Chrys asked as she stared in the same direction.

"Michael?" I mumbled, stepping closer to the tree line.

There was just enough moonlight to see a large dark void in the trees, but not enough to make out any defining features.

What is he?

Unable to help myself, I inched closer, the fallen leaves and branches crunching under my feet. A warning growl escaped the beast's lips as I stepped just inside the tree line. My heart nervously thumped inside my chest. I tightly clenched my teeth together, slowing its acceleration. The beast inched closer to me and let out a frustrated huff. I looked around, there was no one other than the five of us in sight and that included the beast before me.

Everything around me seemed so clear. I could hear an owl hooting among the trees, crickets chirping with in the brush and the wind whistling through the trees, but the thing that stood out the most was a heavy – almost violent – breathing accompanied by a thundering heart beat coming from the beast before me.

Michael.

His neon blue eyes seemed to pierce straight through me, looking beyond me to Chrystal. Another low growl crawled through the night towards us.

I took in a deep breath to steady my heart rate and a mesmerizingly wonderful scent consumed me – a scent that somehow reminded me of Gabriel. I closed my eyes and let myself be enveloped by the intoxicating scent. How one man could have such a hypnotically wonderful scent was beyond my comprehension.

He must be here.

I let out a sigh of pleasure and a vibration of ecstasy pulsed down my spine as the scent touched my skin. It was almost as if I could taste it – a sweet hypnotic vanilla that gave off a calming feeling the moment it hit the nose.

My heart began to accelerate once again as I thought of Gabriel and his perfectly chiseled face – the way his hair swept just across his face in the most irresistible way. I could barely contain my thoughts when a gentle hand touched my shoulder, brushed down my arm, and grasped my hand – an electric current pulsating over my skin.

"Michael, come forth from the shadows where we can see you."

Shock consumed me. It was the voice. I hadn't heard it for awhile, and now it was here right behind me and touching my hand. My heart began to quicken as he gently began to lead me backward toward the car. My vision began to blur and goosebumps rose upon my skin as he tightened his grasp upon my hand.

I wanted to know who this mystery man was, so much so that it hurt to breathe, but I couldn't bring myself to look.

What if he wasn't who I wanted him to be? What if he isn't Gabriel?

Slowly, hesitantly, I opened my eyes. And there, smiling down at me, was Gabriel.

CHAPTER THIRTEEN

REVEALED

Slowly the beast tromped forward, small trees crashing violently to the ground as he made his way closer to us. Chrystal's eyes widened and her heart began to aggressively thump as she slowly stepped backward, never taking her eyes off Michael.

I placed my hand upon her shoulder, causing her heart rate to spike all the further, "It's alright Chrys …"

Her breathing became shallow as she turned and looked at me and red pulsed in her eyes. She shook her head.

"It's t-too la-late," she said, her bones shifting and jig-sawing out of place. She raced for the cover of the trees on the adjacent side of the road, clipping me with the back of her hand. I fell to the ground, my vision momentarily going black from being pelted in the face. The romping of the beast behind me quickened. Out of the corner of my eye I saw a dark blond shadow leap over me and race into the trees where Chrys had fled.

A strong hand helped me to my feet as I heard the commotion of snarling and hissing of a battle taking place in the trees. Fear consumed me.

Michael was going to tear Chrys apart!

A hand brushed across my face and turned my head.

"I will stop them, he will not hurt her," Gabriel said as he turned and raced toward the trees where Michael and Chrys where fighting.

It was him! He was the voice that I'd been hearing all this time! Not the voice of My Strength, but the comforting voice who'd helped me in class and encouraged me during the early days when the transformations had first come about. I'd wanted it to be him, but now that I knew it was him it was a little unnerving.

Gabriel ran toward the trees and quickly disappeared into the foliage. I listened to the crashing of trees and the snarling of beasts hidden behind the trees. There was a loud yelp and squeak, almost simultaneous. Then silence filled the air – not even the crickets were chirping. I listened for a heartbeat, a growl, anything, but no matter how hard I tried, silence still filled the air.

I ran toward the trees, only to be halted by Raphael.

"You should stay here," he said as he shook his head and nervously ran his hand through his hair.

"But what if … he could need help …"

"Gabriel can handle this," Raphael said matter-of-factly.

"I know but I … I can help …I want to help."

Tears welled in my eyes as Raphael pulled me into a side-hug.

"I know Alex … but I cannot allow you to … I'm sorry."

A moment later Natalya came to my other side and wrapped her arms around me, as well. I felt oddly emotional, and a tears started to well into my eyes. Then suddenly a throat cleared somewhere near the tree line, immediately commanding our attention.

A moment later, Gabriel emerged from the trees holding Chrystal limp body in his arms.

"WHAT DID MICHEAL DO TO HER?!" I exclaimed as I raced to Gabriel's side. I quickly gave her a once-over to asses the damage done to her. The left side of her face looked as if it were completely smashed and blood covered her entire left side. More blood spewed from her smashed face with every beat of her heart. There also looked as if there were jagged bites in numerous areas of her body – arms, stomach, and legs. It was a horrifying sight. I turned to Raphael and pleaded with him, "Help her!" Gabriel walked around me and placed her in the back seat of the car.

I began to walk toward the car when I heard a rustling coming from behind me. I turned to find Michael walking from the trees.

"Hey…" He said as he finished buttoning up his shirt and gave me a wink.

Anger boiled inside me when a cocky half smile made it's way on his face. I angrily walked up to Michael and grabbed him by the hand and began to pull him in the direction of the car.

"I didn't know that we were at the hand holding stage in our relationship," he said, a slight grin resting on his face.

I glanced back at Michael with a hateful glare, knowing that if looks could kill I would not be holding the hand of a pompous, arrogant jerk – I would be dragging one instead.

Shock and pain consumed his face as if he knew what my look had intended.

"If you think it ... it has already been done," My Strength said.

Shame consumed me and my elevated heart rate slowed.

"I … I'm sorry …" I mumbled. "I just got angry when I saw what you did to her." I stated as I shoved him toward the car.

Michael stared at Chrystal's limp, lifeless body in horror.

"I didn't … I wasn't …" Michael anxiously ran his hands through his hair. "Is she going to be okay?"

He stepped slightly closer to her with an outstretched hand, almost as if he wanted to touch her.

"She's going to be fine," Gabriel said as he walked to my side and ran his strong gentle hand down my arm, causing electric pulses to vibrate over my skin.

I shook my head, not wanting to be distracted from the situation at hand.

"Going to be fine? Going to be fine? You have got to be kidding me. She is not fine. Just look at her! Does she look fine to you?"

I smacked Michael upon the back of the head.

Michael's heart rate spiked and he turned to me, anger boiling in his neon blue eyes.

"You really need to stop smacking me."

His teeth were tightly clenched as the angry words escaped from his lips.

"And who's going to stop me?" I stepped closer and smacked him upon the back of the head once again.

Did I really just do that?

I could hear Michael's heart begin to pulse and I knew he was going to transform again. Before it could happen, however, Gabriel stepped between Michael and me and said, "Go."

Then he turned his head in the direction of the trees. Michael turned and was gone in a flash, letting out a howl of pain just before entering the trees.

"Why did you let him go and not at least try to stop his transformation? And why won't you guys help her? She's covered in blood."

I glanced at Raphael and then back toward Gabriel to search their faces for answers.

A soft smile touched Gabriel's face and he sweetly grasped my hand, causing my knees to feel as if they would buckle. Gabriel opened the car door and nodded his head toward Chrystal as she laid motionless on the seat. Slowly I slid into the car next to her, causing her breathing to become rapid, almost as if she couldn't get enough air.

I gently rolled her over where I had seen the gaping open wound and crushed bone to find a loose bandage had been placed over it as well as her other wounds. Gabriel had doctored her up. I turned to him as if to ask if it was alright to check them. He nodded his head in approval and I turned my attention back to Chrystal.

Gently I worked the adhesive off so as not to pull or tug at the wound. Shock consumed me. I stared unbelieving at her laceration as it healed itself.

Watching in amazement it rebuilt itself. The section of her skull that had been crushed reconstructed right before me as if it hadn't been smashed into hundreds of tiny pieces. That was followed by rebuilding of the muscles. I turned away – it was all too graphic for me, I couldn't handle it a moment longer. Gently I placed the bandage back on top of the repairing wound and faintly made my way out of the car. I looked up into Gabriel's eyes. The culmination of so many confusing things all at once finally overwhelmed me, and unable to steady myself any longer I clumsily stumbled from the car into Gabriel's chest, causing us both to topple to the ground, wrapped in each other's arms. Every time he touched my skin, shivers of pleasure danced over me. I closed my eyes and took in a deep breath of his sweet hypnotic scent, listening to his erratic heart rate as it pulsed high and fast, matching my own.

I waited for the pain to come as I knew it would with the acceleration of my heart, but it didn't. A smile worked its way on my face as I listened to our thunderous hearts beating as one. The warmth between our bodies seemed to calm our hearts, slowing them in unison. Reluctantly I began to gather myself and rise to my feet, but Gabriel tightened his arms around me – almost as if he didn't want to let me go.

Suddenly there was an awkward throat clearing. Quickly I slipped off of Gabriel and flipped to my feet.

"We … w-we … w-weren't doing anything," I nervously stuttered as I stared awkwardly at the ground, allowing my hair to fall into my face.

"I didn't say you were."

It was Michael's voice. He was back again, once more calm and almost affable.

"I saw you fall and I assumed that Gabriel caught you … however … as to why you're lying on the ground I really don't know because Gabriel is far more agile than I and I'm not that clumsy. I totally would have caught you only with a little more flare."

Then he purposely tripped me, causing me to clumsily fall into his arms. He smiled and his eyebrows almost danced across his forehead as he gave me a throaty laugh.

"See. I told you that I would catch you."

I rolled my eyes and pulled myself from the awkward embrace.

"Yes, but only after you tripped me. What is wrong with you? I mean, first you hate me, then you injure Chrys …" I nodded my head in the direction of the car. "… and now you're hitting on me?"

Michael slowly walked to the car and stared at Chrys' bloody body as I continued.

"I mean, seriously – what's wrong with you? It's like you have some sort-of disorder …"

I continued spewing out words of malice when the voices of My Strength and Gabriel said my name simultaneous, both of them sounding disappointed.

"I'm sorry," I said as I nervously bit my lip. "He just gets on my nerves and I don't understand him … or you for that matter – either one of you."

Gabriel stood up, ran his hand down my arms, and looked at me.

"What is it about us that you don't understand?" He asked as my heart rate raised and shivers danced over my skin. Unable to look Gabriel in the eyes, I stared down at the ground and gave my answer.

"Well … I don't understand how you guys don't get along with Chrys and her friends … I mean you guys are the same … aren't you? Because I keep hearing you guys say that we are the same … and if we are then aren't you and her?"

I glanced up at Gabriel, who nodded his head.

"It is time you knew."

"Knew what?" I questioned, trying to hide my excitement for what I knew was coming.

"It is time you knew what you are and where you come from."

My heart fluttered with anticipation as Gabriel let out a slow, steady breath and continued.

"Well … first things first – I should probably show you what you are. At least … part of what you are."

"What do you mean *part* of what I am?"

His bones began to shift as he further explained.

"Meaning there is more to you than what is seen, which I will explain, but for now I am going to step b-behind the t-tree line so as n-not to embarrass myself." Gabriel turned as his mass enlarged and bones jig-sawed further out of place – his shirt tearing from his back just before disappearing behind the trees.

I waited to hear him holler out in pain as Michael, Raphael, and Chrystal had, but heard nothing when there came Gabriel's voice beautiful and hypnotic.

"I am going to come out so do not be afraid."

"I'm not afraid of you," I stated.

Michael looked at me with a strange look upon his face.

"I didn't say you were," Michael said, as if confused.

"I was talking to –" I began.

"They cannot hear me Alex," Came Gabriel's voice inside my head. ***"Only you can at this moment."***

Michael, Raphael, and Natalya stared at me with curiosity as we silently continued our conversation.

"Why?" I thought, sending out the words toward a vague awareness of Gabriel somewhere in the trees.

"Oh, Alex it is good to hear your voice this way," Gabriel replied. ***"It has been so long since I have been able to speak with anyone telepathically like this – unless we're both in our***

Guardian forms, and that's simply because we're connected in that form. But never Guardian-to-human … except for one, and I thought that I had lost that connection with everyone when I lost Zander."

Zander was the guy from my dream, no I mean memory, no I mean vision. Regardless of whatever it was what was he to me?

I looked into the trees and found a pair of neon blue eyes staring back at me, ***"Who is Zand –"*** I began when suddenly Michael wrapped his arms around me and began to pull me back from the tree line.

"Here he comes … you might want to step back," Michael said, unaware of the silent conversation taking place in my head.

I pulled Michael's arms off me and glanced at him.

"I'm not afraid of Gabriel," I said. "I know no matter what he is he will never hurt me."

Gabriel stepped to just inside the tree line and hesitated.

"What's wrong?" I silently asked.

"Nothing I just … I just know that the moment you see what I am everything for you is going to change."

A sadness filled his words that almost broke my heart.

A soft smile worked its way upon my face.

"It wasn't that normal to begin with."

"What are you smiling about?" Michael asked.

"Nothing," I said. "I'm just excited about how my life is about to change."

I took a deep breath to prepare myself for what I might see. I listened to Gabriel's slow, steady heart beat – its rhythmic beating seemed to calm me as I listened to it.

"How is that possible?" I whispered.

"How is what possible?" Raphael asked as he placed his hand upon my shoulder.

"Well …" I glanced at Raphael and continued. "Just listen to Gabriel's heart beat."

I paused to allow him to listen for a moment to Gabriel's steady pulse.

"And what does that have to do with anything?"

"Listen to how slow it is …"

"Oh … that's something that only Gabriel can do. He can control how and when he transforms. His heart rate has nothing to do with his transformation. He can transform whenever he wants to."

"Alex …"

The way Gabriel said my name made my knees buckle and goosebumps cascade over my skin.

"… I will tell you all about me, but you need to prepare yourself for what is happening right now."

He took in a deep breath and inched closer to the edge of the tree line.

What is he waiting for?

Gabriel's heart rate spiked, "***I just … I haven't … I've never shown anyone – other than Guardians and Betrayers – my transformed form. So you will have to give me a moment. I'm sorry …***"

"Oh … I'm sorry, too. I forgot that you can hear my thoughts. I didn't mean any disrespect. Would it be easier if I came to you? You know – behind the tree line, just the two of us?"

"NO!" Gabriel almost shouted as his heart rate soared, thundering violently inside his chest.

There was an awkward moment of silence, and then hesitantly Gabriel made his way out of the trees. A moment later a large beast was standing at in front of me. He was the most beautiful wolf I had ever seen. His radiant fur was white as snow and as the moonlight glistened off of his fur it reflected the color of the night in an almost sapphire blue hue. His eyes were the most dazzling neon blue I had ever seen with hints of sapphire throughout them and they seemed to shine with an innocence I hadn't seen before. The beautiful beast stood at least six inches higher than me as I stared into it hypnotic eyes.

"Gabriel?" I whispered.

The wolf like creature nodded its head and said, ***"Yes …"***

My heart raced with excitement as I stared at the beautiful wolf before me. His scent was even more intoxicating than before – I couldn't contain my excitement.

"WOW! I can't believe it. This is totally awesome!"

I slowly encircled Gabriel, running my hand over his silky smooth fur, his heart rate jumping nearly every time my hand touched him.

Unable to stop myself I blurted out, "This is what I become?"

"Yes and n-no," Gabriel said as he struggled to keep his heart rate in check.

"What do you mean yes and no? Either I am or I'm not, it can't be both ways. Can it?"

I glanced in Raphael's direction, hoping he would give me a better explanation. I'd completely forgotten that he couldn't hear our silent conversation.

Gabriel shook his head as if to remind me that Raphael couldn't hear us. Then he nudged me in the cheek with his wet black nose, causing me run the back of my hand across my cheek to wipe it off and to look up at him.

"I have so many questions," I said, not knowing where to start.

Gabriel nodded his head.

"I know you do, but it might be easier to talk face-to-face instead of nose-to-face ... if you know what I mean."

He waited for my nod of approval, then once again disappeared behind the coverage of the trees.

I turned my attention back to Michael, Raphael, and Natalya, Chrystal still lay motionless in the back seat of Raphael's car.

"So ..." Raphael began, breaking the uncomfortable silence. "Is there any questions you might have?"

He placed his hand consolingly upon my shoulder.

"Why would you even ask me that? Of *course* I have questions! Hundreds of them!"

How can he be so naïve?

I stared at Raphael as he bit his lip, not really sure how he might proceed from here, when Gabriel's voice chimed in from behind.

"So ask your questions and we will answer them to the best of our abilities. No question is off limits."

When I turned to look at him, he had returned to his natural form, but he wasn't wearing a shirt. I stared at him in stunned silence with what I know must have been the stupidest smile upon my face. My awe of him must have been obvious because he nervously smiled at me as he got closer.

"You'll have to excuse my attire," he said, glancing over at Michael with an irritated look upon his face. "… I had to give my extra shirt to Michael the last time that he transformed."

His face turned slightly red as I continued to stare at him like a moron with my mouth hanging open, I couldn't help myself. He was so unbelievably breathtaking it made it difficult to think.

Gabriel closed his eyes, took in a deep breath as if to build his courage, and walked to my side.

"Ask your questions," he said.

I still stood in awe of his beauty. How one man could look so incredibly sculpted was more than I could comprehend. His chest was perfect – though there was a faded cross-like tattoo just over his heart. I looked a little closer and realized it was a scar in almost a perfect cross-like shape. I placed my hand on top of my shirt where my cross shaped scar was.

It's just like mine.

Even with that one blemish – if you could even call it that – he still looked as if he were cut from the same mold as angels. That's when it hit me – he had said they were guardians.

He's an angel! A guardian angel!

"You're an angel, aren't you? All of you are angels, I'm right aren't I?" I blurted out, my excitement getting the better of me.

Gabriel, Michael, and Raphael laughed to my response.

“Yes, we are angels, but we have been cursed to walk among humans.”

“I heard about the curse, that’s why we have pain when we transform right?” I questioned as I began to bite my nails.

“Yes, that’s why there is pain when we transform it’s also why we transform into wolves.” Gabriel sweetly pulled my hand from my lips and continued. “When Mephistopheles decided he was more powerful than the Creator he was cast out of heavy. During the first battle with Mephistopheles he placed a curse upon stripping us of our immortality and causing us to morph into the beasts that you saw. It’s very difficult to control our actions when we transform. I’ve had thousands of years to practice mastering my transformation and I still have trouble at times. So you can understand our amazement with you and how you are handling yours.”

My cheeks flushed pink with his flattering words.

I am finally getting some answers.

“So I am an angel too, right?” I questioned as I clumsily tripped over my own feet.

Causing me to fall awkwardly into Gabriel’s chest; breathing in his intoxicating fragrance and the side of my mouth whispering against his chest. “Sorry,” I whispered. His breathing was shallow and rapid as I began to pull away from him. I looked up at him as a gentle breeze began to blow, that's when I smelled it a sweet citrusy scent.

"She's here."

"Who's here?" Gabriel questioned as he began to look around still holding me in his arms.

I looked up at as I placed my hand upon my scar.

Almost as though he knew what I was thinking he wrapped his arms around me, "Don't worry Alex I won't let her hurt you."

I tightened my arms around Gabriel as I took in a deep breath of his scent to make to make the smell of citrus disappear.

"Alex …" he quietly whispered, almost as if he were out of breath.

"Yes, Gabriel?"

"I … I can't…"

"You can't what, Gabriel?" I asked as I tightened my arms even more, excited at the sound of my name spoken on his lips.

"I can't b-breath … I think … that … you are going … to break my …" At that moment I heard a few cracking sounds echo though his chest and a wince of pain escaped his lips. "… my … ribs …"

I unwrapped my arms form his chest.

"What was that sound?" scared at the answer I would get.

"Did you just break his ribs?" Michael interrupted, a half smile resting upon his face. "That is totally awesome!"

Michael could barely contain his excitement.

"No it's not!" I screamed. "I'm sorry, I'm so sorry." Tears began to well in my eyes as Gabriel placed his hand under my chin and sweetly looked me in the eyes.

"It's alright Alex, my ribs will heal, but what I need you to do for me is tell me what direction she's in. Can you do that for me?" He asked.

I nodded my head and pointed in the direction from which the scent had come.

"Good now I need you to wait for us here. We will be back shortly."

I nodded my head as I watched Gabriel, Michael, Raphael and Chrystal all head off in the same direction; the direction of *her*.

CHAPTER FOURTEEN

GUILT

Natalya walked over to my side, “It’s going to be okay, Alex.” She comforted as my heart began to rumble inside my chest.

My scar began to burn the closer the scent would come to me and my stomach churned with the thought of having hurt Gabriel. Slowly I began to back into the trees hoping they might hide me from the murderous woman.

“Where are you going, Alex?” Nat asked as I turned and disappeared into the trees.

I ran for several minutes before crumpling to the ground and leaned against a large oak tree. Tightly I clenched my shaking hands into fists as I prayed, “Please don’t let her find me and please let Gabriel to be alright.”

When someone placed their hand consolingly upon my shoulder, “Alex, are you okay?” Eros questioned as brushed the hair from my eyes.

"Eros? Where did you…" I began when he wrapped his arms around my shoulders and pulled my head into his chest.

"Alex, why are you trembling?"

I hadn't realized that I was trembling.

"She coming after me," I whispered.

"Who's coming after you?" Eros questioned as I shook my head.

"I don't know…I just can feel her. Always watching, always hurling murderous thoughts towards me."

"Don't allow your fear of her cloud your vision, Alexandra. If you are to become the woman that I created you to be then you will need to learn to control you fear and the reaction that you have when you are afraid. You must channel that fear into courage." My Strength said as a warmth touched my heart.

I know you're right.

Eros pulled me away from his chest to look me in the eyes. "Alex, I will never allow anyone to hurt you."

Eros placed his hand upon my face and looked me in the eyes. His eyes were kind and gentle as he looked at me.

"You know the fact that someone is trying to kill me isn't…"

"What?! Someone is trying to kill you, why would you say that?" He interrupted concern in his words.

"That doesn't even matter because I can handle it, I know I can" A soft smile touched my face as thought about what My Strength had said but quickly faded as I continued, "But what the worst part is I allowed my fear of her get the better of me and did something that was truly terrible."

"So what did you do that you think is so terrible?" he asked.

I tightly clenched my teeth together, not wanting to tell him as he sweetly ran his hand down my arm, kissed the back of my hand, and a strange smile made its way on his face.

"I didn't mean to hurt Gabriel, but I did," I said as tears began to well in my eyes as I recalled the pain in Gabriel's voice.

Excitement shined in Eros' eyes and his awkward smile widened.

"Why are you smiling? It's not a good thing that I hurt Gabriel," I whispered ashamed with myself and having let my fear get the better of me. I nervously massaged my fingers across my forehead.

"I'm not …"

I gave him a questioning glance as I raised my eyebrows.

"… I mean … I am … I just…" Eros stuttered on unable to come up with a reason why he was smiling.

I pushed Eros away.

"I'm sorry." He said as he placed his hands upon my shoulders and turned me to face him.

"So what did you do to him that is so terrible?"

"I … well I …" My pulse nervously bounced around, both high and low nearly at the same time.

"Nothing you can say will make me feel differently about you … so come on and tell me …" He cupped his hot hand upon my cheek.

I took in a deep breath and slowly let it out. "I … I broke … broke Gabriel's ribs."

Eros' eyes widened.

"You broke his ribs?"

"Yes …"

A look of awe and wonder painted Eros' face.

"How did you break his ribs?"

I shook my head.

"Does it matter?… I allowed …" I looked at Eros as I choked back the tears that pooled in my eyes. "Allowed my fear to get the better of me…" I licked my lips and took in a shallow deep breath. "What's wrong with me? And why can't I control it?"

"Control what?"

A dark look seemed to swell in his eyes as he stared intensely into my eyes.

Suddenly My Strength spoke to me.

"Do not go into detail," he said. "There is much you need to know before you speak to him about this."

"Well?" Eros questioned. "Your, what?"

I took in a slow breath to catch my bearings before continuing.

"My emotions they seem to be all over the place," I said, changing what I'd originally been about to say. "I just can't seem to get it under control."

A confused look pulsed in his eyes as I continued.

"Why?" I asked to cover the moment of uncertainty when My Strength has spoken. "What did you think that I meant?"

"I just … I guess I thought that you were talking about what you did the other day in the hall, on campus. You know, when you stopped me and Raphael from fighting."

"You mean when I stopped you from transforming?"

I looked at him expectantly, waiting for him to get angry.

Instead of addressing what I'd just said, Eros completely changed the subject – almost as if nothing strange was happening at all.

"So I was wondering if you would like to go out this evening," he said, completely catching me off-guard.

Why is he changing the subject? Why now? I just let him know that I know everything.

Not quite sure how to react, I looked away and suddenly noticed that the sun was beginning to paint the sky a light shade of purple.

Is it morning?

"What time is it?" I asked as Eros kissed me on the top of my head.

"About 6 in the morning," he said as he tightened his arms around me. "So … yes or no?"

"Yes or no what?"

"Will you go out with me this evening?"

"Oh … I guess we can hang out … but I first have to see Gabriel and I'm not really sure how long that is going to take."

He pulled me from his chest.

"Why?" he growled, red anger burning in his eyes.

"Careful," My Strength whispered.

"Because … I have some questions that I need to ask him."

"Questions about what?" he asked, his expression unreadable.

"Tread carefully," My Strength stated. *"Tell him very little."*

Eros pulled me closer and stared expectantly into my eyes. I let out a slow steady breath as I continued

"Well … I don't know just … things … okay."

Eros' jaw tightened.

"Okay … but there is something that I need to show you before you make a decision."

"Decision?" I asked innocently, pretending I didn't know what he really meant.

"Gabriel wants something from you, Alex" Eros said. "You'll have to choose between him and me."

A flutter of anger bubbled inside me.

"HE DOESN'T WANT SOMETHING FROM ME!" I snapped.

"YES HE DOES," Eros yelled as red began to pulse in his eyes.

The look that flashed across his face was so terrifying that I literally froze. I knew I'd seen something truly evil within him and everything in me wanted to get away. Fear grabbed me.

I've seen what Gabriel becomes but what Eros was? Something about it was ... dark. If Gabriel was angel then that must mean that Eros is a demon.

My heart began to violently thunder inside my chest, as the red in Eros' eyes burned with complete hatred.

"You need to calm him down!" My Strength urged.

Eros' body began to enlarge as his heart thundered inside his chest. Not knowing what else to do I stared at him in fear.

Seeing the fear in my eyes, Eros took in a deep breath and forced himself to calm down.

"I'm sorry," he said. "I didn't mean to scare you. I just … well when it comes to you I get a little jealous … I can't help it." Anger was still dominate in his voice as he spoke.

He shook his head and ran his hand through his hair.

"I can only remember one other time when I have felt like this about anyone … but that was just distant memories from a past life."

He placed his hand upon my cheek.

"Alex, I can see that I've been going about things with you in the wrong way. So let me try again."

Still uncertain as to how to react to him because there was something in him that changed, but trusting in My Strength, I nodded my head in encouragement for him to continue.

"I know that you have seen what Gabriel is and now I want to show you …" his jaw tightened as he continued and his heart rate spiked ever so slightly. "…what I am."

"But aren't you and Gabriel the same things?" I blurted without thinking even though I knew that they were not the same.

His eyes narrowed, "No," he said flatly. "Not anymore … I am a προδότης *(include pronunciation).*"

"A what?"

"A προδότης … it is the Greek word that means …" He hesitated, almost as if he didn't want to tell me or maybe it was that he was ashamed, I couldn't quiet tell. He let out a slow breath and continued.

"It means that I betrayed the creator and my best friend," he said. "I am a Betrayer."

Shame consumed his face, making it difficult for him to look at me.

"Wait … you are a Betrayer?"

Eros nodded his head.

"Yes."

"So who is this best friend that you betrayed?"

When he looked up at me anger consuming his eyes once again.

"Gabriel, is the one that I betrayed," He said, hatred dripping from every word.

"You were friends with Gabriel?"

"Yes," he said his voice still flat. "We were an unstoppable team once. I can still remember it as if it were yesterday – the look on his face the moment that I betrayed him, the pain and agony of my betrayal written all over his face."

"So why did you do it?" I asked, amazed that he was telling me all of this. "Why did you betray Gabriel?"

"Because I was compelled to obey my master's wishes," Hatred and anger still burned in his eyes, though his voice remained emotionless.

Fear pulsed over me when I remembered something that the woman with the smell of citrus had said. She had said something about her master, but what it was I couldn't remember for some reason.

Could she and Eros be working together?

My hands began shake when My Strength spoke up.

"I am with you Alexandra, you have nothing to fear."

I nodded my head and pressed further for answers as I tried to remain calm. "What do you mean?"

"It doesn't matter …"

As he said it, there almost seemed to be a moment of remorse and regret on his face – as if he were remembering something. It was a surprisingly human look, but he brushed it aside almost immediately – as if to hide his pain by adopting a truly evil grin.

"You should have seen Gabriel's face as I plunged my sword into his chest," he said.

The scar on Gabriel's chest, that was from Eros?

"I really was shocked that he got up from that one, I thought for sure that the poison from my betrayal would kill him and send him back into his spirit state, but I was wrong. I should have known that he was too close to the Creator for anything to happen to him. He always was the favorite."

His heart rate spiked and his body once again began to pulse with anger, red swirling in his eyes.

"How could you do that to your friend?' I blurted out as flashes of Gabriel's face pulsed through my mind.

Anger boiled in Eros' red hateful eyes as fear overwhelmed me. I slowly stepped back, not wanting to be too close to him when he transformed into whatever evil beast he would become.

"Are you scared of me Alex?" He growled, the darkness in his voice seemed to bleed through every word that he spoke. "You should be."

My heart began to race as Eros intimidatingly stepped closer. The hairs on my arms began to stand up as his body pulsed larger and larger with every rapid heartbeat.

Then, as if he were two different people, he said, "You have to get out of here Alex. I'll hold off my transformation as long as I can, but you m-must leave n-now!"

I moved backwards, backing into a tree. My breath wheezed in and out of my lungs. My heart raced, and I could feel my own transformation beginning to come about. I wanted to cry out in pain, but my fear crushed the scream before it even entered my throat.

Eros morphed into a large black void as he hollered, "RUN, ALEX! RUN!!! I CAN'T HOLD IT BACK ANY LONGER!!!"

Pain flooded my body. I couldn't run. My body was changing. I knew that I was changing and I couldn't stop my transformation either.

"It's alright Alex," My Strength said. *"Everything is going to be okay. Gabriel is on his way."*

That's not going to help. I am transforming!

"You are ready," My Strength replied. *"Do not fight it. Become what I made you to be."*

Eros' large dark void made its way toward me and back-handed me across the face. My pulsing body flew through the air, crushing into a tree. Anger moved over me, burning from the inside out.

"You are ready to handle your transformation, but do not do it if you are angry," My Strength warned.

My vision turned red as I searched for Eros. I set my eyes on the large black void that I knew belonged to him, but just before I lunged for him a snow white void tackled him first.

What was that? Gabriel. He had come to protect me? But he can't fight Eros by himself. I must help him.

"Now you are ready," My Strength said. "You are of the right mind and heart. Become what I have created you to be."

I closed my eyes and bright light flashed before me, my soul bursting forth as I became what I was created to be.

CHAPTER FIFTEEN

TRANSFORMATION

A strange ringing echoed through my ears as I laid flat on my back. A soreness covered my body, and yet I felt completely relaxed – content with just staying in the moment. A peace resting over me.

Eventually I opened my eyes, wanting to know where I was. But when I opened my eyes, all I saw was darkness. My heart began to thunder inside my chest. Fear pulsed over me as I shouted, "I'M BLIND! I'M BLIND!" My breaths rapidly raced in and out as I began to panic. My hands reached out, trying to find anything that might seem familiar as the pain began to once again roll over me.

"Alex, its okay," came Raphael's voice from out of the darkness. "Everything is going to be fine. Trust me."

I felt his hand rest gently on my shoulder.

"What do you mean it's going to be okay? I'M BLIND!"

Silence filled the space around us as I choked back the sobs that lingered in my throat.

"What happened?" I finally managed to ask as I controlled my breathing. "Is Gabriel alright? And what about Eros?"

I heard Raphael shuffle and his hand left my shoulder.

"I was actually hoping that you might be able to tell me what happened."

"What do you mean?" I shook my head and continued. "The last thing I remember is speaking to My Strength and a bright light … and then … nothing … I just woke up here, blind."

Raphael let out a slow, steady breath.

"Alex, when I came upon you, Gabriel, and Eros, you were covered in blood," he said quietly. "You were lying between Gabriel and Eros. I assumed that you …"

"Wait a minute …" I interrupted. "Who's blood was I covered in?" Tears began to pour down my face. "I didn't hurt them … did I?"

"I don't know for sure, but …"

"BUT WHAT!?" I yelled.

"… but it does look that way. You were covered from head-to-toe in not only your blood – but theirs."

My head fell in shame as I covered my face with my hands.

"Did I k-kill them?"

I waited impatiently for the answer, simultaneously wanting him to tell me, but also not wanting to know at all what I had done.

Could I really have killed them?

Raphael didn't answer right away, instead he placed his hand back upon my shoulder. I pulled his hand from me and tried to sit up, only to lose my balance and fall clumsily to the side. Raphael's arms tried to steady me but I pushed them away.

"Just tell me!" I demanded. "Did I kill them?!?"

"Oh, Alex …" He wrapped his arms around me tightly, folding me into his chest. "You didn't kill them …"

"Yes I did …" I said, not truly believing him. Tears ran down my face as I slipped from his arms, collapsing back into the bed.

"No, Alex, you didn't," he repeated, this time more insistently. "You didn't kill them. Gabriel is actually here – in his room, recovering."

"So is he okay?"

"I won't lie to you, he is not well," Raphael said hesitantly. "He had so many wounds upon his body that in spots it looked like ground beef. I've never in all my time seen him with so much damage. I mean, we've fought together for a long, long time and he has never been this bad. And the amount of poison pulsing through his system is more than I have ever seen. We've all had our fair share of scars over the years, but none of them have ever been as bad as this.

As he continued to talk about the wounds that I'd inflicted, I could feel bile working its way up my throat, and a flash of the cross-shaped scar on Gabriel's chest flashed in my mind.

"Please take me to him …" I requested as I touched my exposed scar a gentle warmth seemed to pulse through it as my hand rested upon it.

"Alex, you need to rest … you've been through quite an ordeal."

I reached out and somehow managed to grab him by the collar of his shirt.

"I asked you to take me to Gabriel," I said angrily. "I won't ask you again."

The words hissed threateningly from my lips. I could feel the anger boiling through me as if it were a dark cloud covering the light. Guilt swelled over me, I could almost feel the shocked expression that I knew was upon Raphael's face.

I have to know he's okay.

"I'm sorry," I said, backtracking quickly. "I just …I need to know that he is okay." My face tightened up as tears tried to present themselves. "Please. Please take me to Gabriel. I have to see – I have to know that he's okay. Please."

I tightly clenched my teeth together as I waited in anticipation for his answer.

Silence filled the space surrounding me and just as I was about to say something more, I could feel him stand up from the bed. Then someone grabbed my hand and began to lead me out of the room. Silently, we walked for several minutes. I heard what sounded like the ding of an elevator and with a few more stepped we entered the elevator. When the elevator doors opened I took in a deep breath and the sweet scent of Gabriel overwhelmed me as we entered the room, causing my already impaired senses to blur all the more. Slowly I was led to Gabriel's bedside.

"Here," said Michael's voice as he grabbed my other hand and placed both upon the bed. "I'll give you a minute." Michael said as his almost woods scent made its way towards the elevator were he exited the room.

For a moment I just stood there, listening to Gabriel's rhythmic heartbeat.

"Gabriel …" I nervously whispered as I slowly moved my hands across the bed, finding his arm. My hands followed his chiseled arms up to his shoulders. I could feel bandages as I gently traced over his arm. Moving my hands to his face and running my fingers through his hair. "Gabriel please … speak to me."

All I could do was think about how sorry I was for what I'd done to him. I gently placed my hand over his heart, the warmth from his bare chest sent electrical pulses cascading over my skin. Unable to help myself, I buried my head in his chest, my tears soaking his bandaged wounds.

Silently I cried, until suddenly a gentle hand touched the top of my head.

"It's not your fault what happened to me," Gabriel's voice whispered as he sweetly touched my cheek, wiping my tears away.

"Yes it is … I nearly killed you and Eros."

"No … honestly I'm fine …."

"What do you mean you're fine? You are not fine … I can feel your bandages!"

He stopped my hands as I began to run them over his bandages.

"Wait," he said. "What do you mean you can feel them? Can't you see them?"

I shook my head.

"No … I can't … I can't see anything."

"What? How?"

I bit my lip.

"I'm really not sure," I replied. "All I remember is hearing you and Eros fighting, then speaking with My Strength and him telling me that I was ready to transform. And as pain from transformation seized my body I saw a bright light. The next thing I remember was waking up here, unable to see anything."

Gabriel placed his hands upon my cheeks and ran his thumb across my lips. He began to pull me close when he paused.

"Wait – who is this strength that you're speaking of?"

I pulled away, embarrassed that I'd revealed that to him.

"Oh … um … it's nothing. I don't know what I was talking about. I'm just …"

"Alex, it's not good to lie," My Strength interrupted. *"Tell him the truth."*

I let out a frustrated huff.

"That's not really the truth."

"What do you mean?" Gabriel asked as he grasped my hand.

My heart violently pounded, thundering loudly upon my ribs. I pulled my hand from Gabriel's, hating every moment of it, but if I was going to tell him anything then I needed to have my wits about me and no matter how much it hurt I couldn't do that with him holding my hand. I took a deep breath to build my confidence and continued.

"I hear voices in my head."

"I know," he said immediately. "I've been speaking to you telepathically."

"Not just you," I said in a rush. "I've been speaking with a voice and he helps me control my transformations. You know … he gives me the strength to stop my transformation. That's why I call him My Strength." My face turned red as he once again grabbed my hand.

"I hear the voice of your strength as well, only I call him something different."

"But he is a voice in my head how…" I began when it clicked.

The voice that I have been hearing is the voice of God.

"Never mind I just answered my own question." I whispered a little embarrassed that it had taken so long to realize who he was.

My Strength, My God.

"Where is Raphael?" Gabriel asked there seemed to be a smile in his words as he spoke then and sweetly moved me to the side of the bed.

"I don't know," I replied. "Michael is the one who brought me to you, I think."

"Alright, give me a minute and I will see." Silence filled the darkness as I waited for Gabriel to finish his silent conversation with Raphael. "Alex?"

"Yes?"

"You are sure that you saw a bright light after speaking with your strength."

"Yes."

"Okay … that's good news."

"Why is that good news?"

"It's good because it means that your blindness is only temporary."

"Temporary? How do you know it's temporary?"

"Never mind how we know … just give it a few more days and we'll go from there."

I nodded my head and tightly clenched my teeth together.

"So what am I supposed to do?"

Gabriel scooted closer to me.

"Stay here with me," he said, kindness and hope echoing through his words. "I promise I'll take good care of you."

Butterflies danced in my stomach as my heart began to race.

"How will you take care of me?" I asked. "You have wounds all over your body?"

A single tear slowly ran down my cheek.

Gabriel gently wiped it away.

"I'm a fast healer," he said as he brushed some hair form my face.

"Yes I know that you heal fast, but not that fast."

"Alex, it's been nearly 24 hours – I'm almost completely healed."

Gabriel grasped my hand. There was an almost tearing sound, like someone pulling off a Band-Aid, as he placed my hand upon his bare chest.

"See," he said matter-of-factly. "They're healed. All that remains is a nearly invisible scar where the wound was."

"And you're sure that you're not hurt?"

He sweetly ran his hand down my arm, causing goosebumps to rise upon my skin as a soft chuckle escaped his lips.

"Only my pride," he said. "It's a little demoralizing to be taken out by a girl … a girl who still isn't fully aware of who or what she is." A chuckle escaped his lips, "You really put me in my place."

"So you know what happened in the woods between you, me, and Eros?" I asked as my heart did a flip.

"Yes."

I waited for him to elaborate, but only silence filled the space between us. Unable to contain my nerves any longer I blurt out, "So what happened?!?"

Gabriel let out a slow breath.

"It was incredible," he said. "Your eyes … they weren't red like Eros' or even blue like mine when I transform … They were …"

He paused, unable to describe exactly what he'd seen.

"Then what color did they turn?"

"It's difficult to explain … it was unlike anything … any color I've ever seen. Almost like a neon violet … or a … an amethyst in color."

Gabriel paused, as if he was still in shock of what he'd seen.

"Amethyst?" I questioned, running my hand through my hair.

Gabriel placed his hand upon my cheek.

"Your eyes are beautiful, Alex – and not just in your human form but in your beast form as well."

Warmth worked its way to my cheeks as the room began to spin, I had to think of something else.

"Yes, but what am I? If I'm not what you are and I'm not what Eros is, then what am I?"

Gabriel took a deep breath.

"Well, it's a long story and I'll explain everything to you. But first, why don't we get some lunch?" The sound of his stomach growling came through loud and clear at that exact moment, and we both laughed out loud.

"Okay, let's go," I said, reaching out a hand for him to guide me.

Gabriel grasped my hand, intertwining his fingers with mine.

My heart began to accelerate as he readjusted his position and placed one arm around my waist.

Don't read too much into it. He's just trying to assist you, not flirt with you.

We made our way from the elevator down a long hall, I continued walking as he stopped.

"Careful," he said as he stopped me, pulling me back into his chest.

"What?" I nervously asked, trying to keep my heart rate down.

"I don't want you to fall down the stairs."

"Oh …" I stepped forward hesitantly, wanting to place a little distance between myself and his perfect body. I could feel the heat rising up to my cheeks. Nervously I stepped forward, Gabriel guiding me, until we were at the bottom, where I clumsily tripped over my own feet. Gabriel pulled me close to him once again and I closed my eyes and took in a deep breath – his beautifully hypnotic scent enveloping me.

"I'm s-sorry," I said. "I'm just so clumsy … I can barely stand …"

Gabriel placed his finger upon my lips.

"Shh …" he softly whispered.

I could feel him inching closer and closer – his breath hot against my lips – when suddenly someone cleared their throat from the other side of the room. Gabriel quickly pulled back.

"We were … I just … I mean she tripped and … and I caught her …" Gabriel took a deep breath to steady himself. A moment later he stood completely calm and composed, as if nothing had just happened.

"I must speak with you … in private," Michael said, a worrisome seriousness to his tone.

"Alright," Gabriel said as he readjusted me in his arms. I had no choice but stand their impatiently as they carried on their telepathic conversation.

CHAPTER SIXTEEN

NEW DISCOVERIES

As I stood there blindly, a new fragrance caught my attention. Gently, I peeled myself from Gabriel's strong arms and took a deep breath.

"Be careful Alex, I don't want you getting hurt," Gabriel telepathically said, allowing me in upon part of their conversation as he waited for my answer.

"They are on their way here," Michael's voice said. ***"We must prepare for battle."***

I wanted to listen to more, but My Strength interrupted Gabriel's response.

"You should not listen in upon others' conversation," he said.

I rolled my eyes, knowing that he was right.

"I'll be fine," I replied to Gabriel. ***"You just worry about the battle that you must prepare for."***

Then I started slowly walking toward the scent, leaving Michael and Gabriel to continue their silent conversation.

I took a deeper breath, smelling every scent that filled the room. As my other sense compensated for my blindness, I began to discover a whole new sense of awareness. I could sense exactly where the table was that sat in the center of the entryway, the roses in the center of that table, the stairs that we'd just come down, I could sense everything, it was incredible. I took in another deep breath, assessing which direction I needed to go to find where the tantalizing scent was coming from. Cautiously, I walked through the doorway, adjusting my path as my senses deemed necessary – each step bringing me closer and closer to the familiar smell.

After walking through several rooms I came to the door that would lead me to the scent – it was the kitchen door. I blocked my senses – though I'm not quite sure I did – but it dulled my senses so that I would not be overwhelmed upon entering the kitchen. Even with the dulling of my senses kitchen was still slightly overbearing – with all of scents bombarded me the moment I entered.

My head began to spin and my heart started to accelerate.

"Take it slowly," My Strength said. *"You can handle this. Don't let it overwhelm you."*

I nodded my head, knowing My Strength would never steer me wrong. I could smell so many individual scents all at the same time. Closing my blind eyes, I visualized each one – everything that sizzled, cooked, dripped, and banged, I could see them almost as if I were looking at them with my eyes. I also smelled a person – someone I'd smelled before but who I wasn't completely familiar with. I tried to pinpoint who it was.

Someone from school ... It was Oliver!

He was one of the guys that hung out with Gabriel.

I walked over and stood behind Oliver as he stood in front of the stove, stirring something in a pot.

"Hey Oli," I said, surprising him. "What are you making?"

Oli's heart rate increased and a vibration coursed over his body. I placed my hands upon his shoulders and turned him around to face me. Though I couldn't see his eyes I knew they were glowing with the beginnings of transformation.

"Oli … are you okay?"

"NO!" He shouted.

I could feel anger pulsing through him, accompanied by an accelerated heartbeat. Without thinking, I placed my hand upon his chest and focused on the anger burning inside him. I let out a slow, steady breath and let a pulse of light burst from within myself, forcing it into Oli's chest. As I forced my light into his chest I followed it with my consciousness, seeking out any darkness that was causing his transformation.

Within a matter of seconds my light had traveled completely through him, extinguishing all traces of the darkness and returning back into my body, Immediately Oliver collapsed to the ground.

"Are you okay Oliver? I'm so sorry. I didn't mean to hurt you."

I could feel Oliver shake his head.

"No," he said sorrow in his words. "I'm fine. But it seems I hurt you. I'm sorry."

He reached up and cautiously touched my cheek. Pain flashed across my face, and as I ran the back of my hand across my cheek I felt blood. My fingers traced a gaping wound that made a line from the bottom of my temple to the top of my chin. I hadn't even realized that I'd gotten cut.

"ALEX! Are you okay?!" Gabriel almost shouted as he raced to my side.

I could feel Gabriel's heart rate accelerate as if in anger as he examined me. I pulled away from his grasp.

"I'm fine," I stated as I took in a deep breath. Gabriel was beside me, the stove there, Michael was standing in the doorway, and there behind Oli was the sink. I walked around Gabriel and Oli almost as if I could see them and headed to the sink to wash off my cut.

"Alex, Raphael needs to examine you," Gabriel said, placing his hand upon my shoulder.

"I'm fine," I once again stated, I could feel my cut beginning to heal itself as we spoke.

"Please, Alex … I have to know that you are …" Sadness filled his words as he spoke. "If you got that cut from Oliver's claws you could have poison coursing through your body."

I softly shook my head.

"No, I don't think so," I said, turning around to reveal my completely healed wound.

Gabriel softly touched where my wound had been.

"It's incredible!" he exclaimed. "You're incredible! There isn't even a scar, almost as if there wasn't even a cut there. If I hadn't seen it with my own eyes I would have difficulty believing it."

"What?!" Michael shouted, tramping across the kitchen. "That's impossible …even wounds form our own kind leave a scar, and I saw that nasty slash. It had to have left a scar."

Michael grabbed my face and began turning and twisting it in every different direction, but no matter what direction he twisted me in he still could not find a mark.

"No, it's impossible," he said. "I don't understand why she doesn't have at least a hint of a wound. In fact, her skin is completely flawless, perfect, even better than it was before. How is that?"

Placed my hand upon the cross shaped scar upon my chest.

Nope it's still there.

I shrugged my shoulders.

"I don't know."

Someone sweetly grasped my face.

"So how did you do it?" Gabriel asked.

"Do what? Heal myself? I should think that you would know by now. After all, I am what you are, aren't I?"

"No … you're something different," he said, and the room fell silent. Instead of explaining further, he changed the subject.

"How did you make it into the kitchen without leaving a mess behind?" he asked. "Did you get your sight back?"

"No," I said. "I relied upon my other senses – especially my sense of smell. I can pinpoint just about every smell around me and it almost feels like seeing, but in a different kind of way … it's hard to explain."

"Try," Gabriel said. "We want to understand."

I let out a frustrated huff.

"Well … I can smell each and every individual scent – and the exact direction that those smells are coming from." I bit my lip, trying to think of how I might word the next part. "I knew where I wanted to go, and the various smells gave me a kind of map of how to get there."

"You can do that?" Michael asked, with a tone of disbelief in his words. "Wait … we can do that?"

“I’m really not sure any of us have ever had to try that before,” Gabriel said, an odd mixture of curiosity and wonder in his voice.

“Alright, if we’ve talked about my senses long enough there is something that I would like to know. I would really like to know what that smell is.”

“I thought that you could see everything with your sense of smell,” Michael sarcastically belted out.

My jaw tightened in irritation as I let out a slow steady breath to slow my now accelerated heart rate.

“Yes…but…”

“Is it the meat that I have been cooking?” Oli asked as he placed the still sizzling pan into my face, nearly burning me as he waved the pan back and forth in front of my face, making my stomach churn and ache for it all at the same time.

I took in a deep breath, the scent of the rare meat overwhelming me.

“Yes, that’s it.”

Instinctively I knew that it wasn’t the meat that lured me, it was the blood pooling in the bottom of the pan that was causing my mouth to water. I had hoped that I was wrong, but with how many times I had been drawn to the scent I knew.

"It's the blood I've been smelling." I said. "I think I've known for awhile, I just didn't want to admit it. I don't want to … to crave the taste of blood. But every time I smell it … well, can't help but long for it."

My head fell in shame once again

"Alex, it's alright," Gabriel said. "You have nothing to be ashamed of. It's rare – exceedingly rare, in fact – but there are those like you who share this … peculiar … trait."

"Like who?" I pleaded.

"Me …" Oliver said, placing his hand upon my shoulder. "I know what it's like to … to hunger for blood, but that's because I once was a Betrayer. Our animalistic trates are far more dominate that that of a Guardian."

Confusion consumed me.

"What? Why is that?" I asked.

"Why don't we grab a bite to eat and then talk," Gabriel said as his stomach once again growled.

I nodded my head – millions of questions racing through my mind faster than I could have ever imagined.

The meal around the table was infuriatingly silent, but I tried to be patient as I waited for Gabriel to choose his words. Once we had all finished eating, he grabbed my hand and led me from the dining room. We walked for several minutes before going outside and walking through the brush as if he was leading me way from any and all signs of life.

A low growl echoed off of the trees.

"What was that?" I whispered.

I could feel Gabriel's body tense up as his grip upon my hand tightened.

"What was that?" I repeated, this time telepathically.

"Eros," Gabriel replied, anger tainting every word.

A moment later, Eros emerged from the bushes behind the house.

"So, you've already decided which side she's going to be on?" Eros hatefully questioned. "She's female – you know she can't be a Guardian."

"Yes, but if you haven't noticed, Eros, she's no ordinary female," Gabriel ran the back of his hand across my cheek. "She's different. Besides everyone has a choice, even you."

There was a rush of wind and Eros bumped into my side, his hot sweet scent collided with Gabriel's cool hypnotic scent, making my head spin just a little.

"I know that she's different," Eros said as he forcefully grabbed my hand and intertwined his fingers with mine. "That's why I chose her to be my girlfriend."

He pulled my hand up to his lips and pressed his hot mouth upon my hand.

Eros stumbled slightly back, I assumed that Gabriel shoved him ever so slightly, and then both Gabriel and Eros let go of my hands. I could feel their heart rates rise as vibrations began to roll off of them. I knew that I had to stop them.

"STOP!!" I shouted, placing my hands upon their chests and sending my light coursing rapidly through their bodies.

Almost simultaneously a gasp of pain escaped their lips.

"I'm sorry," I said to Gabriel telepathically as my light worked its way back to me.

"No, I'm sorry," he replied. ***"I shouldn't have let Eros get at me like that."***

"You know that she has to choose," Eros said. "So let her choose. You've shown her what you are now – it is time for me to show her what the Betrayers are."

"She can't even see her own hand," Gabriel retorted. "Wow do you expect her to see anything?"

I could feel the anger burning inside Eros as he stood beside me and the heat from his anger seemed to roll in waves off of his body. I tried to disconnect from the conversation, not wanting to hear another argument between the two of them. In that space, My Strength spoke with authority in his voice.

"You have been in the darkness long enough," "he said. *"It is time that you see the world for what it is ... but you must choose wisely, for one choice will draw you closer to me and the other will lead you to eternal darkness."*

Hesitant, but eagly, I slowly opened my eyes. Everything was blurry and every color ran together. I vigorously rubbed my fists over my eyes and opened them again. Gradually my vision cleared, and I immediately noticed both Gabriel and Eros staring at me.

"My vision has returned," I said, smiling at Gabriel before turning my attention to Eros. "Show me what you are."

Eros furrowed his eyebrows. Then he shrugged and gave me a meaningful look.

"You might want to back up," He hissed in an almost dark voice as his eyes pulsed a bright red in color.

Nervously, I complied, slowly inching backward toward Gabriel. Immediately Eros' bones began to jigsaw and enlarge.

"I'm here," Gabriel said quietly, stepping slightly in front of me. "I won't let him hurt you."

Blue flashed in his eyes as he glanced back at me.

I looked over at Eros and noticed something cross his eyes – a fleeting feeling of something. He looked hurt, and I realized it was because of me and Gabriel. He felt betrayed. I tightened my jaw and stepped around Gabriel.

“I know that he won’t hurt me,” I said as I stared up at Eros.

When he saw my actions, a peace seemed to pulse over him and his angry, hateful red eyes turned a soft, beautiful crimson color. I stared intently at Eros as his shirt began to tear from the expansion of his chest and arms. His jaw tightened in pain as he crumpled to the ground and worked his way behind some foliage.

I began to follow him when Gabriel grasped my arm. “He’s fine, but it would be best if you stayed here with me. Our transformations can be quite violent and he is only trying to protect you.”

CHAPTER SEVENTEEN

REVEALED

A heavy, almost violent breathing, came from the direction in which Eros had hidden. I closed my eyes and tried to focus on my other senses. Then, curiously – not knowing if it would work or not – I spoke telepathically with Eros.

"Eros…are you okay?"

"What? … How?" Eros exclaimed.

"How what?" I asked.

"How are you speaking to me inside my head?"

I heard some rustling coming from the brush as if he were stepping closer.

"Why do you ask?"

"Because the only one I knew who could speak telepathically, other than Gabriel, was Alexander. And even he could not speak to me if we were not in the same form."

"I don't know I just …"

I paused for a moment, not really sure how to proceed. My mind began to dance all over the place, going over every possible explanation – most of them not making any sense. Suddenly, Gabriel crumpled to the ground.

"PLEASE! STOP!" Gabriel and Eros shouted telepathically in unison.

"I didn't do anything … I didn't even touch you guys," I said out loud, startled by their extreme reaction. I crouched down beside Gabriel and placed my hand on his back.

"You didn't have to … to touch us," Gabriel stuttered.

"What did I do?" I asked as a tear worked its way out of the corner of my eye.

"You are much more powerful than I –"

"NO!" Eros interrupted. ***"More powerful than we could have ever imagined."***

"What do you mean?" I questioned again, glancing at Gabriel and toward the brush were Eros was.

"You … I don't … well … for starters you are able to speak telepathically to both Eros and myself," Gabriel nodded his head in the direction of which Eros was hiding.

"… and you're able to telepathically link us all …" Eros stated, almost as if he were picking up where Gabriel had left off.

Gabriel nodded his head in agreement.

"What does that have to do with anything?" I asked as my eyebrows crookedly furrowed in confusion.

"Alex ..." Gabriel turned me to face him, our hearts accelerating the moment that our eyes met. ***"None of us can do that … none!"***

"It just doesn't work that way," Eros added.

Confusion flooded my mind.

"What do you mean?" I asked as question after question flitted through my head. A wince of pain escaped Gabriel's perfect lips, followed closely by a whimper of agony from Eros.

"PLEASE, STOP!" Eros growled as a neon red flashed angrily among the bushes.

"WHAT?!" I asked, hurt filling my voice. I looked back and forth from the brush to Gabriel and from Gabriel to the brush, awaiting an answer.

"You just … I mean …. what you did was … was … I don't even know how to explain it!"

Gabriel pulled me closer and placed one hand upon my cheek and the other around my waist.

"Alex, what were you just thinking a moment ago?"

I shook my head, trying to concentrate.

"I don't know …" I said hesitantly. "Everything! It's all just a jumbled mess right now! I still fell like I don't understand anything!"

I took in a deep breath. "I'm thinking of multiple things at once, I guess." I bit my lip and continued. "Does that make any sense?"

A moment later we were interrupted by a loud noise and then suddenly Michael was there.

"What did you do?!?" he huffed, staring into the bushes where Eros was concealing his transformed identity.

"I didn't do anything!" Eros telepathically stated, a low growl rolling from deep inside his chest.

"I KNOW YOU DID BETRAYER!"

"NO I DIDN'T!" Eros growled.

"I know you did YOU STUPID CAT!"

Michael made his way menacingly toward the trees, only to be halted by Gabriel placing a hand upon Michael's chest.

"You can hear him?" Gabriel asked, confusion coloring his words.

"Of course I can hear him!" Michael retorted. "Why wouldn't I be able to, even if he is a filthy cat. Look at him cowering behind the brush. It won't save you."

I watched in shock as Gabriel further explained.

"Because Michael, Eros is not in his human form."

"What do you mean?" Michael asked, neon blue fading from his eyes.

"He's transformed Michael! He's in his Betrayer form!"

Shock flooded Michael's face.

"Then how am I hearing him?"

Gabriel looked over in my direction.

"… Because of her."

"What? I didn't do anything!" I said, cowering back toward the closest tree.

"Not possible …" Michael said.

"No it's not," Eros said in all of our minds. ***"And yet here she is doing it … connecting all of us as if we were all Guardians or all Betrayer."***

"So how is she doing it?" Michael asked blankly, staring at me.

"I don't know," Gabriel said, placing his hand upon Michael's shoulder.

"How long have you known she can do this?" Michael asked, a slightly irritated look on his face.

"Her being able to link all of us telepathically?" Gabriel asked sarcastically. "I just found out only a few moments before you! … But…I have known about her telepathic abilities a little longer …"

"How much longer?" Eros asked in an angry growl that echoed off the trees.

Gabriel bit his lip as if he didn't want to continue.

"Well … remember when the professor asked her a question from chapter 8 when we were only on chapter 7?"

"Yes …" Eros and Michael said in unison, the same tone present in both of their voices as they spoke the word.

"I kind-of … well I sort of …" Gabriel let out a huff and continued. "I gave her the answer."

"YOU WHAT?" Michael shouted.

"You cheated," Eros stated, an almost arrogant tone in his words. ***"It would appear that she is bringing out a darkness in you, Gabriel, which could be the reason that the master is so interested in her."***

"No I didn't … I mean I did but …" Gabriel nervously ran his hand through his hair. "I couldn't help myself, I had to help her … and the Professor was only asking that question to be mean … I know it was wrong, but seeing the panicked look in her eyes and hearing her heart rate accelerate … I just … I couldn't help myself … I had to help her."

"Don't be too disappointed with yourself. I would have done the same thing, but I am a Betrayer it is kind-of my thing." Eros stated.

"I'm not like you, Betrayer. I would never allow myself to be controlled by Mephistopheles. It just shows how weak you are."

There seemed to be a pain in Gabriel's voice as he spoke of Eros' betrayal.

"Shows how much you know, stupid mutt. Mephistopheles doesn't make me do anything that I don't want to do." Eros' words were dark and hateful as the blood chilling red of his eyes darkened.

I could see the anger building in Michael's eyes as I stood there, "Don't call him a stupid mutt you vile, insidious cat."

"Don't you dare speak to me like that mongrel!" A dark, evil growl rumbled from the brush that concealed Eros' transformed form.

I needed to change the subject to relieve some of the awkward tension.

"Alright Eros, you've stalled long enough – it's time that you show me what you are."

A soft rustling came from the brush before me.

I wonder what he will look like.

"Do not be drawn in by what you see," My Strength said. *"Great darkness is often hidden behind great beauty."*

I started to respond in skepticism, but my words were halted as Eros stepped from the brush. He was – incredible! It was difficult to describe such beauty. I stared at him in awe. The light from the sun peaked through the thick, dark trees and reflected off his ebony black fur, highlighting the sapphire tones throughout the fur around his face. I inched forward with my hand outstretched and gently placed it upon his thick beautiful mane. The crimson red of his eyes were only being brightened by his black fur. The moment that I touched Eros, a purr of pleasure whispered across his lips. He like Gabriel in his transformed form stood nearly six inches taller than me in my human form. He had jagged, murderous looking claws upon his paws and his hind and front legs were nearly twice the size of what they had been. Even in this form I could feel the heat pulsing off of him.

I glanced in Gabriel's direction and began to encircle Eros as I had Gabriel in his transformed form. His heart rate spiked every time I touched his fur, just as it had with Gabriel. He was beautiful – even more beautiful in his transformed form than Gabriel.

I silently examined him further – he resembled a black lion, but his size had to be twice as large as any lion ever recorded. I stepped back to further examine him, excitement and fear battling within me.

He had a scar just above his eye, though with his fur as black as it was, it was nearly impossible to see. Gently I ran my hand across the scar when a white mark upon his flawless black fur caught my eye. I leaned over to better examine the marking, touching it with the tips of my fingers.

"Some scars never completely heal, even in our transformed form," Eros stated with a malicious tone and fiery red anger in his eyes as he as he glanced in Gabriel's direction.

Flashes of Gabriel's scar upon his chest washed through my mind. The scar upon Eros' chest was in nearly the exact same shape as Gabriel's. I placed my hand over my own scar, they were all the same shape.

"That's impossible …" I whispered as I continued to trace the scar with one hand and my other resting upon my own. I straightened up and walked over to Gabriel.

"What are you doing?" Eros asked, stepping closer to my side.

"I have to see something," I stated, staring up into Gabriel's irritated brown eyes as if to ask him if what I was about to do was okay. I took in a deep breath, both Gabriel and Eros staring attentively at me. I placed my hand upon Gabriel's shoulders and with a sweet smile I slowly moved them to his chest.

"Take your shirt off," I said.

Gabriel smiled knowingly and Michael made a groaning sound of disapproval.

"Okay, this is getting a little too weird for me" Michael said, turning back toward the house. "I think that I am going to be leaving, now and Alex since you have now learned to use your telepathy you can call me anytime this Betrayer forgets his place." An ornery smirk touched his face, "Which of course is beneath my boots, you filthy cat."

A dark growl vibrated deep from within Eros' chest as he began to step forward, ***"Don't think I won't tear you to pieces, mongrel."***

"I'm so scared I'm shaking in my boots," Michael said as he disappeared behind the trees.

"And don't you think that I won't do everything that I can to stop that from happening." I stated as I gave Eros an almost commanding stare. Fear flashed in Eros' eyes, "Yes you know what I can become, don't you?"

Gabriel stepped closer and placed one hand around my waist and the other one upon my cheek. Then he pulled me close to his chest.

My heart began to nervously thunder inside my chest as my cheeks heated.

"Don't touch her," Eros angrily said; anger billowing off of him and he stepped from behind a tree where he had quickly transformed back into his human form.

Gabriel stepped between us and placed his hand upon Eros as his body vibrated with his own transformation. As he started to change I stared at the white cross-shaped scar on Eros' bare chest.

Then I turned my attention over to Gabriel, subconsciously hearing what they were saying but not really registering that the conversation was getting a little heated. Gabriel's shirt was unbuttoned about half way down his chest. I saw a dark, almost black scar – similar to the mark on Eros. Without really thinking I stepped closer to him and pulled back his shirt, halting their heated conversation.

"What happened?" I asked, pulling Eros closer and placing my hand over his scar. I looked up into Gabriel's eyes and then Eros'. Silence filled the space around us. "Why do you both have the same scar?" I pointed at each of their scars, pulling back Gabriel's shirt as I did.

Gabriel and Eros glanced at each others' scars.

"And, why does it ma…" I began when Eros interrupted.

"It's nothing, just a coincidence," Eros said. "Nothing more. Enough of this talk! Which side do you choose? Mine or Gabriel's?" Red flashed in his eyes. "Betrayer or Guardian?"

"I … I don't … I mean, I'm going to have to think about it … I don't want to hastily jump into anything."

I nervously bit my lip and tangled my fingers through my hair.

"Is that okay?"

Anger boiled in Eros' eyes, causing them to pulse a neon red in color.

"IS IT OKAY? NO IT'S NOT OKAY! I WANT YOU TO CHOOSE NOW!"

Immediately Gabriel began to show signs of transforming, and I knew it was out of concern for me. So I quickly placed my hand on Eros' chest, interrupting his outraged words, while simultaneously putting a hand on Gabriel's chest. Then I sent a burst of light racing into them. A gasp of pain escaped Gabriel's lips and vibrated over his body. Eros' eyes rolled back into his head and both Gabriel and Eros began to violently convulse, their bodies jerking in all directions.

CHAPTER EIGHTEEN

HELP

As I looked down at their convulsing bodies, wondering what it was I'd done, I started to panic.

"What do I do?" I pleaded with My Strength.

"Help is on the way," he responded immediately. *"In the meantime you must neutralize the poison coursing through their bodies."*

Shock flooded me.

"Poison! What poison?!?"

"The darkness in Eros is like a poison to Gabriel," My Strength said. *"The same is true of Gabriel's light to Eros. You have both light and darkness within you and when you tried to stop their transformations you forced your light into Eros and the darkness that resides in you, you forced that into Gabriel. You need to remove your light and darkness from them."*

I placed my hands upon their chests, one on each, not knowing what to do next.

"If you don't remove the poison from both of their bodies then all will be lost," My Strength said.

Horror swelled over me.

"They're going to die if I can't do this?!" I exclaimed, pulling my hands off their chests.

"They won't die Alexandra," My Strength said comfortingly. *"But they will be in a kind of a deep sleep as long as the poison continues to pulse through their veins."*

"So they will be prisoners inside their own bodies?"

"Yes, in a matter of speaking."

Gasps of pain escaped both Gabriel's and Eros' mouths as the air gargled inside their chests.

"Alex, you must hurry," My Strength said. *"There is not much time before the poison completely consumes them."*

"I can't do this," I stated, terrified that it wouldn't work.

"You can do this," My Strength said, warmth touching my heart. *"I believe in you."*

I took in a deep breath and prepared myself for what I was about to do.

"You must remain true to who you are," he continued. *"You must understand that there is both light and darkness – it's what*

makes you who you are. Don't let the darkness take over. And remember, I am here – always. All you have to do is ask."

I nodded my head, confident that My Strength would help me stay true to who I was. I placed one shaking hand upon Gabriel's chest, Black lines had worked their way through his chest and up his arms, sweet beaded across his pale clammy forehead. I turned to Eros to place my hand upon his chest. He looked so much worse than Gabriel. His tanned skin was pale – in fact it had become so pale that in nearly matched my own. A large snow-white scar shaped like a star was in the center of his chest where his heart was, and the mark spider-webbed out as if it were growing. Growls echoed inside him as if his body was desperately trying to fight off the poison.

I placed my hand over Eros' heart, trying to concentrate as I began to notice Guardians and Betrayers in their transformed forms making their way toward me. Angry growls and roars rang out all around us.

"I can't do this," I whispered to My Strength.

"But I can," he replied immediately. *"Believe in me and what you can do through me."*

I could feel my own transformation coming as my heart began to pound violently inside my chest.

Oh no! This can't be happening – not when they need me so much!

"Let it come Alex," My Strength said. *"You're more powerful in mid transformation than in human form. So let it come."*

I nodded my head in compliance and embraced the transformation, while still keeping my beast form at bay.

My jaw tightened in concentration.

"I can't do this with all of the growling, snarling and roaring!" I said to My Strength. *"It's too much for me to handle and there isn't enough time."*

A tear rolled down my cheek for fear of not being able to save them.

"Then I will give you the time that you need and the silence that is required."

Then, as if My Strength had placed me inside a bubble, all noises ceased, I couldn't even hear Eros and Gabriel breathing, though I could still see their chests moving up and down with each difficult breath. I placed my hands upon their chests again, allowing a partial transformation to begin. My bones began to shift within my hands, enlarging and tearing through my skin, the black flesh once again appearing. Claws grew from my fingers though they weren't the same. The claws on my hand that I had placed upon Gabriel's chest were thick and sharp and the claws upon the hand on Eros' chest were hooked, almost demonic looking nails, as the pain of the partial transformation pulsed over me my muscles tightened causing my nails to tear into both Gabriel's and Eros' chest.

No!!!

Agony touched their face as my nails tore into them.

"It's alright, they will heal just stay focused upon the task at hand." My strength said as tears began to fill my eyes.

I took in a deep breath and refocused pushing my light through their veins. Instinctively I split the light in two halves and pushed one half into each of them. A sick feeling washed over me as I continued to move through their poison-riddled veins, a nasty taste filled my mouth.

What is that?

"It's the poison," My Strength stated.

I could feel the bile rising up into my throat as I worked further into their veins.

"You must focus on containing the poison."

I nodded my head as I let out a slow steady breath, increasing the speed of the light. Every bit of the poison that I came across I swallowed with my light. Finally, after what seemed like an eternity, I could tell that their blood was free of all poison.

"Now comes the hard part," My Strength said.

"What do you mean hard part? That was hard."

I could feel the sweet beginning to bead across my forehead as I tried to contain the poison from contaminating their blood streams again, when the scent of their tantalizing clean blood overwhelmed me.

"You can do this," My Strength reassured. *"You must absorb the poison, so that your subconscious can leave their bodied, but you must do it quickly."*

I could feel the presence of the poison with in me.

Wait, this poison is my poison. I can just allow it to become a part of me.

"You can't just absorb it that way. Your poison has absorbed some of their essence it must be purified before you can absorb it."

And just how am I supposed to do that?

"Trust in the abilities that I have given you." My Strength stated.

I allowed my light to burn brighter and brighter until it was so hot I felt as though lava were burning me from the inside, but the most difficult part of allowing my light to burn at such an intense level was keeping it cool around the edges so that it would not harm Gabriel or Eros. Finally my light completely consumed every last bit of the poison.

I let out a sigh of relief and as the air escaped my lips all sound and motion came back in a crashing wave, and I realized I was in the middle of a battle between Guardians and Betrayers.

"You must stop them." My Strength insisted.

"How? I'm just one person." I tightened my jaw frustrated that I didn't know what I was to do.

"Use your telepathy," he said. *"But you must be stern and commanding for them to listen to you."*

Okay.

"Alex you have nothing to fear," My Strength said. *"You can handle this. Trust me. Look at what you have already accomplished."*

I looked down at Gabriel and Eros as they peacefully rested on the ground – the black and white spidering veins now gone and the color of their skin beginning to return to normal. I closed my eyes to focus and let out a steady breath.

"Please be quiet everyone," I said, using telepathy.

Nothing happened. They continued battling as though I had said nothing.

"Be stern!" My Strength said with authority.

"STOP!" I telepathically shouted, linking all of the Betrayers and Guardians, causing all commotion to cease immediately. Looking at me with curiosity the Guardians and Betrayers separated into their own respective groups. I could feel the blood pulse heavily through my veins as my heart seemed to beat roughly inside my chest. My head began to swim as I slowly stepped between the Betrayers and the Guardians.

"Why are you fighting?" I demanded telepathically, trying to retain the stern voice that My Strength had encouraged. Silence filled the space between us as they all stared at me in shock. I could feel my irritation with them growing as each second silently ticked by. Darkness began to build inside me as I stared at the creatures that stood around me.

"Well?" I angrily growled, my bones slightly shifting and enlarging, beginning the feeling of tearing flesh.

"Calm down!" My Strength whispered, an urgency in his words.

I DON'T WANT TO CALM DOWN!

"Alex …" Gabriel's voice whispered weakly beside me, and I felt his hand grab mine. I wanted so badly to be angry with him, but when I turned around my anger dissipated and the pain from transformation left.

"Are you guys okay?" I asked as tears began to escape the corners of my eyes. "I thought you and Eros were going to die."

I pulled my hands from his weak grasp, placing them upon his face as I glanced over at Eros.

"I'm fine …" Gabriel said, placing his hand upon the back of my arm, still weak from the poison that had coursed through his veins. "Are you alright?"

"I'm fine," I said as I looked around at the beasts surrounding us and began to search for Raphael.

They all look alike. I'm never going to find him.

"Find who?" Michael telepathically asked as a large blond wolf stepped up beside me.

"Raphael," I replied immediately, not giving a second thought to the increasingly comfortable method of communicating with these beings that I knew I now belonged to somehow. ***"Gabriel needs to be examined by him."***

"I'm here," Raphael said a moment later.

I searched the beasts before me, but not one was him.

"Where?"

I questioned as he stepped from behind some trees in his human form, still buttoning up his shirt.

"I'm fine," Gabriel said as he pushed Raphael's hand away from his forehead.

I placed my hand on Raphael's shoulder.

"Could you do something else for me?" I asked

A soft smile worked its way upon his face.

"Sure."

I bit my lip and took a deep breath, knowing that what I was about to ask him would be very difficult for him to do.

"Will you examine Eros as well?" I asked, looking over at Eros' wheezing body as his chest erratically moved up and down. "Please?" I pleaded.

Raphael swallowed hard and his jaw tightened.

"Yes," he said. "I will – but I'm not sure what good I'll be. I haven't studied the biology of Betrayers before, so I'm not guaranteeing anything."

"Okay …" I nodded my head and moved to his side.

Horror washed over his face as he began his examination. "Not good …" He shook his head.

"What? What's not good?" I asked, "All you've done is touched his forehead."

"Michael?" Raphael said as the large golden wolf stepped closer and nodded his head. "I need your help. We must get Eros into the house. We have to get his body temperature up – he's cold as ice."

An irritated growl rumbled from deep within Michael's chest.

"Why do I have to do it?" Michael asked telepathically, taking advantage of the link I was continuing to establish with every little effort.

Before Raphael could answer, a woman's voice interrupted their conversation.

"You're not touching him!" the voice said telepathically.

I know that voice.

I placed my hand upon the scar upon my chest and began to search the crowd of beasts before me, but I couldn't pick her out of the crowd of beasts. Then there came the familiar scent of citrus as the crowd of Betrayers parted and a woman gracefully worked her way toward us, hidden by the shadows of the trees. She stepped just behind the cover of the shadows, making it difficult to fully see her.

"Who is that?" I whispered as Gabriel rose to his feet and steps between her and me.

A soft chuckle escaped her lips.

"Gabriel, you haven't told her about me, yet?"

A vibration of anger pulsed over his back. I stepped forward and placed one hand on his shoulder and the other on his forearm, holding him in place.

A soft smile made its way on his face.

"Why would I?" he said, the sneer on his face echoed in his tone. "She already knows who you are and that you're not a threat to her. So why would I?"

"Really?" She said, stepping from the shadows.

Shock consumed me as I laid eyes upon the beautiful creature before me. She had the body of a woman – an hour glass shape. Her face was human, yet also resembled the face of a cheetah. Blood red was the color of her eyes, which were lined perfectly with long beautiful lashes. She seemed to have short velvet-like fur covering her entire body – a body that was almost in full view thanks to her extremely risqué choice of wardrobe. Her fingers had wicked-looking cat-like claws, and as she stepped slightly closer her bare clawed feet scratched across the ground in a haunting way. As she smiled, she revealed large, razor-sharp fangs.

A shiver of fear coursed over my skin.

"She thinks there's something threatening about me," The cat beast said as she ran the tip of one of her claws down my cheek.

I could smell the blood spill over her claw as she drug it down my cheek to just below my chin.

"Can't you smell the fear on her? She reeks of it."

A low angry growl rumbled through Gabriel's chest, followed by the echoes of Michael and Raphael, I held him tighter as the line her claw had traced on my cheek began to sting. I wanted to reach up and touch it but resisted the urge – not wanting to let go of Gabriel for fear of what might happen.

"I would have thought that stabbing you with the sword of death would have ended you, but it appears that you are much more resilient than I anticipated."

She began to walk circles around us, almost as if we were her prey; Gabriel following her with his eyes.

She stepped closer to me and whispered in my ear, "I may not have killed you, but," She pulled the front of my shirt down revealing my black cross shaped scar, "I have placed my mark on you." Her lips dance across my ear as she continued. "A reminder that you will never be able to rid yourself of me; I'm a part of you now." She ran her tongue over my cheek licking the blood from it.

Instinctively I pulled away from her, "Are you done with your perverse gestures and gloating?" I asked as I wiped her saliva from my cheek.

"How dare you talk to me like that, you should be less worried about what I have been saying and more worried about the tiny cut I placed upon your cheek. I'm sure you can feel my venom working its way through your body as we speak."

Her eyes burned with hatred as she stared at me.

"Alex!?! What are you doing? We need to have Raph..." Gabriel began to questioned telepathically, panic in his thoughts.

"It's alright," I replied quickly, though I wasn't sure if that was true. "I can handle this."

I closed my eyes and focused on using my light to heal the sleight injury the cat woman had inflicted. My Strength interrupted my concentration, however.

"Eros needs help," he said. *"He must get warm. You must not let Catrina make you lose focus about what has to be done – for if you do Eros will be lost to us."*

I nodded my head in compliance and hesitantly released Gabriel from my grip. Then I walked to Eros' side.

"I told you not to touch him!" Catrina's voice growled.

I shot her a dirty look and kneeled down beside him anyway.

"If you want to get technical, Catrina, you told Raphael not to touch him," I said, not masking the disdain I already had for her.

I really don't like her.

A moment later I felt a gust of wind followed by an intense heat hovering behind me. Irritation with Catrina began to course over me.

"So, has he mentioned me ..." she asked, obviously taking every ounce of self-discipline to hold herself back.

I slowly turned around – my eyebrows furrowed in agitation as a look of shock consumed hers.

"No. He's never mentioned you, but I do know who you are and that you have been watching me. You know your scent is..." I shook my head in disgust and wrinkled my nose as I continued,

"So completely disgusting that it would turn my stomach every time I would smell it." I said flatly before turning my attention back to Raphael. "Raphael, will you please take him to the house? Michael, will you assist him?"

"No. I won't –" he began, but I wouldn't let him finish.

"Let me rephrase that – Michael, you will help Raphael take Eros up to the house," I sternly stated, staring Michael directly in the eyes.

"DON'T TOUCH HIM!" Catrina shouted as heat began to billow off her in waves.

I let out a frustrated huff.

"You are really beginning to annoy me," I said, turning to face her and looking directly into her eyes in the same way I'd just done to Michael.

A smirk worked its way onto Catrina's face.

"Good," she said, not backing down.

I turned my attention back to Raphael and Michael as Gabriel stepped over to my side.

"I don't want you hurt," his lips whispered against my ear, sending shivers cascading down my back. Letting out a slow breath I steadied my heart rate and continued with what I was saying.

"Raphael, Michael, take Eros to the house and get him warm, please."

Michael started to protest one more time, but a sharp look shut his mouth. As he leaned down to pick up Eros, Catrina started to growl. My jaw tightened and my bones began to jigsaw slightly as I allowed myself to begin to transform.

"I will deal with Catrina," I said, nodding to Michael and Raphael. "You just worry about saving Eros."

Catrina began to step around me to prevent them from moving Eros when there came a soft throat clearing and a smile worked its way upon her face. She ran her hand back through her hair as the smile widened, "What do you say we make a trade."

"A trade, don't make me laugh you have nothing I want." I stated as I folded my arms across my chest.

"Really?" She said as a Betrayer came from into the clearing dragging Chrystal by the hair.

Horror washed over me, "Chrystal!"

"I guess it would appear I do have something that you want." Catrina said as she savagely grabbed Chrystal by the arm.

"I'm so sorry, Alex. Maybe if I was stronger, like you I could have fought them off." Chris said as tears streamed down her beaten face.

"What did you do to her?" I demanded staring angrily at Catrina.

"Nothing really, we just ruffed her up a bit after all she is a traitor and the penalty for betraying her own kind is death, so this only the beginning of her suffering." Evil pulsed in her eyes and radiated from her sinister grin.

"Don't you dare lay another hand upon her!" Anger began to burn hot with in my chest causing my scar to throb.

She ran her claw down Chrys' cheek causing her blood to spill over her finger and pain to consume Chrys' face. I stepped forward wanting to tear her apart only to be halted by Gabriel.

"I'm terribly sorry. We have no other choice, but to torcher and kill her, unless," She licked Chrys' blood from her claw, "Unless you are willing to make a trade; Chrys for Eros."

I glanced over at Eros then back at Chrys they both needed help, and if I didn't give Eros to them then they were going to kill Chrystal.

"She's lying…" Chrys telepathically whispered.

Acting upon impulse I spoke up, "She's not going to kill Chrys she's one of them, so take Eros immediately and get him warm."

Raphael and Michael nodded their heads and ran out of sight as Catrina spoke up, "You think I'm bluffing?"

"Yes."

She nodded her head and then in a flash she raised Chrys over her and plunged her hand through her chest. A cry of complete agony escaped her lips as Catrina pulled her bloody hand from Chrys' body dropping her to the ground.

"CHRYS!" I shouted as tears poured down my face and I ran to her side. "I'm so s-sorry Chr-Chris I d-didn't t-think th-that she w-would actually k-kill you…" I said as I turned her to face me when there came Chrys' voice from the trees.

"She didn't…"

I looked up as Chrystal walked into the clearing.

"Then how…" I began as I looked down to find Oliver lying in my arms. "Oli…"

"It's okay…" He coughed as blood spilled from his lips and he gasped for air, "I-I g-get to g-go home now a-and spend th-the r-rest of m-my life w-with the c-Creator." He wiped a tear from my cheek. "S-so d-don't cry f-for m-me." He grasped my hand, "C-can I s-see one l-last s-smile before I l-leave t-this world?"

I nodded my head and smiled to the best of my ability, "One day I'll see you again Oli."

A faint smile touched his face, "T-thank you." He mumbled as his eyes closed and his last breath wheezed from his blood stained lips.

I tightly hugged him into my chest as his body began to glow as if his soul was coming forth.

"Alex, please allow me to take my child home," My Strength said.

I nodded my head and let go of Oliver as his body was raised up in the air and his soul began to pull away from it. Once his body released his soul the body fell lifeless to the ground returning to dust. Oli smiled and waved at us, "Goodbye." He eagerly said as he disappeared into the clouds above.

CHAPTER NINETEEN

HOW?

I ran to Gabriel as he wrapped his arms around me. "It's okay Alex, h-he's in a better place now." He said as he tightened his hold on me.

"Oh, Boo, hoo, hoo. 'It's okay Alex because he's in a better place now.' Hah! All this blubbering makes me sick." Chrystal said as she walked over to Catrina's side.

"Chrys what are you doing?" I questioned as Gabriel let go of me and I turned to face Chrys and Catrina. "And how did you switch places with Oliver."

"Oh, you didn't know? Well then let me enlighten you." Catrina said as she wrapped her arms around Chrystal, "You see Chrystal here, she works for me and as far as her switching places with Oli well she didn't but she did bring him to us, he was a traitor after all." Catrina nonchalantly shrugged her shoulders, "So I dealt with him."

I fell to my knees in shock.

Chrys betrayed me.

Tears began to pool in my eyes as Gabriel leaned down and wrapped his arms around me once again, "But that doesn't explain how you pulled off such an allusion."

An evil look consumed Chrystal's face, "That's because Mephistopheles bestowed his blessing upon me giving me the power over allusions. So it was quite simple to pull a wool over your eyes so to speak." A shiver of displeasure vibrated over her skin and she shook her head turning to Catrina, "Do you know how disgusting it was trying to pretend that I liked her, she kind-of smell like those filthy mutts."

"Well that is bound to happen when one hangs around them as often as she has."

"Chrystal's vison is being clouded right now." My Strength said an almost pain in words, *"You mustn't hold it against her."*

I thought about the words that My Strength had said as Chrystal and Catrina talked about how much they hate me and the Guardians. Nodding my head I took in a deep breath, "I'm okay, Gabriel." I said as unfolded myself from his arms and standing up.

The warmth of My Strength touched my heart as I spoke, "It's okay Chrys. I forgive you, for everything." A soft smile touch my face.

Shock consumed Chrystal's face, "Don't lie." A painful anger filled her words as she spoke them through her tightly clenched teeth.

"I'm not lying, I do forgive you. No matter what you have done," I said as a peace washed over me.

"Why?" I hatefully questioned as tears pooled in her confused eyes.

"Because you're my friend Chrys and…"

"STOP!" Catrina shouted, "Stop filling her head full of rubbish."

"I'm not I…" I began when Catrina flew to my side grabbing me by the arm her claws tearing through my skin.

"Stop her," My Strength said. *"You don't want another battle to break out, not now it's not the right time."*

I tightened my jaw, "I've had just about enough of you, Catrina. It's time for you to stop." I said as I took in a deep breath and placed my hand on Catrina's chest, sending the darker of my two lights rapidly coursing through her body. I was surprised how quickly I could move – so fast that she didn't have to react. One moment she was clawing my arm, the next I had escaped her grasp and was pushing my light into her darkness, overcoming every shadow of transformation she had within her.

"Stay focused only on the darkness that comes from transformation," My Strength said. *"Don't worry about the other darkness that resides within her."*

I nodded my head again and focused my light on her dark transformation, working my way through her veins. The same sickness that had crept into my stomach when pushing away the poison from Eros began to overwhelm me.

"Remember, I am here," My Strength said. *"You can do all things through me, and this is only a temporary fix. Her abilities will return, but it will take some time."* I nodded my head as an extra pulse of light and strength rolled over me, giving me the extra push I needed to extinguish Catrina's transformation.

Catrina fell to the ground – a roar of pain rolling from her chest.

"What did you do to me?" She demanded in a weak voice as she struggled to get to her feet, another Betrayer assisting her.

"I extinguished your transformation," I stated as she rose to her feet.

The short fur that covered her body had disappeared, revealing her almost shimmery olive-colored shin. Her claws and fangs had shrank back to normal as her hair shortened into a jagged pixie cut and her build shrank to a thin, almost toothpick-like build. She looked like she could be a model – tall and slender with long legs. Her head hung as she rested against a large black leopard that stood next to her, its lip raised in anger as it showed its razor sharp teeth.

"How?" she asked, looking up at me as her red eyes changed into a beautiful dark brown and all eyes staring at me in disbelief.

I stared at her for a moment, not quite sure how to explain what I had done.

"I turned off your transformation," I said. "… Kind of …"

Anger and hatred filled her dark brown eyes.

"What do you mean you turned off my transformation?" she questioned as her heart rate spiked from her anger.

"Exactly what I said – I turned it off."

"She can't do that can she?" Chrys questioned disbelief in her eyes.

"OF COURSE SHE CAN'T DO THAT. SHE'S LYING!" She shouted as she stumbled backward.

"If you don't believe me, then transform – right here, right now."

"Alex you can't let her –" Gabriel began.

I raised my hand, stopping his protest.

"I won't stop you," I said, almost encouraging her to try.

Catrina looked up at me, confusion plaguing her face.

"You won't?"

I shook my head.

"I won't."

She nodded her head and closed her eyes. I could see the concentration on her face as she let out a slow steady breath.

Nervously I watched as her bones slightly shifted.

"Be confident in your abilities and what you are capable of with my help," My Strength said. I let out a slow steady breath, knowing I can always trust My Strength. I focused my attention back on Catrina. Her face had a slightly red tint to it as she held her breath. A moment later she looked up at me with fear in her eyes when I tapped in on a telepathic conversation that I had not initiated.

"Plan B has been completed and awaiting your orders captain."

"Good then make haste we are leave, immediately." Catrina telepathically said as she turned at race for the trees.

We stared after Catrina as she raced behind the covering of the trees in a frantic sprint.

"Where are they going?" Gabriel asked.

"They are retreating," I said, glancing in his direction.

"How do you know?"

"I read her mind …"

Roars rang out all around, followed by hundreds of pounding paws racing over the ground. I could feel Gabriel's fear growing as the pounding continued. I placed my hand upon his cheek as his body began to pulse with transformation.

"It's okay," I said. "They're leaving."

A smile worked its way on my face.

"Stopping Catrina's transformation put the fear of God in them," I said. "They're running in fear."

"Are you sure?" Gabriel asked with a tightened jaw, trying to control his transformation.

"Yes, I'm sure," I said. "They're not coming back. Trust me. I know what they're thinking about."

Gabriel's heart rate normalized and he sweetly placed his hand upon my cheek.

"I can't imagine what it must be like," he said. "Hearing them inside your head like that – it must be terrible."

He ran his hand through my hair.

"It's alright," I said. "But it's going to take some getting used to."

I smiled at him comfortingly and then turned toward the house, wondering how Eros was doing.

"C'mon," I said, boldly grabbing Gabriel's hand and leading him back toward the house. "Let's go check on Eros."

A moment later we entered the room where Raphael and Michael had placed Eros. The room was chaos. People were frantically trying to keep Eros from hurting anyone, including himself, as his body violently convulsed in and out of transformation. His roars of agony echoed through the halls.

Without thinking about it, I made my way over to a cabinet full of medicines and pulled out some vials. Trusting my instincts guide me; I mixed the medicines and then made my way over to Eros. Amidst all of the commotion no one had even noticed me get into the cabinet.

"He's too strong, we can't hold him down," Raphael shouted, glancing in Gabriel's direction while trying to hold down Eros' legs as Michael unsuccessfully tried to hold down his arms and chest.

"What happened?" Gabriel asked, stepping closer to all of the commotion.

"He's seizing!" Michael said, making the sarcasm very apparent in his words.

"I know, but he seemed fine when we sent him with you," Gabriel replied.

Acting quickly, I maneuvered unnoticed around the jumble of people surrounding Eros. Taking in a deep breath to gain my courage, I plunged the syringe quickly into his chest.

The room fell silent as his body slowly stopped seizing and his rapid heart rate calmed, stopping his involuntary transformations.

“What did you do to him?” Raphael breathlessly asked, releasing Eros’ legs.

I shook my head.

“I’m not sure,” I said. “I just … I don’t know … I knew he needed it, so I gave it to him.”

“So what did you inject into his chest?”

“I … I don’t know. I just knew it was the right thing to do.”

Gabriel placed his hand upon my arm.

“How did you know that it wouldn’t kill him?” he asked.

“I …”

I could feel the blood rising in my cheeks as my voice lowered.

“I just knew,” I said. “Like I felt it deep inside … in my soul.”

Michael’s face wrinkled with irritation.

“That’s ridiculous!” he retorted.

Raphael let out a slow steady breath.

“It *is* ridiculous,” he said. “But I also believe every word of it. After years of working at the hospital and helping regular humans every day I’ve seen all kinds of miracles. But when it comes to my own kind it seems like I can never do anything to save them. I thought there was no way to save Eros from the fate that awaited him.”

What does he mean?

Michael stared down at Eros he pulled a knife that he had concealed within his boot and placed it upon Eros' throat, "We should just kill the beast now and put him out of his misery."

"It was not his time," My Strength said inside my head.

"No, you can't!" I exclaimed.

I placed my hand upon Michael's hand and turned my attention to Raphael.

"Is he going to be okay?" I asked as Raphael examined his body.

"He's stable for the time being, but we don't know how long the medication you gave him will last.

He turned to me and there was a note of wonder in his eyes. It was somewhat discomforting, but I smiled at him as best I could.

"I haven't seen a guardian or anyone for that matter do that – or anything even remotely close to what you did," Raphael said. "And I'm over 2,000 years old!"

Gabriel grasped me by the shoulders and placed me square in front of him.

"Alex, what you did outside, when you turned Catrina's transformation off – well, none of us are able to do that," he said.

"Look I'm not entirely sure how I did it just know that with out My Strength I wouldn't have been able to do it." I said my cheeks turning slightly pink from embarrassment.

"Don't you think that's a little cocky? I mean really you may be strong, but to be honest I think that I could take you." Michael said with a crooked smile.

Raphael walked up behind Michael and smacked him upon the back of the head.

"Hey! What was that for?"

"She was talking about God, you moron." Raphael stated as he rolled his eyes.

"I knew that." Michael stated as he pursed his lips.

"Sure you did, you just keep telling yourself that."

"How dare…" Michael began as he shoved Raphael.

"That's enough!" I sternly shouted, "It's been a long day and we all should get some rest." I said as I turned to exit the room. Clumsily I tripped over my own feet and just before I hit the floor Gabriel caught me. Holding me in his arms, we stared deeply into each others' eyes. I hoped that he would kiss me, but just as he began to pull me closer we were interrupted by someone clearing their throat.

Startled Gabriel quickly straightened up and dropped me upon the ground.

"I'm sorry!" Gabriel said, surprised at himself for his reaction. "I didn't … I mean we didn't … we weren't …"

Gabriel nervously babbled as he and Raphael helped me to my feet.

"No I'm sorry," Raphael nervously ran his hand through his hair and continued. "I didn't mean to interrupt … whatever that was…"

Sweet began to bead across Gabriel's forehead as he tried to explain what had happened.

"It wasn't … we weren't … she just …"

I placed my finger against his lips to silence his babble.

"I tripped and he caught me …" I said. "Why did you clear your throat like that?"

Raphael stared intently at Gabriel, I could almost feel their heated telepathic conversation.

"You know it's not nice to have a telepathic conversation with me standing right here!" I telepathically stated, interrupting their serious conversation with a half-smile upon my face.

"Yes … she might be able to help," Raphael said, nodding his head.

"No!" Gabriel said sternly.

"I just thought that she …"

"No, it's too dangerous … I won't let her."

Anger swelled inside me. "You won't let me? How dare you think that you can order me around or tell me what I can and cannot do!"

I poked Gabriel in the chest and continued.

"I can decide for myself what is and what is not too dangerous for me," I continued, my anger starting to rise. "I'm a lot tougher than I look."

Gabriel grabbed me by the shoulders.

"I know you can, but I don't want you hurt," he said. "If anything happened to you, Alex … I just … I couldn't bear it."

I let out a slow breath.

"Well … what's this thing you think is too dangerous for me to do?"

Gabriel nodded his head as if to give Raphael consent to tell me.

"Well, you see it's … well it's like this … I mean you see Eros is … I mean we …"

Raphael let out a frustrated huff as Gabriel rolled his eyes and continued where Raphael had left off.

"It might be better if we just show her what we're talking about."

"Yes … you're probably right."

Gabriel shot me a soft sweet smile, grabbed my hand and led me from the room, closely followed by Raphael. We made our way through the halls and down the stairs to the basement. Working our way through the basement we came to the last room – it was a type of library, with books lining every wall from ground to ceiling. Michael was on his knees in the middle of the room, pain consuming his posture.

"Michael!" I exclaimed, rushing to his side. "Are you okay?"

Michael didn't respond, as if he couldn't hear me. He remained kneeled in the center of the room, mumbling something under his breath.

"What's wrong with him?" I asked, turning to Gabriel. "Why is he ignoring me?"

"I'm not ignoring you," Michael answered suddenly, standing up rapidly and turning to me with a smile. "I was meditating – or praying, if you will …"

"Praying?" I asked. "About what?"

Gabriel stepped up beside me and placed his hand on my shoulder.

"Alex, you know that we are Guardians," he said, pointing to himself, Michael, and Raphael. "And you know that Eros, Crystal, and Catrina are Betrayers."

I nodded my head and he continued.

"Well … we're more than that. In fact, those are just fancy names for something else. Something … greater. We're angels of light and goodness – Guardians are, anyway. The Betrayers are angels of darkness and evil. You might know them as demons. And Eros …

"Hold on a minute," I interrupted, raising my eyebrows. "So you're saying that you, Raphael, and Michael are all angels of light?"

"Yes."

"… and Eros is a demon?"

Gabriel bit his lip.

"Yes and no," he said.

"What do you mean, yes and no? Either yes he is or no he's not? It can't be both."

"Just that he is a demon and … isn't …"

I let out a frustrated huff.

What is going on?

Michael also seemed frustrated with the slowness of Gabriel's explanation, and so he began to speak in earnest.

"Eros was a Guardian," he said, his words coming out in a heated rush. "And during a battle between angels and demons Eros – still on the Guardians side and in his half-transformed form – battled toward Mephistopheles."

Gabriel stepped up beside me and put a hand up to stop Michael's tirade.

"Calm down Michael, there's a better way to tell her this tale," he said.

Michael looked at Gabriel curiously for a moment, and then nodded as he realized what his friend was suggesting. Gabriel's then turned to me and placed his hands on either side of my head, his palms flat against my temples.

"I need you to relax," Gabriel said as he stared into my eyes.

I signaled my agreement and prepared for what might come next by closing my eyes and emptying my mind.

CHAPTER TWENTY

AGONY

After a moment the darkness behind my eyes began to form into the strikingly crisp vision of a battle. Soon it was as if I was right in the middle of the action, with fighting raging around me. It was terrifying!

Suddenly a horrifying Betrayer beast raced for me. As if my body wasn't my own I leaped into action, my body moving in ways I didn't even know was possible. The Betrayer demon didn't have a chance of taking me down. I was like a machine taking down the Betrayers one by one with a sword that I held in the style of a samurai. It was disturbing how good I was as I continued plunging my blade into one Betrayer after another – their flesh tearing violently open the moment my blade sliced against their skin. The blade of my sword seemed to cause their skin to bubble and blister and left gaping wounds wherever it had touched them.

Their bodies began to convulse, foam and crimson, black blood spewing from the mouths of Betrayers as I passed.

Shrieks and roars echoed all around me. Though the body I inhabited continued to fight, all I wanted to do was curl up in a ball. I began to feel the familiar sensation of pain as my body began to morph into the beast. Through the pain I could faintly hear Gabriel's voice.

"Alex, it's not real," he said, panic in his voice. "You're not really there! You're with me in the library."

My head began to spin, causing everything around me to blur. Unable to steady myself, I felt myself slip to the floor, but strong hands caught me before my head hit the hard concrete.

* * *

Gabriel's heavenly scent filled my nose as I massaged my hands over my eyes. When my vision cleared I began to examine my surroundings. I was back in the library, only it was completely demolished – as if a hurricane had torn through.

"What happened here?" I asked as I continued examining the room. Blood and dust polluted the air.

Gabriel's jaw stiffened.

"You happened." Michael angrily said as he jabbed his finger in my direction.

"What do you mean?"

"Alex," Gabriel said, a note of interest in his words, "how did you know where to find this?" He held up a large, beautiful diamond white sword with a large sapphire stone at the end of the handle – the same sword I'd had in my hands in the vision.

"That's my sword," I said immediately, without thinking. "Or, I mean, the sword I had when you teleported me to that battleground. I thought I was going to die. How did you do that anyway?"

Concern crossed Gabriel's face and his eyebrows furrowed in worry as he looked at me.

"Alex, the only one other than myself who knew where this was is someone that is no longer with us."

Tears seemed to fill his eyes as he held the sword out before him and went on.

"But you grabbed it as though you have known all along where it was."

Confusion consumed me.

"So you didn't teleport me anywhere? I was here all along?" My voice sank to near silence as I looked around the room. "I did all of this?"

Gabriel placed his hand on my shoulder.

"Yes, but I don't think that you're to blame."

"Not to blame? Really?!?! Look at this mess!"

"That's not what I meant at all," Gabriel said, cutting me off before I could get any more agitated. "Let me put it another way. There's no way you could have possibly known where this sword was unless you were there when it was placed in hiding."

"What are you saying?" I asked as I shook my head, trying to clear away the last of the cobwebs.

"I'm saying that you were here 23 years ago when I placed it there," Gabriel said matter-of-factly, pointing to an area of the library that had a small cubby hole where apparently I had gotten the sword.

"That's impossible," I said, not fully understanding what my ears were hearing. "I'm only 20 years old, soon to be 21 … There's no way that's correct …"

Everyone stared curiously at Gabriel as he further explained his words.

"You *were* here that day – or rather your father was here and since I was showing you a memory from which he was present in your sub conscious was placed inside his body. I believe that that is how you knew where the sword was hidden."

Shock flooded over me.

"You ....you knew my father?"

"Yes ..."

"But how? How did you know him?"

My eyes pleaded with him to tell me something – anything! I clung to this hope that if I could just know a little more about him it might help my clouded memories of him, my mother and the person that was always there as a child come flooding back.

"I knew your father for many, many years before you came into his life," Gabriel said as he stared down at the sword. I could tell by the look on his face that he was remembering something. "We fought alongside each other in many battles. I knew that I could always count on him to have my back. When he first met your mother he knew that she was the one he was meant to be with. It was love at first sight. After many years of being on the run they settled down right here in Iola Kansas. I knew that eventually you would be drawn back to where you were born, drawn here in your search for answers so I step up a base of operations. I have watched over you since the day your parents die and wanting to get you as far as I could from where your parents died I took you to India."

"Wait so this is the town where my parents died?" I questioned.

Gabriel nodded his head.

"So what happened to them, was it a car accident?"

“No your parents were murdered.” He said as anger and pain filled his eyes.

My jaw tightened in frustration, “By who?”

Before he could answer there was a loud wail of pain that echoed through the walls, I pressed my finger against his lips.

“What *was* that?” I asked, confusion in my expression.

“It sounded like Eros.”

Another cry rang out, this one even more insistent than the first. I turned to Gabriel, a fierce look in my eyes.

“What were you going to show me down here before I went beast on this place?” Gabriel nodded his head and made his way around me to a demolished shelf and placed his hand firmly upon a small, nearly unnoticeable cross that was formed from a natural depression in the wood. As he pressed it the wall began to shift, revealing a secret passage. As soon as the door opened, the blood curdling screams of pain flooded the library. A pulse of anger washed over me.

“What are you doing to him?!”

“We’re not doing anything to him,” Raphael said insistently. “It’s just – the medicine you ejected him with has worn off, and no one can get close enough to even touch him, let alone give him another dose.”

“Take me to him,” I said, nodding my head in the direction of where the cries were coming from.

“Of course,” Raphael said, stepping out in front of me and making his way down the dark, damp hall.

I studied the halls as we slowly made our way to Eros. The further we moved into the dungeon the more I became disturbed with what I saw. Rooms lined the hall, each one more disturbing than the one before.

“What horrifying nightmares go on here?” I whispered as my stomach churned.

“These rooms were made for interrogating the Betrayers,” Gabriel said.

“That’s a lie,” I whispered as a tear escaped the corner of my eye.

“No, it’s true – we really do interrogate Betrayers in theses rooms,” Raphael said as we continued down the dim shadowy hall.

“Yes, but that’s not all we do … is it?” Gabriel muttered in a hushed tone.

Guilt haunted Raphael’s face.

“No, that’s not all we did …” He seemed to be completely disgusted with the words coming out of his mouth. “… we …” He stopped his trek down the hall as his gaze fell to the ground in regret. “… we tortured them … We told ourselves that it was to find out where their headquarters were, but I don't believe that anymore … not when I would see the ways that we coerced the information out of them … It was and is quite disturbing … and I am ashamed to say it, but I was participating in the interrogation process along with everyone else." He looked up and turned his attention to Gabriel. "But not you … you never participated … why?"

Gabriel let out a slow, steady breath.

"Why would I?" he asked. "You may not remember, but we were once all on the same side – before Mephistopheles decided that he was more powerful than Jahovah."

Another cry of agony rang out.

"Yes, but –" Raphael began.

"But now is not the time to discuss this matter," I grabbed Raphael by the elbow. "We need to get to Eros – NOW!"

Raphael nodded his head and continued moving further through the halls. The cries of agony were nearly unbearable as we came to the end of the hall. Just before we entered the room Gabriel grasped my hand.

"He won't be himself," he said.

"What do you mean?"

Gabriel shook his head.

"You'll see what I mean," he replied, opening the door and stepping to the side.

Slowly I entered the room, not fully prepared for what I would see. Terror washed over me as I stared panic-stricken at Eros. He was practically unrecognizable – his skin blackened as if he had stood by a sulfur-burning furnace. The whites of his eyes were blood red and the irises were as black as night. His body violently jerked around as if it were trying to break free from his chains, which had to be nearly five inches thick. And yet every time his body convulsed it put strain upon the brackets that had been drilled into the stone.

"That's not going to hold much longer," I said, pointing at the brackets as they turned white from the strain. I looked around to see if there were any other exits from the room.

Raphael made his way to my side.

"Here," he said, shoving a syringe into my hands. "You're the only one who can do it, but you're going to have to hurry."

As if confirming his words, Eros convulsed again and one of his arms ripped free from its constraints. Raphael and Michael along with two other guardians; whose names escaped me, ran to his side to hold him down as I bolted to Eros to inject him with more of the medicine I'd created. Eros lashed out and somehow all of them were flung violently to the opposite wall. Eros ripped his other arm free and clutched me in his hands, raking his claws murderously down my back. A wheeze of pain escaped my lips.

"We've grown tired of you getting in the way, girl!" He shouted, his voice sounding dark and villainous – as if possessed by pure evil. He grabbed the hand holding the syringe and wrenched it back. A moment later the bones in my wrist cracked and splintered with a sickening sound. The pain was so excruciating that it made me sick to my stomach, and my vision began to cloud. I could feel myself starting to pass out, as the blood spilled from my open wound.

"You have to transform," My Strength said. *"It will help you to heal."*

"How?" I whimpered.

"Focus, Alexandra – focus," he replied.

Everything seemed to be moving in slow motion as I bowed my head in compliance. The stink of blood only made it that much more difficult as I tried to focus.

"ALEX!" Gabriel shouted, making his way to my side. Eros gave him a wicked glare and flung his hand in Gabriel's direction. The moment that Eros' fist collided with Gabriel's chest, a bone-crushing sound echoed through the chamber followed closely by a growl of agony. His body flew swiftly through the air and slammed into the wall, air escaping his lungs with a gasp.

The red in Eros' eyes darkened as he grabbed me by the throat. Standing up, he raised me over his head. I closed my eyes as my vision blurred more.

"Focus, Alexandra – Focus," My Strength whispered once again.

I released all of the air from my lungs, my breath wheezing through my numb lips, as blood spilled from the corners of my mouth and the pain of transformation flooded over me immediately healing my shattered arm and then going to work upon my back

"THIS ENDS NOW!" Eros roared – his evil, shadowy voice echoing through the halls.

My jaw stiffened and I tightened my grip upon the syringe that I still held in my once broken hand. My eyes flashed open as my transformation continued my bones enlarging, and fear consumed Eros' face; I stared down at him. I glanced over at Gabriel – awe consumed his face as he stared back into my eyes. I turned my attention back to Eros' terrified face.

"You're right Eros, this *ends* NOW!" I thundered as I plunged the syringe into his chest.

A gasp escaped his mouth and he released me, his body collapsing to the ground below as the medicine immediately went to work.

CHAPTER TWENTY-ONE

DAMP DARKNESS

I rubbed my sore chest as my bones manipulated back into place.

“Are you guys okay?” I asked as I looked at Michael, Raphael, and Gabriel. Michael and Raphael still lay stunned on the ground as if they couldn’t comprehend what just happened.

My eyes felt heavy as I staggered a few clumsy steps in his direction before collapsing to the ground in a puddle of my own blood.

“ALEX!” Gabriel hollered as Raphael, Michael and himself made their way to my side.

“I’m f-fine,” I stuttered as my body continued to heal itself, the tears in my back stitching themselves together. I sat up and continued. “Really – I’m fine,” I said as Gabriel grasped me around the waist to help me to my feet.

My heart flipped as he ran his hand tenderly up my arm, across my shoulders, and over my back making flutters of pleasure cascade over my body.

"It's incredible ..." he said as he continued to tenderly examine my back.

"What is?" I muttered as I unsuccessfully tried to keep my heart rate in check.

"It's just ..." he turned me around to face him. "... I have never seen a Guardian – or a Betrayer, for that matter – heal as quickly as you have. There's not even a scar to suggest an injury of any kind. It's incredible!"

Raphael stepped slightly closer.

"And did you see her eyes," he asked, awe in his voice. "They were amazing!"

"Yeah," echoed Michael as he pulled himself off the floor. "They were totally AWESOME!!!"

"Don't you guys know it's rude to talk about someone when they're standing right there in front of you," I said, slightly miffed. "What's so extraordinary about my eyes?"

Gabriel placed his hand upon my cheek.

"They're beautiful."

"They're extraordinary!" Raphael echoed, followed closely by Michael.

“THEY’RE AWESOME!!!”

I let out a frustrated huff and Gabriel nodded his head.

“They were the most dazzling shade of amethyst I have ever seen.”

“You told me that before.”

“I know,” Gabriel said, then nodded his head toward Raphael and Michael. “I didn’t tell them, though.”

“So you have seen her totally awesome eyes before and you didn’t tell us?” Michael asked, shock consuming his face.

“Well, it was on a need-to-know basis, and you didn’t need to know,” Gabriel said evasively. “Anyway we need to discuss what we’re going to do with Eros. We can’t keep him sedated forever.”

“My vote is to end him while we still have the chance.” Michael said as he glared down at Eros with malice in his eyes.

I walked over to Eros’ body as it lay in a puddle of my blood.

“Can you please place him up on the bed?” I looked over at the mattress where Eros had been. It, too, was drenched in blood. “Never-mind, let’s take Eros upstairs and place him on a real bed.” I stared at Michael and Raphael to indicate that I wanted them to do it.

“We can’t risk it getting loose,” Gabriel said hesitantly. “It has to be contained.”

"What do you mean *it*?" I questioned, wondering if he was being intentionally evasive so as not to help Eros any more than he had to.

"Eros is no longer a part of that body," he said, immediately dashing my doubts. "If I would have been there that day, just a little sooner maybe he wouldn't be going through this torcher."

I placed my hand on his shoulder.

"Gabriel, you couldn't have stopped Eros from becoming a Betrayer." Raphael stated, "Believe me I have struggled with the same feelings of guilt." Raphael turned to Michael, "Anyway we really should do as Alex has asked and take Eros upstairs." A look of hurt touched his face, "From the looks of him, he doesn't have much time left."

"What do you mean, not much time left?" I fearfully asked.

"Let's take him upstairs and I'll explain what I mean." Raphael said as he grasped Eros by the arm and hoisted him upon his shoulder.

"Michael can you please help Raphael?"

Hatred burned in Michael's eyes, "I'm not touching that thing again." He hissed through his tightly clenched teeth. "It just won't happen!"

"How can you say that? I thought that you were supposed to be Guardians?" I felt a warmth touch my heart as the My Strength were using me to speak with them. "It doesn't matter how you feel about Eros you need to ask you're self if the Creator would approve of how you are acting."

Michael angrily stepped forward a neon blue flashing in his eyes, "I have known the Creator long before you were even born so…"

"So you should know better and know that how you are acting is not according to the will of the Creator. We can't let our hurt cloud our vision and calm down and listen we will know what it is that he want us to do." A sadness filled his words as he continued, "I know what the creator has is asking of me and even though I may not understand it he does and I choose to trust the creator and go forward knowing that everything will work out according to his plan."

Michael bowed his head and a moment later he walked over next to Raphael to assist him in carrying Eros. "You're right," he said looking at Gabriel. "I allowed my own foolish thoughts and feeling get in the way of what I know the Creator want us to do.

"Good then we need to get Eros in a room that has a lot of natural light, because I believe that the light will help the serum work a little longer if it is in the light." I said, turning back to Raphael and Michael. "So are there any rooms like that in this house?"

I could see the wheels turning as Michael and Raphael tried to think of a room that might fit that description.

"We can take him to my room," Gabriel said, his voice strained.

A moment of shock passed across for Raphael and Michael's faces, but then they nodded silently and lifted Eros, carrying him out of the room and down the hall. We walked through the dungeon to the basement, then proceeded to the main floor where we made our way to the end of a hall. Gabriel stopped and ran his hand slowly across the wall where the wooden trim – about halfway up the wall. Suddenly the wall split open to the sides, revealing a large elevator.

"After you," Gabriel said.

Michael and Raphael nodded their heads and maneuvered their way into the elevator awkwardly with Eros' body, only to roughly smack his upon the wall as they entered."

"Be careful," I said as their faces scrunched in awkward remorse.

The ride up to Gabriel's room was silent, and a moment later the elevator doors opened. Gabriel's room was magnificent – unlike anything I'd ever seen before. The ceiling had a large skylight window, allowing natural light to flood the room – almost making it blindingly bright. Large windows lined two of the walls around the massive room. The floors were a coffee brown in color and the other walls were an almost icy blue hue. There was a grand wooden bed in the center of the room, topped with white frosted pillows and a silvery alabaster comforter. At the head of the bed there was a wall of cocoa-colored bookshelves and a small sitting area in front of a large stone fireplace. Everything was in perfect order, except for one corner where there was a hamper overflowing with clothes.

Gabriel's face flushed a deep red when he seen the pile of unwashed close in the corner of the room. "I um…Well you see I… The reason that…" He stuttered as Raphael and Michael carried Eros over to the white bed. He let out a slow steady breath and continued this time much more composed. "The truth is I really *hate* to wash close. Anyway what do you think?" he asked, "Is this going to be enough natural light?"

"This is incredible," I said as I wrapped my arms tightly around Gabriel's chest. "Much better than I could have ever imagined."

"Okay, so what's next?" Raphael asked as he looked down at Eros.

"Well," I said as we all walked over to the seating area, "Has anyone seen Nat, I really think that she should be a part of the discussion of what to do with Eros.

"I'm not sure," Raphael said as he stood up and began to walk towards the door. "But I'll got and look for her. I agree with you that she should be here with us while we are discussing what to do with him."

Just before Raphael left the room Michael spoke up, "You won't find her." Frustration filled his expression.

"What do you mean he won't find her?" I questioned as I intently stared at him.

Raphael walked back towards us, "She asked you a question Michael." Concern consumed his words as he spoke them.

Michael's jaw tightened, "Because she's not here."

"Okay then did she go back to the apartment?"

"No."

Irritation began to boil inside me. "Michael quit stalling and just tell us where Natalya is."

"She was taken," He looked up at me a pain in his eyes as he continued, "By the Betrayers."

I fell to my knees as Raphael angrily questioned Michael, "How do you know?"

"Because when we realized that that the Betrayers were here I had Jordan stay behind to protect Natalya and…" He took in a deep breath, "there were just too many of them they over powered him and took her."

I stood unmoving as Michael and Raphael bickered back and forth.

"I could have stopped them." I whispered as a tear escaped the corner of my eye.

"No you couldn't ha…" Gabriel began.

"You don't understand…" I cried, "I heard them talking with Catrina telepathically talking with her and they said that plan B had been completed."

"You couldn't have known that that was what they were talking about," Gabriel stated as he placed his hand upon my shoulder. "Alex, Natalya being taken isn't your fault."

I shook my head and stood up. "I'm going to look for her."

Gabriel grabbed my hand, "Their long gone by now."

"Then there has got to be someone that know something about the Betrayers and where to find them." I pleaded.

"The only one that would be able to give us any information on them was Oli and…" His head fell and a tear ran down his cheek, "At least he is in a better place now." He took in a deep breath, "Look, Alex I know that it's hard to not do anything, but we need to come up with a plan because even if we do find out where they have taken her, if we don't have a plan we be more likely to fail and if we fail then we won't be able to save her."

I stared at Gabriel when my strength spoke up, *"Gabriel is full of wisdom, what he is saying is true."*

I nodded my head as another tear escaped my eye. "Okay, we will come up with a plan.

CHAPTER TWENTY-TWO

VOID

We sat in the group for hours, trying to figure out our next move and having given Eros several doses of the medicine, but for the most part we just sat there brainstorming options. Every time we thought that we had a solution it turned out to be a failure. Just when I had started to lose all hope, My Strength spoke to me.

"I have a solution," He said.

Excitement swelled inside me.

My Strength! Of course, I should have reached out to you from the beginning. What is your solution? I'm sorry for not having done so.

"You must release the evil spirits that have possessed him causing him this distress. The evil spirits are causing his vision of what's important to become clouded and he can't see beyond their selfish desires. He can help you save Natalya." My Strength said.

Okay, how can I release Eros from the evil spirits that possess him?

"For you to expel the demons from him you first need to realize exactly what you are up against."

I nodded my head and My Strength continued.

"Long ago there was a battle of the spirits, and during that battle he came in contact with Mephistopheles," My Strength explained; visions of the battle Gabriel had shown me before flashed through my mind. *"Most demons do not have the ability to possess angels, but Mephistopheles is the first Betrayer. He has a power beyond those of the others because of who he was before his fall to sin."*

Suddenly I was in a large white, empty space as My Strength fell silent. A young, handsome man stood before me. He had sandy blond hair with sea-blue eyes and a sculpted strong build. I stared at him for a moment – he looked familiar.

That's right he was in my vison or memory or dream, whatever it was he, Zander was in it.

"Where am I?" I questioned as I continued to examine the area.

The Zander moved closer to me.

"You're in the Void," he said to me. "The White Void – the space between life and death. Do not be afraid, you are not dead.

Your spirit is here only. In fact, only a small part of you is here with me."

"And I know you don't I? I mean I've seen you before." I asked

Excitement pulsed in his eyes, "Yes you do know me. I am your Fa…" He paused for a moment and let out a slow, steady breath. "I am Zander, where is it that you know me from Alexandra?"

There seemed to be pain in his words as he spoke them; as though he was praying that I would remember him. "I had a dream with you in it. At least I think that it was a dream though I am not entirely sure. Natalya has this crazy idea that they are memories or visons, but I'm not really sure if I believe that." I bit my lip waiting for Zander to continue; I was secretly hoping that I did know him from somewhere other than the dreams and stand here in the Void with him I felt as though I was closer to him than the dreams let on.

His eyes sparkled with kindness and he nodded his head as he continued. "In the Void one can place their memories upon the walls of the Void. Not everyone is able to project their thoughts upon the walls though, but you are not an ordinary girl so I am sure that in no time at all you will be able to project you thoughts upon the walls of the Void," he said almost as though he was bragging upon me.

My face flushed red, he placed his hands upon my shoulders. It was oddly comforting – as if by being in his presence I would always be safe.

*I **like** this man. There is just something comforting about him.*

I shyly bit my lip as I thought about the comforting presence of Zander.

He bit his lip in the same manner, almost in mirror to me, as he tried to think of how he might explain the way the Void worked.

"The Void is empty space, and if one's mind is powerful enough they can project their thoughts into that space," he said. "It takes someone of immense power to be able to do this. It requires a great deal of concentration, and in most cases years to master. Let me give you an example. Nothing you will see is real, though it will feel that way. It's just a memory. Do you understand?"

"Yes I understand," I said as everything around us began to blur.

Suddenly we were standing in a dark forest. Betrayer and Guardians battled around us.

"It's only a memory," Zander's voice echoed through the forest and he disappeared.

Even with those words bouncing off the trees, fear still gripped me. I couldn't help it – the battle was terrifying. The roars of agony that rang out all around me and the smell of blood flooding the air – how could this be a memory?

It's only a memory. It's not real. It's only a memory. It's not real.

Suddenly a Betrayer raced toward me – its black sword raised over its head. It only took me a moment to realize that it was Catrina, and the hate in her eyes made my heart quiver as she raced towards me. Right before she reached me, Zander's voice rang out.

"STOP!"

I let out a slow, stabilizing breath. Catrina's sword rested at my throat. I could almost feel the tip of her blade upon my skin.

"Alexandra, what are you doing?" Zander questioned as he made his way to where I stood.

"Nothing," I said quickly. "I haven't moved from this spot – I swear!"

"You shouldn't swear young lady," he replied automatically, as if not really thinking about his words. Then he seemed to be distracted by something on my shirt as he pointed to neck. "What is that?"

I stepped back and glanced down at my body.

"What?"

"YOU'RE BLEEDING!" He shouted as he ran his hand over my neck and pulled it back, revealing the blood smeared across his hand.

I placed my hand upon my neck right into the warm sticky blood as it pulsed down my neck.

"That's not possible," he said as he examined Catrina's frozen frame.

"What's not possible?"

"Catrina is here," he said. "How can she be here? It's only a memory."

"How should I know," I said, bewildered. "It's your memory."

"Yes it's my memory, but I don't remember Catrina being there," he said. "But that's not the real problem."

"What do you mean real problem?"

"I mean that you pulled Catrina's spirit – her real spirit – into the void."

"WHAT?!"

A thin smile worked its way upon his face.

"You are far more powerful than we originally thought. To pull someone's spirit from their bodies takes immense powers." He seemed to beam with pride as he spoke to me.

"If you're going to show her what happened to Eros then you need to do it now," My Strength stated. *"I will return Catrina's soul back to her body..."*

Zander nodded his head and let out a slow breath, as if clearing his mind. Catrina disappeared and the memory around me began to move once again, only this time it moved so fast that it was nearly impossible to see anything – as if Zander was fast forwarding to the important part.

After several minutes the memory began to slow, until everything was moving at a normal pace – or at least normal for Guardians and Betrayers. I stood before a very handsome man who was obviously Eros, but there was something different about him. His eyes didn't glow a blood red – they were neon blue like Gabriel's. Yet there seemed to be something more – an almost peaceful feeling seemed to radiate off of him, a peace that reminded me of Gabriel.

He battled a large half-man, half-lion beast that had hulking arms that were at least twice the size of Eros', and his chest was nearly three time the size. The beast's skin was an almost ebony brown in color, and he had blazing red eyes, with thick, flowing, raven-black hair.

Fear rushed over me as I watched Eros and the monstrosity battling, but even with the beast being twice his size Eros still seemed to be holding his own.

And then one lucky swipe from the beast knocked Eros down, and a moment later an evil hand was savagely wrapped around Eros' neck.

Eros plunged his sword toward the creature. As it tore into the beast's side a blood curdling roar rang out. Hatred consumed the beast's charred red eyes as his chest convulsed. It reached its other clawed hand to the blade and tore it from his body. Then he lunged forward and bit with large fangs into the crook of Eros' neck, almost as though he was a vampire.

The beast pulled back slightly and dark shadows spirited into Eros' open wound. Black poison began to stream through his veins and in a matter of seconds it had almost completely dominated his body. The towering creature released Eros, his body falling lifeless to the ground.

"NO!!!" Gabriel, Zander, Michael, and Raphael all shouted in unison. Gabriel rushed to Eros' side, panic in his eyes.

I stared petrified as the scene continued before me.

Gabriel buried his head into Eros' chest and tears began to slip from his eyes as Eros slowly opened his eyes.

"You h-have to g-get away f-from me …" Eros stuttered as he tried to push Gabriel away.

"No … I won't leave you …"

"You … HAVE … TO …" Eros roared as his eyes turned from neon blue to an amethyst. "I … c-can't hold th-them back any l-longer …" His jaw tightened along with the muscles in his arms, as he tried to hold back his demonic transformation.

"Eros … you are my best friend," Gabriel said.

"We are not Eros anymore," a voice said from Eros' lips – a deeply disturbing voice that sounded nothing like Eros. "We are Legion, for we are many."

Tears made their way down Gabriel's cheek.

"Please fight the darkness Eros," Gabriel pleaded. "Please …"

In response, Eros threw Gabriel off of him and his eyes turned neon red in color.

Eros grabbed a nearby Betrayer sword and Gabriel picked up Eros' Guardian sword – and then Legion raced toward him. They drove their swords into each other's chests and everything began to move in slow motion once again.

Mephistopheles grabbed Eros and Raphael grabbed Gabriel with the assistance of Zander, while Michael fought off the advancing Betrayers, buying time for Raphael and Zander to drag Gabriel to safety.

The memory froze as I stared at Gabriel and Eros. I placed my hand upon my scar as I stared unmoving at how they had gotten theirs. It all made sense – the same cross-shaped scars, the hatred, compassion, and disappointment they had for each other. They had been friends and were forced into being enemies by Mephistopheles when he possessed Eros with Legions of demons. But despite all of that there still seemed to be a part of Eros that was good – a part where he still tried to fight the hold that the darkness had upon him.

"Do you know what you must do?" My Strength questioned, drawing me away from the frozen scene before me.

"Yes," I said. "I think so. I must expel the evil spirits from Eros. I must drive out Legion."

"Yes," My Strength replied.

"NO," Zander said suddenly, pleading with My Strength. "Eloi – please, she is but a child."

"I'm almost 21." I said frustration thick in my words.

An almost parental look of irritation settled into Zander's eyes as he waited for My Strengths' response.

"She is ready," My Strength said.

Zander nodded his head and let out a slow steady breath, "I trust you Elio and if you say she is ready I believe you." Zander said.

A moment later a bright light flashed and my spirit was reunited with my body.

"You are ready," My Strength said. *"Trust in your abilities and always know that I am here."*

CHAPTER TWENTY-THREE

SACRIFICE

I tried to steady my nerves by closing my eyes and slowly breathing through my nose.

"Alex?"

Gabriel said my name with curiosity in his voice.

"I know how to cure Eros," I stated as I opened my eyes.

"What?!" Gabriel asked.

"How?" Raphael asked.

I bit my lip, not wanting to go on because I knew what their response would be. I took in a deep breath and rushed forward anyway.

"I can remove the demons from his body," I said, running my words together as quickly as I could.

"Alex, that's nearly impossible!" Raphael said.

"I can do this."

"How do you know…" Gabriel began when Raphael interrupted hi question. "Even if you did somehow manage to remove the demons from him," Raphael glanced in Eros' direction and continued. "Well … that kind of process … it … well it takes a toll on a person. No matter how hard you try, you will never be able to … to …"

"You'll never be able to expel all of the darkness from yourself," Michael said, finishing what Raphael didn't have the courage to finish himself. He looked at me and a tender sadness welled in the depths of his blue eyes. It was a deep emotion, and I was surprised at how fond I felt for this usually gruff Guardian.

A smile worked its way upon my face.

"Is that all you're worried about?"

"Isn't that enough?" Gabriel asked, frustration covering his face.

I looked at Gabriel and ran my hand down his arm.

"I learned a long time ago that there's both good and bad in everyone," I said. "That includes myself. It's just something that we all must face. Gabriel, I know this isn't going to be easy, but I know its something I must do."

He began to protest and I placed my finger upon his lips.

"I know you don't want me to get hurt, but Gabriel – I can do this. I won't be doing it alone. My Strength, the creator of Heaven and Earth and everything in them will be there to help me push through.

I wrapped my arms tightly around his chest, not caring whether Raphael and Michael were looking.

"Please trust me," I said, pressing my cheek against his. "I can do this."

He nodded his head.

"Okay ..." he whispered, his posture tensing as if he didn't really agree with what he said.

I began to make my way towards Eros when Michael stopped me by grabbing my arm, "I have failed to protect you and now Natalya as well, so please," Pain filled his eyes as he continued, "Please, allow me to take on this burden for you Alex. Allow me to battle the demons that have taken up residence in Eros' body."

I shook my head, "I'm sorry Michael but this is something that My Strength has asked me to do. So you see even if I wanted to I cannot allow you to do that."

"I had to try." Michael stated as he released my arm.

I walked over to Eros' ridged body and slowly unbuttoned his shirt, about hallway down his chest I stopped and placed my palm over his heart. I closed my eyes in an attempt to focus.

I could hear every little thing in the room – Raphael's impatient footsteps pacing back and forth, Michael irritatingly clicked the end of a pen, a fly in the corner of the room rhythmically running its legs over its face. Frustration pulsed over me as I tried in vain to focus.

"You need to relax, Alexandra. Focus only upon the task at hand." My Strength said as a warmth touched my heart calming my irritations immediately.

Taking in a deep breath, I once again placed my hand upon Eros' bare chest. His lips had greyed even further and sweat drenched his clammy body. Shaky breaths whispered through his lips, and turmoil seemed to churn aggressively beneath my palm as Eros began to awaken from his medicine-induced coma. I stiffened my hand over Eros' sternum, his heart rate beating so rapidly it felt as if it were a continuous hum, vibrating beneath my hand.

I closed my eyes in an attempt to concentrate. With a slow, steady breath I forced my light into Eros' chest.

His veins were so polluted with darkness that everything surrounding my light was a shadowy black in color. It almost felt as if the blackness that surrounded my light was trying to choke the life out of me. I could feel the darkness pressing violently against my luminous spirit.

An overwhelming sickness seeped into me and my heart began to fiercely beat inside my chest. It began to become difficult to breathe as my spirit seemed to cringe away from the encroaching darkness

I began to feel weak, but just when I started to panic I remembered My Strength's words.

"Let My Strength be your strength," it echoed in the recesses of my mind. *"If you need help, all you need to do is ask."*

A soft smile worked its way upon my face and I whispered, "Please, help …"

I closed my eyes as a peace washed over me. When I opened my eyes, I knew I was going to be better equipped to deal with the weight of the demons.

It looked as if my soul had once again been pulled into the Void, except the walls were not white – they were nearly black. I began to scan the space and a slight movement caught my eye. I turned and my eyes fell upon a large statue-like mass. I moved toward the dark greyish sculpture, but no matter how far I ran the sculpture didn't seem to get any closer.

I let out a slow, steady breath, focused on a partial transformation, where I used my new vision to zone in upon the sculpture. Starting at the base of the statue I carefully examined it – it almost looked as if it was cast in iron. My eyes made their way up the legs and to the chest where there was a dim light shining from the center of the statue's chest. Continuing upward, my eyes came to rest upon the fear-stricken face of Eros.

"EROS!" I exclaimed, my words echoing through the dark space and the light in the center of his chest brightening slightly.

I had to get to him. My jaw tightened and I took in a deep breath as I stepped toward Eros, making sure I firmly placed my foot upon the ground before taking the next step.

The moment I took my first firm step a cascade of energy bounced around me – as though a force field had been placed between Eros and me. The barricade seemed to become stronger with each step toward him. An angry roar streamed past me.

Bit by bit, I inched closer to the Eros statue. It was agony, but with every step came another surge of power from My Strength. Just before I was close enough to touch him, a large dark shadow crashed into me, knocking me to the ground.

"LEAVE!" The shadow roared, a slew of voices echoing at the same time. "Eros no longer inhabits this body."

The voices wailed as the shadow of the black void materialized into a dark evil figure. I knew who this figure was.

"You are wrong, Legion." I said as I looked around the coliseum of Eros' mind. "Eros' presence is still here. I can feel him and his light no matter how dim it may be."

Legion grew even larger and materialized into a beast with six arms sprouting from a massive chest and three heads splitting from one. The center head was a lion with demon-like qualities. The other two heads where human, though so drastically deformed that they looked to come straight out of a horror movie. Jagged teeth overlapped their lips, and snake-like forked tongues slipped in and out through the sides of their mouths. Where their eyes should have been there was nothing but black emptiness.

Fear began to pulse over me as I stared petrified in front of Legion.

"I am here," My Strength whispered, and I felt immediate peace, just from his words.

I closed my eyes and took a deep breath. Legion bellowed with delight, assuming my accelerated heart rate was from fear. I let out a slow, steady breath and began to transform.

"Good," My Strength said. *"Accept who you are. Become who I created you to be."*

I nodded my head as my teeth became razor sharp fangs and my nails became hooked claws. I could feel the dark black skin rip through my flesh. I opened my eyes and fear plagued the faces of the beasts called Legion. Looking as my hand I realized that the black flesh that I had seen was actually short velvet like fur. The black faded into a beautiful snow white color about halfway up my arm and my long blond hair turned silvery white and when the light hit it just right it would reflect the Amethyst color I knew my eyes had turned. As I stood before the best in a partial transformation a beautiful, diamond-white sword appeared in my hand with the word "Truth" inscribed on the side of the blade.

"You will release Eros, for it is the will of the Creator." I stated, standing confidently before Legion knowing that with My Strength's power coursing through my body we would overcome Legion, together.

Legion's body convulsed as if part of him wanted to leave.

"COWARDS!" Legion shouted. "YOU WILL FIGHT! THIS BODY IS OURS! SHE HAS NO POWER HERE!"

The lion-head roared as fear consumed the expressions of the other heads.

"But she has the sword of truth," a different evil voice whimpered.

"No matter, she has interfered too much. Without her around that filthy wolf will lose all hope and give in to the one true master, Mephistopheles. We will crush his will."

I rolled my eyes and let out a frustrated huff as Legion talked to himself. "Look as much as I enjoy you talking to yourself," I said my voice thick with sarcasm. My look hardened as I continued, "I'll tell you one last time, Release him!" I repeated, preparing myself for some kind of retaliation.

Legion stepped closer to me, his hulking body hovering over my own.

"Why don't you make me?" He taunted, venomous saliva spewing with every word. I moved back, careful not to let his venom burn my skin.

"As you wish," I said as another sword of truth appeared in my free hand.

He cracked his neck and his eyes burned a fiery red in color. He let out a deafening roar and six swords appeared in his six giant hands.

I raised my swords out in front of myself as he swung the blades in my direction – my diamond-white blades against his six midnight-black ones. The clash of the blades sent sparks showering down around us.

I moved as though I was born to do this, and yet with every advance I made, he countered, and visa-versa. Neither one of us could gain any ground as the battle raged on.

"Fight smart, not hard young one," Zander's voice whispered to me from out of the darkness. *"Look for an opening."*

He has six arms! There are no openings!

"What is the word of truth?" My Strength questioned.

I don't know.

I knew that I had to be missing something important, but what it was I did not know. I continued to battle as my mind pondered his question. Suddenly, not quite sure how I did it, I knocked two of Legion's swords away. They sailed through the air, landing next to the statue of Eros. The light within his heart shone slightly brighter and expanded through his chest as I gained a small amount of an advantage over Legion.

"Speak the word and end this battle," My Strength said.

Word? What word? How can I speak the word if I don't know what the word is?

"Speak the word," My Strength repeated insistently.

As I frantically tried to understand what he was telling me, the voice of Zander whispered to me.

"Eloi," he said – the name he had used for My Strength when he had brought me to the Void before.

Where have I heard that before? Was it in a book?

Then I remembered – it was something I'd heard in church once. The preacher had been preaching on the crucifixion of Jesus, and in the moment before his death he had cried out something – "Eloi, Eloi. Lama sabachthani."

What did that preacher say it meant?

"My God, my God why have you forsaken me?"

That was it! It had to be for there is power in the name.

I took in a deep breath to speak the word when Legion grabbed me by the throat and plunged his remaining swords as though they were one blade through my chest. I gasped for air as he pulled the blood red swords from my body and continued crushing my neck within his massive hand.

Blood began to spill from my lips as the air gurgled in and out of my punctured lungs. I looked over at Eros as a tear fell from the corner of his hard, statue-like eye.

Legion thundered with evil laughter and my vision began to blur.

I won't give up.

I wrapped my hands around his hulking arms as he began to laugh triumphantly. Then he threw me across the Void of Eros' mind. The air wheezed through my lips and I grasped for the closest item to pull myself to my feet. A faint light rippled through the dark void and a stump appeared to help me hoist myself to my feet.

"Look at you. You are pathetic. How can you help Eros when you can't even help yourself?"

I won't give up.

Staggering to my feet I turned to face Legion.

"There is st-still one th-thing that you f-forgot …"

A cocky look consumed Legion's faces.

"Really? And what is that? Because from the looks of it I could finish you off with four arms tide behind my back." An evil smile worked its way upon his face. "In fact, I think I'll do just that."

He chuckled as four of his arms disappeared along with two of his heads. He was almost more terrifying in a more normal form than he had been as that gruesome beast. Silently he walked toward me. I could feel heat radiating off him as his skin began to boil.

"Have you ever seen a Betrayer's true form?" he asked quietly, his voice more menacing than any shout he could have thrown at me. His skin turned to black as brimstone and his blood seemed to burn orange like lava showing through his black brimstone.

"This form is perfect, and it is immortal."

"Why would I ever care what a Betrayer would look like?" I asked, trying to gather what little strength I had left.

"You really don't know?" Legion questioned. "Don't you know who your parents are?"

I shook my head as he continued, a sneer forming on his lips.

"Your mother was a Betrayer," he said, sending a shock through me. I didn't want to believe it, but it made sense. So many things made sense, in fact, with that one little piece of information.

"Not just any Betrayer," he continued mercilessly. "She was an original."

A crooked smile rested upon his face as he waited for the impact of what he had said to sink in.

"Speak the word," My Strength said to me insistently. *"He's trying to distract you from what you came here to do because he knows that my strength runs through you. Don't let his words scare you. Don't let who your parents were change who you have become."*

I nodded my head and My Strengths love touched my heart giving me the power to overcome anything, even if my mother was a betrayer. So with the help of My Strength Legion's words faded to a mere whisper as I complied with the command of My Strength.

I looked up, placed my hand upon Legion's chest and spoke the word.

"Eloi."

There's power in the name.

A blindingly bright light grew from my hand, I could feel my heart become completely consumed with a power unlike anything I had ever felt before.

The light made its way through Eros' mind, expanding farther than the eye could see. A quiet humming began to pulse over the statue and light began to break through the iron prison that encompassed Eros.

Fear consumed Legion as he tried unsuccessfully to remove my hand from his chest.

"What are you doing?" He demanded, panic filling his eyes as the light began to move over his body.

"Are you willing to sacrifice your life for Eros?" Eloi asked.

I closed my eyes and a tear fell from my eye as I placed my free hand on the open wound in my chest. A moment later, I nodded my head.

"Yes, I am willing," I said.

"Greater love has no one than this," My Strength said, *"that he lay down his life for a friend. Well done, my child."*

I could feel an intense heat radiate from under my hand. The light increased, becoming a fiery white light, accompanied by an agonizingly hot pulse that seemed to radiate from the power throbbing through my veins. The heat and light became so mighty that it became difficult to breath. My hands tensed into fists as my vision began to blur into darkness.

I knew that death was close. I just prayed that I had done enough to save Eros from the grasp of Legion.

I could feel someone's hand pressing firmly on the wound in my chest, but it was faint.

"Raphael!" Gabriel exclaimed, his voice filled with concern. "She's bleeding!"

"I'm here …" Raphael said. "Is she breathing?"

"NO!" Gabriel replied in earnest. "You've got to save her."

Wanting to give him some measure of comfort, I agonizingly took a gasping breath.

"ALEX!" Gabriel shouted.

I opened my eyes and took another gasping breath.

"Is Eros alright?" I asked as I looked into Gabriel's tear filled eyes.

"Alex, we have to get you help," he said. "Y-you're not healing …"

Raphael moved closer.

"I'm going to have to stich you up," he said. "You're losing too much blood.

"Is … Eros … Okay," I repeated, looking pleadingly into Gabriel's eyes. "P-please I have to k- know."

Gabriel lifted me into his arms and carried me to Eros' bedside.

"Please … p-put me down …"

Gabriel placed me upon the bed and I collapsed onto Eros' chest.

"Eloi, please," I said, a gasping sob escaping my lips. "P-please … I am w-willing. Please, Eloi."

Suddenly I felt Eros' chest begin to move as air whispered through his lips.

Thank you, Eloi. Thank you.

"Alex?" Eros said suddenly, coming awake and looking around him curiously. When he noticed me he tightly wrapped his arms around me.

"I saw you …"

I tried to smile, but as he hugged me close it sent horrifying pain cascading over my body.

"You're bleeding!" he said, concern replacing his joy.

A faint smile made touched my face.

"I'm j-just g-glad your o-okay," my words slowly made their way through my weak lips, "You have to p-promise me, pr-promise that y-you will s-save Nat." I pleaded as I grasped his shirt in my weak hands.

Eros nodded his head, "I promise." He whispered as he kissed the top of my head.

"T-thank y-you." I faintly said as I gave in to the pain. My eyes closed and an overwhelming darkness enveloping me as one last breath wheezed through my frail, powerless lungs.

I closed my eyes, completely at peace with myself and the power of My Strength as I felt the soothing presence of death releasing all the agony from my injuries; the quiet of death consuming me, and all else evaporating into silence.